# The Sun Always Sets on The Third Reich

*An Alternate History Novel*

Robert J. Bradshaw

*The Sun Always Sets on The Third Reich*

*First Edition*



Cover Art By Ronnie Jensen at: *Tegnemaskin.no*

ISBN: 978-1-0693247-1-9

# Contents

## Important Terminology:

**Germania:** Formerly Berlin. Hitler planned for the name of the capital to be changed should the Reich have been victorious in the war.

***Führer*:** Leader of the Third Reich and head of the Nazi party.

***Wehrmacht*:** "Defense Force"; the armed forces of Nazi Germany. While it included the army (*Heer*), navy (*Kreigsmarine*) and air force (*Luftwaffe*) under its name, the term is often erroneously used as a shorthand to refer to the Germany Army exclusively.

**SS:** Abbreviation for *Schutzstaffel*; "Protection Squadron." Beginning as bodyguards to Nazi Party members, the SS quickly rose in scope, with its subdivision the *Waffen*-SS becoming an army in its own right. Their competition with the *Wehrmacht* was well known, as the two factions competed for resources and personnel, particularly near the end of the war. Due to their loyalty to the Nazi Party, they often recruited the most fanatical members of German society. At their height they had strict requirements to join, including proof of Aryan lineage dating back over a hundred years and no Jewish family members.

**Brownshirts:** The nickname for the *Sturmabteilung*; "Storm Division," or SA. This paramilitary force served as the Nazi's muscle and enforcers during the early years of the party. More of a gang of thugs than an actual military, they were quickly eclipsed by the SS.

**Hitler Youth**: An all-male youth organization for boys aged thirteen to eighteen. Its primary goal was to educate its members in Nazi ideology and principles. It featured many outdoor activities to build comradery and keep a high level of fitness. A junior version of the organization also existed for boys aged ten to thirteen, known as the *Deutsch Jungvolk* or "German Young People." A similar organization—"The League of German Girls"—also existed for females and served to instruct young women in the duties of motherhood and domestic responsibilities.

**Francisco Franco:** Spanish dictator and general who came to power after the Spanish Civil War (1936-1939) concluded with his faction, the "Nationalists," defeating the democratically elected government and their supporters, the "Republicans." It is well known that Franco's "Nationalists" were heavily backed by Fascist Italy and Nazi Germany, while the greatest supporter of the "Republicans" was the USSR.

**Gestapo:** The secret police of the Nazi state.

***Zollgrenzschutz*:** "Customs Border Guards"; the agency served as the Reich's immigration enforcement officers as well as border patrol at all international airports and land ports of entry.

**Note:** Military ranks of several factions, while mentioned by their correct terms in dialogue, will be referred to by their US Army equivalent in the narrative, for the sake of consistency, transparency and flow throughout the novel.

# Act I

## A Failed Dream by Dead Men

"For a few months I was inclined to believe in National Socialism. I thought of it as a necessary fever. And I was gratified to see that there were, associated with it for a time, some of the wisest and most outstanding Germans. But these, one by one, he had got rid of or even killed. ... He has left nothing but a bunch of shirted gangsters! ... But of our Germany, which was a nation of poets and musicians, of artists and soldiers, he has made a nation of hysterics and hermits, engulfed in a mob and led by a thousand liars or fanatics."

— Kaiser Wilhelm II on Adolf Hitler

# Chapter I

## *Arrival in a Crumbling Utopia*

The art style of the Reich had changed little in eighty years.

The advertisement for the sixty-seventh Hitler Youth World Cup was a series of bright colours and close-cut blond hair. In the stylized image, hundreds of uniformed children marched to the beat of a silent drum. In the distance, the Nuremberg arena could be seen flanked by pillars of light racing to meet the heavens.

The twenty flags of the National Socialist Federation were clasped in the pale hands of the grinning children. My home flag of Spain was among them, and while Spanish pride captured me for a moment, I wished the standard was depicted somewhere far away from Hitler and his so-called thousand-year Reich.

I'm not sure what compelled me to stare at the mural for as long as I had been. It had been on the train's arched ceiling for the entire trip, but I had only begun to process it now.

Tearing my eyes from the advertisement, I turned my attention to the scenery that raced by the window in a blur. Dilapidated buildings pocked the horizon, connected to civilization by fields that were nothing but mounds of dirt after a dry summer and a slow harvest. I knew the train route I was taking was quite far from the autobahns that led into the city, but so far, I hadn't had the best first impression of Germania.

I nestled into the seat, my mind focusing on the meeting I had the next day, which was the reason I had found myself being called to the Volkswagen World Headquarters in the heart of the Reich. I visualized my talking points for a few moments before thinking of my younger brother and the plans we made to get together while I was in the city. I smiled, thinking how nice it would be to have a drink with him after so many years apart.

I turned my head and looked at the briefcase beside me. Inside were the files and projections regarding the *Lebensnetz* which I had been asked by my team lead to compile. The computer-based network had been gaining traction ever since its expansion from solely military usage and was now available to the general public. The president of Volkswagen Spain had sent out a memo decreeing that the *Lebensnetz* was the future of sales, and more importantly, the future of the company. I expected the meeting would focus mostly on how such a piece of technology could be bent to fit the company's needs.

I looked out the window as the train slowed, surprised. The bullet train had not made a stop since Saarbrücken, and that was due to the presence of the immigration station there, where we were all checked.

As we came to a rest, I determined that the designers figured a small stop at a natural braking point wouldn't hurt before the train resumed its journey toward Victory Station, the massive structure that sat at the southern end of the famed Avenue of Splendors.

I turned my attention to an elderly gentleman and his wife as they passed by my seat. The man held a wrapped gift in his hand, while his wife gripped a bottle of expensive champagne. My imagination followed them down the aisle, out into the modest station where their loving family was waiting to take them away to a charming afternoon of pleasant conversation and wonderful food.

I found myself feeling envious, but quickly dismissed the notion.

A group of three women entered from a different car and settled in the seats across the aisle from me.

"Thank you for agreeing to move seats, Melony," a blonde, the thinnest of the group, said. "That couple looked to be from the Eastern Commissariats, and not the colonist kind either." The hate in her voice was plain.

While she had spoken in German, I understood her without issue as I was fluent in the language. This was part of the reason why I was the one tasked with representing Volkswagen Spain on this business trip.

The thin woman's blue eyes darted across the aisle, sizing me up. I suspected she recognized the Spanish gene markers on my face as her mouth twisted into a sneer before she turned her attention back to her two companions.

As the train shunted forward, I took a breath, ready for my travels to end and to experience Germania. Despite what my mother's side of the family said about the Reich, I was excited to see the capital. The phrase, "All roads lead to Rome," may have been true at one time, but in today's day and age, all roads led to Germania.

*Alondra's passion must be rubbing off on me,* I thought as my mind filled with my team leader's smile and excited mannerisms when discussing her visits to Germany.

If anyone else had asked me to go, I probably would have said no and gone on my way. But Alondra always knew just what to say to get what she wanted out of her subordinates.

My mother was no doubt turning in her grave, knowing that I had volunteered to attend meetings in the "cancerous cesspit of an evil empire," just because my pretty boss had asked me to. But if I was being honest with myself, I *was* the best person to represent the company. I was fluent in both German and French, on top of my mother tongue, and could use this to coordinate and schmooze with members of the Volkswagen family of companies all across the Reich and Federation.

I turned my attention to the windows as the outskirts began to blend into the main metropolitan area of the city. What were once two-story estates now became factories and storage yards. The greys of steel and concrete replaced the greens and browns of the countryside.

After several minutes, I became restless again; travel had never agreed with me, and for once I was thankful for the frugal nature of my company having booked my journey via rail. I had only flown in a jet once—eight years prior, in my early twenties—and I had felt similar to how a person going from a horse and buggy to a race car might feel. In a word, nauseous.

I became bored of the passing buildings and the sight of swastika flags and tuned in to the conversation between the group of ladies sitting across the aisle.

"You haven't seen it?" the biggest of the group asked, her blonde hair tied into an oddly styled bun. "It's the best in the Reich. Simply stunning. While you're here, let me get you tickets. It is something you must see. In fact, I heard the travelling Japanese troop is with them this month. I might go with you just to see their set."

"I've heard good things," the thin blonde said. "I heard the Japs contort their bodies at the end of their segment to form a swastika."

"How thoughtful," the fat one said. "I always like the

Japanese—such nice people; always good guests. Never had any trouble with them or their tourists. They bow and take pictures and are so kind."

"Not like the Americans," the small blonde said. "So rude and arrogant and always in the way."

"Don't forget the British. They are always so *loud*," the brunette said, clearly the youngest of the three. "They are always drunk too."

"Oh, I forgot your town is near the military base. You said there is a lot of cross training there?" the large blonde replied, her doe eyes fixed on the brunette across from her.

"Not *a lot*, really ... but when there is they come into town smelling of booze and they chase anything with breasts," the brunette replied.

The big blonde thinned her lips. "But really, dear, can you blame them? They see a German beauty like you or a true Aryan—a whole town of them? I'm surprised the Brits don't invade on that premise itself."

The thin blonde folded her arms. "I still don't understand why the Führers have allowed the existence of the other empires. Okay, Japan? Sure. America? Fine. But does the New Roman Empire even serve a purpose in today's world?" The other women stayed quiet, prompting her to add, "What did they do in the Great War? Yes, the Africa campaign, but they owe every victory to us."

"Listen to you," the brunette said, chuckling to herself. "You talk as if you were there."

"I wasn't, but my great uncles were. Two died for the Reich and they didn't die so that clown Mussolini and his stupid son could turn that part of the world into a circus."

There was a lull in the conversation, and I was about to lose interest when the big blonde spoke up. "So, Gerda, have you met a suiter yet?"

"No, not yet," the brunette said, one leg crossing over the other. "No one has made me think, *Wow I want to see this person every day*, and I doubt that will happen, to be honest."

The smaller blonde put her hand on the brunette's face. "But think of the children you'll have. You're Aryan enough that by mixing with someone suitable—maybe an SS officer or someone who can show you their blood record—the two of you can make beautiful babies. My niece asked her husband for his blood record when they began getting serious. Lots of girls do it; it isn't weird."

The brunette shrugged. "It's not as popular anymore. Most girls my age don't ask. People don't put much stock in the blood stuff anymore."

"What is this world coming to? I can't believe it," the big blonde said, covering her mouth.

Gerda shrugged, her eyes focused on the big blonde, "It's true, Auntie. But ever since they stopped handing out the Motherhood Medals, what's the point?"

The two women gasped before the bigger blonde snapped, "You don't mean that. A medal shouldn't be the only reason to have children!"

"No, but it helps," Gerda replied, her hand moving through her long hair.

There was a moment when the two older women looked equally uncomfortable before the bigger of the two said, "Still, while I would never talk bad about the Führer, ceasing the medals in his second year was not his most popular policy."

"He certainly isn't his father," the smaller blonde said, before adding, "and neither are what the Great Führer was. Of course, Karl was close."

"Karl had good instructors," the big blonde said, and I could see the brunette was losing interest, just as I was. Her head turned to watch the skyscrapers that whipped by. "Think, to be brought up by Dr. Goebbels or Mr. Bormann The amount of knowledge given to you at such a young age."

"Don't forget Heidie Goebbels," the thin blonde said with a warm smile on her face. "He picked the right woman there. I'm sure she kept him on the right track too."

"You know what they say, behind every strong man is an even stronger woman," Gerda said, and each of the ladies smirked and nodded in agreement at the phrase.

The conversation slowly shifted to what attractions the brunette planned to see while in the capital. She mentioned the Schiller Theater before planning to venture to Austria to see the tomb of the Great Führer. It was this statement that caused me to remember my eighth-grade field trip to the Valley of The Fallen outside of Madrid.

Even as a child I knew there was something wrong about the place.

The air at the site was heavy. The Angel of Death watching over the entrance, the dictator buried deep in the floor, surrounded by bodies of those slain in the Civil War. The church could pretend it was a holy site all they wanted, even holding mass every Sunday to keep up the front, but I knew God had never been there.

While I was sure the tomb of the Führer was a much smaller landmark, it would still be impressive from a stylistic point of view. I had read that Hitler had wanted the designs completed well before his death so he could critique his final resting place. I had heard stories that the man had become obsessed with the project, rejecting plan after plan for the most trivial of details. Perhaps he had thought that by prolonging the construction, he could prolong his life as well.

There was an announcement over the loudspeaker, and while I was fluent in the language, I couldn't understand it due to the subpar system. That was one thing the Reich and Madrid had in common.

The train slowed as we entered a tunnel, and I figured it had announced my final stop. The skyscrapers were replaced with a drab wall of concrete for several moments.

I stood and gathered my bags just as the car filled with light. I looked out the window and saw the domed roof of the train station—the sunlight descending through the thousands of glass panes.

"Did you see the *Volkshalle*?" one of the women asked her companions, and I recognized the voice as belonging to the thin one.

"No, did I miss it?" Gerda asked. "I want to do a tour. Do you think they will have anything available today?"

The remainder of their conversation was interrupted by the voices of other passengers drowning them out as people impatiently pushed for the exit. I took a deep breath, my briefcase in one hand, luggage in the other.

I had finally arrived in Germania.

# Chapter 2

## *The Avenue of Splendors*

Victory Train Station was a matted ball of steel, brickwork and train cars. It was crowded by people who all shunted around seemingly endless platforms toward staircases that connected to suspended walkways that led to the exits.

As I ascended the stairs, I could see a small glass-walled elevator moving up beside me. I looked inside and saw a family dressed like tourists. The group moved out of the elevator with a younger woman pushing the fifth member, a man in his forties, in a wheelchair.

I knew the party's policies on cripples, liking to keep the weak extinct in their endless battle against the imperfections of the human body. They hated crippled Germans, but handicap tourists? Sure, they'd take their money.

As I arrived at the suspended walkway, I took a left and intertwined with the thousands of passing tourists, businessmen and citizens of the Reich. I followed the herd as we walked over train after train below. The engines became larger and larger as the types of transport shifted from the bullet model I had been on to the large creeping hulks that shipped those lucky conscripts to the fortified Ural Mountain region that served as the natural border between the Reich and the Siberian wastes beyond.

Pulling my eyes from a massive red engine, I looked up, seeing evidence of where the roof had been modified to accommodate the domed glass it now sported. I remembered seeing the original flat roof design in a history book, but I guessed in the sixty something years since the station was built, some architect had come along and decided the building needed a facelift.

Stairs and more elevators awaited the hoard at the end of the pathway and directed us all downward into a large room. Through the glass wall I could see the path had snaked us behind an identity checkpoint before bringing us to a series of exit doors.

A group of policemen stood to the side, their sharp uniforms catching my eye. They watched the exit doors closely for anyone who attempted to use them as an entrance. It had been close to a decade since a prominent terrorist attack had occurred anywhere west of Kiev, and with the seventy-year anniversary of the Axis victory looming ahead, law enforcement was bound to feel they were due for one.

The doors opened and the light of the day hit me with all its might. I blinked as I attempted to avoid the hundreds of scurrying people.

As my eyes adjusted, they landed on the jewel of the Reich in all its architectural majesty.

The *Volkshalle*.

The massive domed construction had been created to encapsulate the absolute pinnacle of the Nazi ideology. Towering over everything that dared to stand near it, the structure was a projection of power and a display of their victory over all in the Great War. I had seen the newsreels of well over one hundred thousand fanatical loyalists *Seig Heiling* the Führer, who appeared little more than a speck on the raised ledge high above. The ventilation systems worked overtime to prevent the moisture in the air from all the fervent breaths forming into precipitation.

I must admit, it was an impressive sight. I gripped the handle of my bag, my knuckles whitening, memories of my mother's teachings echoing in my brain.

*It's the same trick they use to capture young children. The allure of power, the crisp uniforms and of course a healthy dose of patriotic duty piled behind a phone book of propaganda.*

Despite my many strides, the *Volkshalle* never seemed to get any closer. As I continued to walk forward, my initial awe began to subside. I could see the faults in the building. Certain sections appeared to be leaning. Various scaffolds on the eastern side had been erected in an attempt to repair the damage caused by the sinking structure.

I could almost hear my mother laughing at what she would have seen as poetic irony.

*Too top heavy for Germania's soft wetland. An ideology sinking under its own weight.*

Taking my eyes off the monstrosity, I turned and gazed at the towering artillery pieces that lined the avenue on either side. While I had been excited to see them before, now that I was in front of the pieces, I recognized them for the antiques they were. The protective shrouds that covered the bases were coated in layers of fresh paint in an attempt to cover the graffiti left behind by bored youths.

I felt the aging artillery pieces represented the whole of Germania and its empire well. They were a projection of force to enemies long gone, destroyed by weapons equally as obsolete.

I kept my face neutral as I passed numerous tourists who posed with the weapons from a war long won.

A young man in his twenties stood with his girlfriend and pointed at the sleeping giants. "These are the actual guns pulled from the Eastern Front. Some of them were even deployed for the Archangel offensive." He nodded in a self-congratulatory way for being able to regurgitate the reported history he had read in the *Encyclopedia Germanica*.

"Oh," his girlfriend said, her eyes moving past the guns and up to the sky, where a flock of birds moved farther up the avenue.

"And do you know which Field Marshall was in charge of the assault?" the man asked, his arm sliding over her shoulder. He could hardly keep himself from spoiling the answer.

I walked out of earshot before I could hear if she had gotten the question correct. It mattered little to me. I cared not which so-called "hero" was responsible for one of the last offenses of the war.

I moved into the shadow of the Triumph Arch and marvelled at the sight of it. I had seen the French arch in Paris, and this put it to shame. As I walked through the arch, I could see small, almost invisible etchings in the stone: the name of every German who had been killed in the First Great War. I could almost remember word-for-word the way my teacher described it:

*"A war the Reich, by all accounts, should have won."*

As I exited the arch, I grew tired of pulling my suitcase behind me, knowing that I still had a great deal of walking to do before I reached the end of the avenue. Far ahead I could just about make out the grand plaza that housed the most prestigious buildings of the Reich. I visualized the Reich Chancellery and Army Headquarters flanking the entranceway of the plaza, standing guard for the Führer's Palace, whose façade frowned upon the Reichstag to the east.

I looked at my watch and saw that it was approaching four in the afternoon. While the notion of seeing the changing of the guard was an enticing thought, I didn't want to walk several more kilometres to reach it.

I turned left and passed a group of tourists who were pointing to a collection of buildings to the west. Upon reaching the road, I hailed a cab. A black Audi pulled up to the curb and I greeted the driver upon entering.

As I settled into the seat he asked, "Where to?"

"The Adlon, please."

The driver tapped the meter and replied, "Nice place. Is it your first time in the city?"

I narrowed my eyes, recalling that Germans weren't known for their small talk. His accent sounded proper enough, but I detected a hint of Italian in his facial features.

"Yes," I said, patting my suitcase to ensure it was still beside me. "Beautiful city." I wasn't sure what compelled me to say that.

"Want to take the scenic route?"

"No, the direct route is fine."

The driver took off down the street and gestured to the left. He appeared to hesitate before finally committing to his train of thought and saying, "Something Germania does differently is the lack of crosswalks and stop lights in many areas of the city. Speer hated them."

"Speer? Who's Speer?"

The driver's hairy arm came across the headrest of the passenger seat so he could glance back at me for a moment before his eyes returned to the road. "The head architect who designed the whole city, of course."

I stayed silent, knowing the statement to be ridiculous. One man couldn't design everything. A project of this scale would involve hundreds of architects.

The driver then pointed somewhere else, but I didn't bother to follow his finger. "And then there are the below-ground roads and pedestrian crossings. That was Speer's way around the lack of lights for a while. Didn't last too long though; caused too much confusion, making it impossible to get anywhere once the city really started to grow, and if there was an accident in one of the subterranean roads"—he threw up a hand in vague frustration—"half the city couldn't get to the other half through the traffic."

"When did they add the stop lights?"

"The sixties, I think. The Great Führer was dead, I know that. And Speer was off the project by that time, well into retirement. Still, some parts of the city, like this one, still have no lights. The farther you get from the *Volkshalle,* the more frequent they become."

Seeing the entrance to an underground walkway, I asked, "Aren't those paths dangerous? Especially at night?"

"Yeah, young women never go into one alone." The driver shrugged, his hairy mitt of a hand rubbing the material of the seat. "They were different times when they built them. People were civil; the police had more of a respected presence. Now? Well, I don't know."

The conversation faded and I continued to look out the window. Building after building passed by and I began to feel the white marble closing in around me.

It was suffocating.

# Chapter 3

## *A Night at the Adlon*

I exited the taxi and walked through the rotating glass door. The hotel lobby was heavy on the crystal but light on the gold.

I looked to my right and saw a group of police officers sitting near the fireplace to the right of the foyer. The group laughed jovially as one of them concluded a joke. My eyes shifted to the left as a *Wehrmacht* officer, wearing the insignia of military police, approached the group, clipboard in hand. He placed his hand on the shoulder of one of the seated officers before proceeding to whisper something into his ear.

I turned my attention to the ceiling, noting the intricate plaster work before it gave way to an exquisite chandelier that looked to have been liberated from the Palace of Versailles. I was aware that the hotel had at one time been considered the finest in Germania and how many Reichsmarks it would cost to stay here, even for a single night. Alondra's words came to me from memory:

*"The company frequently gets deals on rooms. You'll love it."*

I walked toward the reception desk as a soft-voiced hotel employee behind the counter asked, "May I help you, sir?"

I detected an Austrian undertone to her German.

"Yes," I said, before clearing my throat. "Checking in, please."

"Excellent." She looked down at her black book, flipping the page over as she said, "ID please."

I handed over my driver's licence. She took it, holding the card under a UV lamp to check the security features. Her brow furrowed. Having encountered a similar problem at the immigration checkpoint at Saarbrücken, I said, "It's a Spanish document. Not as many security features."

She looked at the card for a moment more before ensuring my face matched the picture, then quickly let out a quiet laugh. "That would be it." She leaned forward in the chair, saying, "You know, I thought I picked up a slight accent, but your German is quite good."

She began to jot down the information into the book before adding, "Other than Spain, only the British Empire have yet to adopt the recommended security measures."

While the receptionist was simply making small talk and not seeking a reply, my mind spun an answer all the same.

*Behind the times as always, that's the legacy of Franco's Spain for you. As for the Brits? Just stubborn to change, I think.*

The receptionist proceeded to check the roster of rooms, finding my name. "Okay, Mr. Domínguez, I see you are staying with us for two nights. Are you part of the police convention by chance?"

As I shook my head no, she added, "Oh, okay. It seems like everyone is in town for that." She looked over a piece of paper to her right, and as her finger found my name once more, she nodded to herself. "Oh yes, Volkswagen Spain. Excellent, your bill will be mailed to the head office, so no need for a deposit."

She looked up, scratching her cheek as she added, "Will you need help with your bags?"

I lifted my briefcase while looking at my luggage behind me. "I'll manage."

The receptionist grabbed a key from the wall behind her. "Room four-fifteen. Grand view of the city," she said, sliding the brass key across the desk.

I nodded in thanks as I pocketed the key. I moved around the reception area and over to the hallway where a trio of elevators stood before me. I pressed the elevator button and waited, listening to the soft chimes of the elevators going between floors. The sound of a piano playing from the dining room caught my ear.

*Fancy place,* I thought, before smiling at a German-looking woman who passed by in an elegant dress, ignoring me completely.

I heard the door of the elevator to my left opening and moved toward it. I was about to enter when I saw a group of people, all of which were of African descent. Two wore blazers and earpieces, the butt of their handguns visible inside their underarm holsters. These two men stood in front of an older gentleman who wore a much more expressive suit, the pin on his lapel showing the colours and outline of an African nation with a black Swastika overtop of it. I wasn't familiar with the country itself, but it mattered little; the pin had done its job identifying the man.

Beside him was a woman who was much younger than her paramour. I estimated her to be on the cusp of her thirties, and she was visibly pregnant. Her expensive jewelry eventually drew my attention up to her neckline.

One of the bodyguards went to say something, but the gentleman behind him said, "Let him on," in perfect German.

The bodyguard nodded before making more uneasy eye contact with me and asking, "Going up?"

I stepped in, mumbling something in vague agreement. I pressed the button for the fourth floor. I could see the option for the penthouse was selected and this helped finalize my suspicions. The man must have been a politician from the Reich-controlled zone of Africa, for it wouldn't be possible for him to afford such luxuries without it.

I had seen Africans before, but they were few and far between. I also knew that these two guards likely represented only a fraction of the security detail at his disposal while he toured the Greater Germanic Reich. The remainder of his entourage were most likely in the underground parking garage, standing watch over their armoured limousine, cigarettes dangling from their mouths. No telling what nearly a century of propaganda and delusional rhetoric would cause people to do, if they saw him and his family out alone on the streets, even if he was a sympathiser and on official Reich business.

The elevator stopped at my floor, and I exited. I thought of wishing the man a good trip, but the idea of meeting the wild eyes of his bodyguards told me to keep my head forward and comments to myself.

I walked down the hall, the rumbling of the elevator doors closing behind me. A serving tray, littered with the remnants of lunch, sat outside the door of a suite midway down the hall. As I walked past the scrapings of food, the sound of buzzing flies entered my ears. I was a little disappointed that the staff at the world-famous Adlon hadn't bothered to remove the trash.

I continued on, pulling the key from my pocket in preparation. As I passed another door, I could hear the sounds of a woman moaning in a Slavic dialect. Either someone had used false identification to smuggle her out of the Eastern Commissariats, or someone high up in the party had a Slavic bride and paid off anyone who asked about her origins. I figured it was the latter and found it humorous that some high-up official had a fetish for the type of girl that could get them expelled from the party.

My keys found the lock just as the moaning morphed into a stream of Slavic profanity. I opened the door and switched on the light. My room was quite elegant, with golden wallpaper and red curtains. The wood finishing served as an attempt to create a sense of nostalgia for the hotel as it had been during the reign of the Great Führer, but I could tell it was not original.

The TV was large, and the bed looked soft and welcoming. Still, my eyes lingered on the cracked plaster on the ceiling, which looked like it had been in that state for several years. I knew I would find nothing as grand in Madrid, but I suppose I had expected more.

I looked to the bed and the duvet, the design of which would have been considered quaint thirty years ago, and thought about taking a nap, as I was weary from the journey. I moved to the window, my hand pushing aside the curtain as I looked out to the city beyond. From where I stood, I could truly see how much the *Volkshalle* was beginning to lean.

I could hear sirens in the distance coming from somewhere in the heart of the concrete jungle.

My eyes drifted down and to the left. Next to the entrance to an underground walkway was a tattered individual lighting a spoon with a lighter, his back pressed to the wall.

*Disgusting,* I thought, and if I was being honest, I wasn't sure if I was directing the hate toward the drug habit or the knowledge that local law enforcement hadn't removed this individual yet.

As if I had summoned them, a police cruiser turned the corner and drove past the entrance to the walkway. Their speed was not excessive, and if they had been paying attention, they would have seen the drug-addled mess of a man plain as day. Perhaps they had seen him but didn't want to do the paperwork.

As the police car disappeared from view, I thought about how far removed from reality the images of the clean streets and safe cities I remembered from my childhood were.

I found myself shaking my head at the laziness of these officers and watched as the man ceased lighting the spoon. He pulled a syringe from his pocket, and I grimaced.

*In a world where addicts are given the death penalty, people still let themselves get to that level.*

I closed the curtain, letting the world capital exist as it was outside, the thin layer of fabric offering me a small sense of security that Germania had, so far, failed to provide.

I retreated to the bed and removed my suit, hanging it in the closet before changing into more comfortable attire.

As I sat on the edge of the bed I thought, *I miss Spain.*

---

The air was cold around me, and I was a child once again.

Karl Hitler, son of the Great Führer, was dead. His funeral procession was on the television, and I knew I was dreaming. I had to be, as I had been in my late teens during the original broadcast.

"Good riddance," my mother said, her arm extended toward the ashtray, the smoldering ruin of a cigarette long smoked hanging between her fingers. It was the very thing that would kill her not even six years later.

I felt delighted to see her again, even though I knew she was nothing but a memory.

I looked at her, noting how alive and full of life she appeared—a stark contrast to my last memories of her. I had been afraid to hug her near the end, the fear that she would snap in my arms an all too real paranoia. The bandana around her head was absent as well, and her flowing brunette hair was as vibrant as I had ever seen it.

I turned back to the TV, realizing now that the broadcast was in black and white. I did not question this and kept the dream alive, maintaining my role as a passive observer as the swastika-draped coffin was loaded into the back of the hearse.

An era had ended.

I felt the dismay of the people, the tears being shed, the line of veterans that saluted as the vehicle left the Führer's palace and headed down the Avenue of Splendors.

It was said that the Führer worked tirelessly until his last day, even attempting to dictate letters from his death bed, though his stomach was riddled with ulcers.

I remembered thinking at the time: *He worked himself to death, and for what? He is dead, the orders and file work left to be completed by someone else.*

The camera panned to the three children of the Führer, who were positioned on the balcony at the front of the palace where their grandfather had stood so many times. The echoes of his speeches still reverberated through the halls of history.

"Someone should just shoot them all," my mother said. "Save the world a whole lot of trouble." I knew the sour face she was making, for she made it any time someone dared to discuss the Reich in her general vicinity.

"You shouldn't say those things, Mom," my brother Ernesto said as he entered the room, wearing his school uniform.

I remembered then that the school had dismissed the students early, as so many teachers were distraught by the Führer's untimely death and wished to watch the procession in a self-imposed exile.

On the broadcast, Otto, the oldest of the Führer's children, stood between his siblings. He looked depressed and terrified by the heap of responsibility that was hurtling toward him. The camera stayed on him, showing that he was struggling to hold back tears. The loss of the Führer had affected the nation and even more so the entire National Socialist Federation in a way it may never recover from. If even someone as strong as Otto, the heir, was crying, then surely you, the citizens of the Reich, were allowed to weep as well. In truth, it was encouraged.

The camera zoomed out once more, to reinforce that the other siblings stood on either side of their brother. The trio of siblings standing tall, shoulder to shoulder in their pristine party uniforms. The minister of propaganda had her money shot.

I looked to Magda, the second oldest, and could see a fire in her eyes. A determination for a future knowable only to her. As she stood tall above the masses who watched her father head for that cold hole in the ground, she looked almost pleased.

Her stare turned and she beamed directly into the camera. Looking at me.

The television was no longer there, only Magda and those black beads that served as her eyes. Always watching...

I awoke in a sweat.

My eyes scanned the ceiling as the dream melted away, my heart thundering in my chest, the alarm clock sending out a dull chime from the end table beside me. I rolled over and saw that I had been sleeping through its soft call for several minutes.

*I should have turned it up louder*, I thought, perturbed by how quiet the alarm had been.

I arose, blinking again. The image of Magda still lingered, but the details were quickly becoming lost as the seconds eroded the shaky memory. I got up and headed to the bathroom, running the tap and splashing water on my face before looking at myself in the mirror. I fixated on my brown eyes, but I could only see Magda behind them, peering out from somewhere in my subconscious. She looked the most like her grandfather.

I showered and dressed, trying to keep my mind on the meeting and the various discussion points I had prepared. I knew I would have no time for the lazy morning that I originally planned. I would be late for my meeting if I didn't pick up the pace to make up for my oversleeping.

I ventured downstairs, and after the receptionist pointed in the direction of the dining room, I took a seat and ordered a small breakfast of eggs, sausages, toast and a coffee. I smiled at the server as she presented the bill, but internally was agape at the price of such a pedestrian offering of food. I tucked the remaining Reichsmarks into the black leather holder before returning to my room.

I freshened up and grabbed my briefcase. Checking my wristwatch, I noted that the meeting started in half an hour. I knew I wasn't far, but would still have to hail a taxi.

I returned to the lobby in a hurry, and as I moved through the rotating door, the attendant smiled at me. The seams on his crisp green uniform were perfectly pressed. "Taxi, sir?"

"Yes, please," I said, out of breath and feeling sweat begin to slick my back.

"Right away." The man nodded before stepping out to the curb and raising a gloved hand.

He watched as one taxi sped by before a second one proceeded to do the same. I moved closer, hoping this would probe him to be more aggressive.

"Busy day," the doorman said before moving out into the first lane of traffic.

I could see the Brandenburg Gate was lit up in a shade of orange by the early morning sunlight. I turned my attention back to the attendant and watched as he waved to an unseen vehicle before stepping back. A black taxicab pulled to the curb in front of me.

"Help with your bag—" the doorman began.

"No. I'm fine, thank you." I reached into my wallet and handed the man a ten Reichsmark bill. He took it with a courteous bow, but I noticed the hesitation.

As I entered the taxi, it dawned on me that while in Madrid that amount would have been a sizable tip for something so simple, here in Germania I might as well have insulted the man's mother.

I sighed. *Another reason to hate this city.*

The attendant shut my door with a delicate touch, prompting the driver to switch his indicator to the opposite direction.

"Volkswagen Headquarters," I said. "It's on Ganz *Straße*—"

"Yes, I know where it is," the driver said before putting the taxi in gear.

I came to appreciate this driver as he weaved in and out of traffic. Perhaps he had seen me tip the doorman and pegged me for who I was: a tourist in a big city that I had no business being in.

# Chapter 4

## *History is Curated by the Victors*

The meeting ended just before four o'clock. As I walked down the congested street, I reflected on how the vice presidents spoke with the representatives from the Eastern Commissariats, harping on the same points over and over. They considered the *Lebensnetz* to be little more than a fleeting fad, something that would come and go with little fanfare, hardly impacting the methods of how we conducted business. Due to their position of power, everyone else blindly agreed with them. Only the French representative and I felt differently.

I looked at my watch, cognizant of the time and knowing that if I wanted to achieve my goal and visit the Museum of the Great Wars, it would have to be soon. I thought of taking a taxi back to the hotel to change and drop off my briefcase, but by that time I would be hard-pressed to fit in the museum and eat something before I had to meet my brother at the beer hall like we had arranged. Not to mention the cost of the fare.

I knew the museum was closer to me now than the hotel, so I decided I would walk. Doing so would also give me a chance to take in more of the world capital's atmosphere.

As I walked, I realized that while the sites were impressive, the smells certainly were not. Everything reeked of emissions, and every alley stunk of urine. I was in the real Germania now; there was no reason for a tourist to be walking through this area.

I felt like my mother's shadow lingered over me as one of her opinions pierced my frontal lobe.

*You're witnessing the reality that is the third generation of National Socialism. Dirty, oil-laden and covered in a thick film of grime.*

I arrived at the bridge that connected to the famous "Museum Island" and crossed over, taking a moment to appreciate the clear water that flowed lazily below me. I took in the view of the Egyptian museum off in the distance, and while I felt a ping of excitement at the idea of entering it, I knew it would be a waste, as I had seen my fair share of Egyptian exhibits in both Madrid and Paris.

I followed behind a group of children in their *Jungvolk* outfits. The boys jumped up and down with excitement, ready to conquer any destination their *Gruppenführer* of a father led them to.

Groups of tourists passed by as they headed in the opposite direction, each speaking of the various museums or architectural marvels. I heard several people speaking Spanish, but their accent was so far removed from my own that it sounded like a different language. I figured they were from somewhere within the American sphere of influence and continued on.

I moved down the street, becoming aware of just how immaculate the cobblestone avenues had become once again. The only piece of trash came from the page of a newspaper that the wind had stolen from someone's hand. The paper moved across the street and tumbled out of sight into a crowd of tourists, their cameras capturing the facades of the various museums.

I arrived at the Museum of the Great Wars a little after four o'clock and noticed there was no line to enter. All the black stanchions were empty, a path through them leading directly to the entrance door. I could see cannons were mounted on the corners of the roof and respected the design choice.

"Is this your first time at the museum, sir?" the eager attendant behind the glass asked as I entered the building, approaching the ticket booth.

"Yes," I replied, a touch of excitement in my voice as I started to anticipate all the history contained within its walls.

The man's face soured, but he nodded all the same. "Well, sir, I must suggest that you come back tomorrow as we close in less than an hour. You could never see all the great pieces and exhibits that the museum has to offer in such a short allotment of time. I recommend at least two hours at the minimum for a first-time visit." He paused, his face returning to a more pleasant expression. "To come today would be a waste of money."

"I can't come tomorrow. This is the only day I can see it," I said, annoyed.

"Are you sure?" the employee asked, his voice sounding as if he was nearly pleading. "Perhaps before your flight or?"

"Yes, I'm sure." I bit my tongue, holding back that my train would be departing just after the museum would be opening tomorrow.

The employee opened the till and added the Reichsmarks I had handed him to the stack. He gestured for me to extend my hand, and as I did, he stamped the back of my palm. "Enjoy your visit," he said, his exasperation clear as he pointed vaguely toward the right, where a golden-trussed entrance awaited me.

I passed a security guard and showed him my stamp. As I moved around him, I looked at the ink, seeing that it was a picture of the exterior of the building. I peeled my eyes from my brand and stepped forward. My eyes immediately focused on the enormous eagle that hung from the skylights above, sunlight shining down upon the reef and swastika in its clutches.

My attention was brought from the towering bird of prey to a group of patrons exiting the exhibits from the left side of the foyer. Each babbled to one another about their impressions while a pair of children scurried under the stanchions toward a small exhibit that guarded the entrance. A relic of the Great War, a halftrack draped in the *Wehrmacht* flag.

"Yes, you two saw that on the way in," one of the mothers said before turning her attention back to her husband, who was going on about the Japanese victory over the Soviets at the battle of Khalkhin Gol and why the curriculum should spend more time on it.

A voice from the ticket counter caused me to look back.

"What do you mean it closes at five?" a woman said. Her German was good, but I noted the French undertones. She was tall, with thick brunette hair that hung down to the centre of her back. She wore a tight black dress and ankle-high boots, and a small black purse hung from her shoulder.

"It closes at five, *Fräulein*," the employee said, his voice taking on a more hostile edge than he had with me.

"I didn't know everyone in the world capital closes up shop at five. I thought this was the city that never sleeps."

"No, that would be New York."

"Just another way the Americans are more efficient than the Germans, I'm afraid." She sounded almost disappointed in the Reich.

"Are you coming in or not?"

"Yes, I suppose so." An air of tiredness clung to her words as she reached into her bag and collected a wad of Reichsmarks before passing them over to the red-faced employee.

I turned forward to avoid her notice that I had been staring, instead pretending to gaze up at the eagle in all its might. The woman passed by me a few moments later.

"Oh, another eagle—how original," she muttered, her hand burrowing into her purse to produce a maroon-coloured lipstick and small pocket mirror.

"I liked your city that never sleeps comment," I said, watching her as she applied the lipstick.

She examined herself quickly before folding the mirror and returning it to her bag. "Thanks. That's the thing with the Germans: confuse something of theirs with America and you'll get great service." She strolled forward, ignoring the halftrack exhibit and walking straight into the first room.

"How do you know *I'm* not German?" I asked, struggling to keep up with her.

A sliver of a smile appeared at the corner of her mouth. She gave me a once over before saying, "Oh dear, you're not German." She sounded hurt that I had even asked.

We walked past the exhibit that was dedicated to Charlemagne and the Holy Roman Empire. I remembered from classes that the party considered this to be the First Reich.

The woman looked at a display case of lances before turning and giving the same bored expression toward the armoured mannequins. "I've seen this. Just like the ones at..." she trailed off, seeming to slow her step as if waiting for me to catch up. As I followed, I heard her mumble in French, "God I would kill the Führer's dog for a smoke."

"Filthy habit, you know," I replied in her mother tongue.

She turned, a genuine smile on her face this time. "Your

French accent is better than your German." She gave me another once over.

"My Spanish is even better," I said, still speaking French.

"Oh, that's what you are. I was going to guess Greek, but..." She tilted her head before breaking into Spanish, "I see it now. What part? Valencia?"

"Madrid, actually."

"Oh, yes. I went to school there for a little bit."

I gave a face to show that I was impressed, both by her schooling choice and her pronunciation of the words.

"Which program?" I asked as we moved past a series of maps that depicted the expanding empire. A collection of gold plaques hung underneath with black stencils upon them signifying the year they represented.

"Painting. I always admired Spanish art. I didn't take it for long though before I had to move back to Paris. My father's um, how should I say it? His *nagging* got the better of me." She paused. "I guess I could have said *bitching*. That might have been a better word." She laughed before turning to me. "You know, if we are going to keep up with the small talk I should know your name."

"Eduardo," I said after a momentary pause where I forgot my own name. While less than a second had passed, to me it felt like an eternity.

"Meriam," she replied simply, then walked forward, heading toward the section of the room dedicated to the Seven Years War.

She ignored the Prussian equipment, instead stopping to gaze at the Napoleonic era French uniforms displayed. Her eyes drifted to a trio of cannons, each from a different faction. She stood there for a moment before pivoting and walking toward the exit of the exhibit.

I took two long strides to catch up to her and said, "You seem bored being here, or is that just me?"

"Oh, sorry. This is my third museum today; I guess I'm over it. But..." She trailed off as we entered the hall dedicated to the First Great War, her eyes lingering on the artillery pieces that pointed toward the ceiling to the left of us. "What was I saying?" she asked vaguely, studying the wall-sized map. Her eyes appeared to study the French lines.

"You were saying you were bored because it's your third—"

"Oh, yes. Bored of the Prussian stuff, anyway. A lot of similar pieces in the Germanic Museum. But this *this* is why I came."

She walked onward slowly, her eyes moving past the various racks of rifles, early grenade prototypes and bayonets before stopping at a display case showing a vintage French soldier's uniform.

"My great grandfather died in the battle of the Somme. I try to see any museum that has French pieces in it. Makes me feel closer to him. I never met him, of course, but I heard a lot about him."

I stayed silent, not sure what to say. We walked on. She moved with a deliberate pace, studying the German uniforms before turning to face the other side of the room and taking in the machine gun position that sat behind various sandbags and mock barbed wire.

"Imagine the war if both those inventions hadn't come to be," Meriam said, her eyes going to the floor before moving on.

We spent some time looking at the few pieces of British equipment as well as a display of helmets from ten different nations in the conflict, the German ones having the central spot.

We reached the end of the building and took a left to enter the next section of the museum. An archway overhead informed us we were entering "The Hall of the Second Great War."

Seeing this, Meriam muttered, "Nothing great about it."

The first room was dedicated to several small exhibits depicting the invasions of Poland, Denmark and Norway. Maps behind the equipment and uniforms showed the ever-increasing land mass of the Reich in black. Meriam walked through without a second glance. She mumbled something, but I did not catch what she said.

As we entered the next room Meriam beelined toward the area dedicated to the Invasion of Belgium and France. She read over the plaques with intensity. I left her alone to read as I studied the French weapons. That was until my eyes landed on the train car to the right side of the room. I approached it, knowing full well what it was.

The very train car where France had signed their surrender.

My eyes moved over the contours of the carriage, and I was amazed by just how much history could be contained in such a thing. My mind flickered with pages of text I had read in school. Germany's surrender in the First Great War had been in a train car, and Hitler, in an act of unrivalled pettiness, had his people bring the same carriage for the French representatives to surrender in.

In front of the display was a plaque that explained this with a note at the bottom that I read quietly to myself: "Originally housed in the Soldiers Hall of the Army High Command complex until 1974 when, by order of the Führer, Karl Hitler, the train car was moved to this spot, allowing more citizens of the Reich and elsewhere to view such a powerful piece of history."

"No mention of the French forces that continued to fight

on after the surrender order, I see," Meriam said from beside me.

I didn't show it, but she had startled me.

"I've never heard of that," I replied, shifting my gaze to look into her brown eyes.

"Of course not," she said, sounding unsurprised. "Many French soldiers kept fighting against the Italians. We may have been beaten by the Germans—we could handle that—but the Italians..." She grimaced before walking on, adding, "The Germans had to bail them out that time too."

We moved on. Meriam was taking everything in, and I could tell she was becoming depressed.

*It's interesting that the same items rouse nationalistic pride in some people and sadness in others,* I thought as I walked behind her.

As we left the room Meriam said, "We should have fought harder."

The next room smelled of oil and lubricant and I could see it had been designed to house the vehicles of the conflict. The wall to the right contained numerous bay doors, allowing the vehicles to be paraded on the streets for the most special of holidays.

The enormous hall contained captured British and French tanks on the left side of the room, with the German and Italian weapons of war on the right. The vehicles pointed their barrels at each other, locked in an endless standoff. I looked at the plaques that listed the dates of service, notable battles and various specifications.

Further on, a large photo of Field Marshal Rommel hung above the four German vehicles, dedicated to the Africa theater of war. His eyes focused forward, appearing to study the anti-tank piece pointed at his amour, an Australian flag that had been captured during the victory of El Alamein was draped behind the weapon.

We exited the room soon after, leaving Rommel to smell the remnants of diesel fuel for eternity. I suspected that deep down it would have killed the man to know that the remnants of his great Panzer legions were stuck in a garage in the capital, forced to grow old and obsolete.

The next area contained more vehicles, and I could see these were pulled from the Eastern Front. I was tempted to reach out and touch the contours of the mighty Tiger tank that sat behind a loose red rope, but I held my hand back and instead marvelled at such a massive piece of machinery.

The large sign in front described that this specific tank participated in the battle of Kuybyshev, citing a dozen confirmed Russian T-34 kills. I knew that this battle in particular had been important as Hitler had thought they would be able to capture Stalin there, but the Soviet dictator had escaped into the Ural Mountains during the battle, similar to how he had fled Moscow some months prior.

We moved on and I could tell Meriam cared little about the Eastern Front, however it was my turn to linger. I passed a massive shrine dedicated to the two battles of Moscow as well as the furious fighting in Kiev. While Meriam paused to read about the sieges of both Leningrad and Stalingrad, I used this opportunity to head to the right side of the room. I passed an exhibit devoted to the Caucus oil fields and studied the troves of information dedicated to the battle of the Ural Mountains.

The number of men and equipment stated by the plaques to be involved were absolutely staggering. I moved on after several minutes of reading and looked over my shoulder to see Meriam was admiring a captured Soviet flag that was said to have been found in Stalin's empty bunker.

A wall mounted mural showed the various air assaults that

smashed the area past the Urals into submission. Photographs and models of the planes used as well as deactivated bombs sat on stands nearby. I had heard that one of Hermann Göring's properties had been turned into a museum of its own and that he had several planes from various eras in a hanger adjacent to the mansion. I thought it would be interesting to see someday.

Meriam had already exited the room by the time I noticed she was gone. I took one last look around before moving on and saw she had sped through the next area, which was dedicated to the battle in the Atlantic and the victory there. A small section was devoted to the recalling of the U-boat fleet and the implantation of new code systems after the enigma machines were compromised. These new codes stumped the allies, leading to their inevitable defeat.

Toward the end of the room a moderate-sized exhibit showed the renewed bombing blitz of the United Kingdom in mid-1944. Several photos of the English surrender in November of the same year marked the official end of the war. The exhibit concluded with the famous photo of Hitler standing in front of Big Ben shortly after attending the Coronation of Edward VIII.

Meriam sauntered into the adjacent section, and I took that as my cue to leave. The next area was dedicated to the post-war conflict against the remnant Soviet forces in the eastern wastes. A large exhibit was full of captured Siberian Free Corps memorabilia dating from the 1950s.

As I moved closer to listen to an overhead television explaining the fighting to subdue the continued resistance movements past the Ural Mountains, a guard strolled in from the foyer and said, "The Museum is closed, sir. Please proceed to the exit."

I nodded with a soft smile, prompting the guard to move on. I heard him say the same thing to Meriam, but she didn't reply, instead walking toward the exit with a deliberate pace. As I followed her out of the exhibit, I felt a sense of satisfaction that despite the ticket agent's assurances to the contrary, I had managed to see everything worth seeing inside the museum in under fifty minutes.

I moved out of the way as a group of people muttered in Italian to each other. Judging by the little bit I could pick up, they hadn't liked that they had been asked to leave while inspecting the Africa Corps exhibit. No doubt they would continue to talk about their hurt pride at the hotel bar over a bottle of French wine.

As I entered the lobby, I could see Meriam standing, arms folded, waiting for me. A woman in a cream-coloured uniform approached her and said something, but Meriam waved her away. Unphased, the woman approached me, extending a small piece of paper in front of her. Without thinking, I accepted it. The paper had hardly touched my fingers as she said, "Please fill out our survey to tell us what you liked."

I stayed silent and moved toward Meriam. I could see a group of people hunched over a chest-high ledge, scribbling away on their identical pieces of paper. A wooden box sat next to a small tin of pencils toward the head of the ledge.

I looked down at the ballot and read over each question. Seeing the disgust in Meriam's eyes, I scrunched the ballot in my fist and lobbed it with delight into a nearby trash can. I stopped at the coat check and picked up my jacket and briefcase. Placing my jacket over my arm, I walked outside to see Meriam standing at the bottom of the steps.

"How did that one compare to the other two on your trek today?" I asked, my eyes adjusting to the sunlight.

Meriam lit a cigarette before crossing her right arm under the other to support her elbow.

"It was okay. I just wish it turned out differently for the

French." She paused, her eyes darting across my face. She chuckled, taking a drag of her cigarette before saying, "Sorry, that's not what you asked."

"No, but that's okay."

"I would say it was better than the Etymology Museum, less impressive than the Germania Museum." Seeing my contemplative face she said, "I don't mind when the Germans are proud of their history, just not when it's at the expense of other cultures."

"Like the French."

She took another drag of her cigarette. "Like the French."

We stood in silence for a moment and watched the cars pass by.

"How was the Führer room?" I asked for the sake of conversation, since she had mentioned the Germania Museum. "I've heard good things."

"Eh? You've seen one photo of old Adolf, you've seen them all. But the brush work on Karl is as good as they say." She continued to smoke for a moment before adding, "I'm sorry I walked through there so fast just now. I could tell you were excited to see the stuff in there. I know we skipped some exhibits."

I shrugged. "It's okay, we ended just on time, so it worked out." I omitted that I had seen the tanks and that was the main topic of my interest anyway.

I looked at the time, and seeing that it was a little after five, I knew I needed to depart if I was going to be able to eat before seeing my brother. I contemplated inviting Meriam to dinner, but seeing how perturbed she looked about the exhibits inside, I figured she would want to be left alone.

"I best be going," I said. "I have plans with my brother."

"Oh, sounds fun," she said, snuffing out her cigarette on the sidewalk under her boot. "What district?"

"He said to meet him at Hindenburg's Beer Hall. So, wherever that is."

Meriam shook her head. "I don't know it. I don't think it's a touristy place."

"Knowing my brother, it's probably a little run down," I replied with a laugh. As Meriam adjusted her bag, I added, "I make regular trips to Paris. If you give me your number ... maybe I can see you again some time?"

"Eduardo, are you asking me out?" Meriam's face brightened. "I would like that." She pulled out a pen. As she looked for something to write on, she said, "Give me your number; I'll write it on my hand."

I gave her my phone number and watched as she scribbled down the digits on her palm. I must admit I had always been the one writing down women's phone numbers, but I was open to this reversal.

Putting the cap back onto the pen she smiled, saying in Spanish, "There, see you around."

She pivoted and I watched as she moved down the street in the direction of the Museum of Asian History.

I knew I was less than two kilometres away from the hotel and decided to walk it. The thought of paying for a taxi for such a short distance brought a pain to my wallet. Still, I chanced another look at Meriam as she walked away. I looked forward to her call. I just hoped she would transfer the number to a piece of stationary before my digits got washed down the drain and our meeting faded to memory.

# Chapter 5

## *A Clash of Ideologies*

The sirens wailing from the next block over made me question why I had agreed to meet my brother in the first place. I watched as the taxi disappeared around a corner, and with it, my final connection to the hotel, leaving me stranded in the underbelly of Germania.

I looked up at the sign over the weathered door to ensure I was in the correct spot. The red lettering on the suspended sign informed me that I was standing in front of THE WORLD FAMOUS HINDENBURG'S

I wasn't sure what world this establishment was famous in, because it certainly wasn't this one. The sound of a smashing bottle from the alley nearby gave me my invitation to get off the street.

I entered the beer hall and took a seat at the bar, noticing the dust collecting on the golden swastika behind the aging bartender. I knew if old Adolf was still alive that totem would have been spotless, but then again, the fervor behind ideologies often become weaker the farther they are from their passionate creators.

After ordering a beer that I recognized on draft, I looked up at the three TVs behind the bar. One was blank, looking as if it hadn't worked in a while, and the other two were broadcasting a static-laden football game. I did not know either team.

A booming laugh tuned me in to the conversation of two men beside me. Their haircuts and pant legs tucked into weathered black jackboots told me everything I needed to know about their political leanings.

"But why even go, is what I'm saying," the man furthest from me said.

"To show the world that we are still something to respect. To show the other empires we still have our balls," the man with his back to me replied.

"But all the Reichsmarks it's costing, and for what? They would be better spending it here, where it would actually do some good." He paused, sipping the remnants of his drink. "If the party asked me, what would I rather: ten-thousand tanks and ten-thousand planes or one moon landing, I would take the tanks and planes."

The man next to me scoffed. He adjusted his arm, and I could see his bicep was clad in a half dozen tattoos of nazi loyalty, the ink broadcasting stolen ideas from superior cultures long in the ground.

"We are talking about the last frontier; the moon is just a gateway to it. The start of a system-spanning Reich. The first in human history. The beginning of a new era." He balled his hand into a fist. "This is science fiction-level of stuff here, hundreds of years before it should be happening." He paused to take a sip from his stein, lifting it with too much gusto and causing several drops of beer to be spilled onto his chin. "If I was the Führer, I would load the Von Brauns with enough explosives to blow a swastika onto the face of the moon. Then every time humanity looked up, we could remember that peace did exist in our time, and this is a testament of it!"

The first man motioned for the barman to bring him another draft before he retorted, "What are you on about? Hundreds of years before what?"

The man closest to me drove his finger into the table, "I've thought a lot about it and we, as a species, are living the best possible timeline. We are hundreds of years ahead. The Great Wars were a turning point, not just for Germany but for the world. If we would have lost and the Bolsheviks were allowed to prosper, we would have entered another dark age like what happened after the fall of Rome." He nodded in self-assurance before adding, "But with our victory, we proved our ideology was superior to all others. We have finally caught the world up, made up for the lost time after the Roman Empire was raped."

"You're repeating yourself," the friend said as he handed the bartender a twenty Reichsmark bill and took his fresh beer with a quiet nod.

"Well, I would hope so ... it's an important point."

"You're drunk," the first man said, looking at the barman who was wiping down the counter a metre away. "Another drink for my friend."

I felt a hand on my shoulder and turned to see my brother standing over me. "Big brother!" he announced with excitement. "You've made it."

Ernesto's hair was dyed blond and his eyes, clad in blue contact lenses, looked like they belonged to a different man. Still, I was thrilled to see my brother after so many years apart. I stood and hugged him.

As Ernesto released me from the embrace, he motioned to my beer. "What are you doing sitting at the bar with these types? You need to be at a table with the real intellectuals."

I looked over my shoulder, worried the two men at the bar

would take offense to what he had said, but they clearly did not hear him as their conversation continued without pause. I grabbed my beer and followed Ernesto as he guided me over to one of the long tables at the centre of the hall. He placed his hands on my shoulders, sitting me down, before taking a seat across from me.

"How was the train ride?" he asked before signaling to the pigtailed waitress to bring him a drink of his own.

"It was, um, good?" I said, struggling to remember a single notable thing from the voyage. I failed to come up with anything other than, "Those bullet trains are impressive."

"Faster every year," Ernesto replied, a touch of pride in his voice as if I had complimented his own creation. "Glad to hear your journey was okay. It's a shame the company wouldn't shell out the Reichsmarks to book you on a jet. You would have been here in a fraction of the time. Plus, the view of the city from the sky ... absolutely stunning." He shrugged. "But whatever, you're here now and I get to see my brother."

"How's Millie?" I asked as Ernesto looked toward the bar, seemingly impatient for his beer.

"Huh? Oh, we broke up. I don't know, a year ago or something."

"Oh no, that's—"

"Life? Save your pity," he replied, his lips curling into something unpleasant. "It was for the best. She wasn't a true believer anyway."

Ernesto thanked the server as she placed the frothy stein in front of him. "Cheers to the Reich," he said as we banged our glasses together, him using much more force than I did.

I took a sip but still my mind lingered on what he meant by Millie not being a "true believer." I had heard she was a dedicated National Socialist like most and had been in the League of German Girls in her youth. Her degree was in Reich Foreign

Policy and Commerce. Something didn't add up and I was worried about uncovering the answer.

Ernesto wiped his lips with the back of his hand and spoke, but this time he used the pet-name my mother had called me in my youth. "Tell me, Edu, do you believe in the expression, 'hard times create strong men, strong men create good times, good times create weak men, weak men create hard times'—that sort of thing?"

I nodded, "Of course; it's proven. I would say it's a fact at this point."

"Good, because I believe it too."

I narrowed my eyes, wondering why he was starting a conversation this way. I had hoped this rendezvous would be reminiscing on childhood memories, not politics. I had been holding out hope that his obsession with the Reich was something he would have grown out of by now, but between his dyed hair and the divorce, it would appear I was sadly mistaken. "I hope we aren't getting political," I said in a last-ditch attempt to steer the conversation from the fiery wreck I was anticipating it would lead to.

"No, no. No politics." Ernesto held up his hands in mock defense. He lowered them before saying, "Do you ever feel like you were born to do more?" He stared through me for a moment, as if taking stock of every action that had led him here. As the seconds dragged on, he added, "Lately I've found myself envying our grandfather more, that he got to fight. I mean *yes*, he was on the wrong side—the Republicans were nothing but communists—but he was a man of action and fought for his beliefs. You have to respect that."

It was at this moment that I looked around the hall and saw Hindenburg's for what it was. The two men at the bar had been the rule, not the exception. Each patron wore some sort of black boots, Great War era camouflage pants, and completed the ensemble with a black or brown shirt. It seemed obvious now that this was not any simple beer hall for regular patrons of the Reich, but instead an echo chamber for those that felt disenfranchised with the current shape of the empire. Every country had places like this, some hidden away in basements, others broadcasting their existence with signs and slogans, but in principle they were always the same.

I gulped as Ernesto continued, "I believe our society is full of weak men and our sacred Reich is slipping further and further from the light that the Great Führer showed us the way with. I think he and Dr. Goebbels, hell, even Reinhard Heydrich, would be spitting on us if they saw the state of their beloved Reich today."

I nodded, not because I agreed, but because I was unsure of what else to do.

"True believers, that's what started this empire. And that is what will keep it going." As I sat in silence, Ernesto added, "This current Führer, he's nothing like his father ... or his grandfather." He looked over his shoulder before adding, "I dare say he is one of those weak men I'm talking about."

I pulled my head back in stunned surprise by the boldness of such a claim, and in public no less. "Watch yourself! That's—"

"Treason? How can it be treason to want to continue the Great Führer's dream?" He paused, rubbing his forehead. "Luckily there are people in his bloodline that still have a grasp on what it is to be strong."

I opened my mouth to change the subject, but Ernesto was too quick. "Now, Magda—I have no aversion to putting my life on the line for her and storming the chancellery right now, tonight!"

His voice was rising now. I reached across the table and put a hand on his shoulder to keep him contained.

Shaking it off, he continued, "She may be his younger sister, but at least she is a woman with vision. Their youngest brother, Wolfgang, stands with her too, I'm told."

"Vision?" I laughed, not able to help myself. "I've hardly heard about the Hitler siblings in the press. Outside of pictures with celebrities, I sometimes forget they exist."

"Oh, they exist, and they have a great deal of support. When she takes over and appoints Wolfgang into a prominent position, maybe the head of the SS, then she will turn this Reich around. Whip all those bottom feeders into shape.

"Take over?" I questioned. My mind pleaded with me to leave, but instead, I asked, "What are you talking about? If the Gestapo overheard this, they—"

"They won't do much. I have it on good authority most of them want Otto gone." He sighed. "Sometimes I find myself wondering what would have happened if Karl had married one of Bormann's daughters instead of Goebbels'. I look at the Bormann family and see one of power. There is talk that they are involved in Magda's camp as well. It's true what they say." He took another sip of beer then, this one the longest yet.

"Who? The press?" I asked, my tone innocent as I felt rather guilty by association that this conversation had been forced upon me.

"The press?" He scoffed. "Don't listen to them; it's all filtered and injected with an agenda. You can't trust it. That's why I keep my ear to the ground." His finger drove itself into the table again. "Conversing with intellectuals, not talking heads or hired actors churning out propaganda." He gestured around him. "Talking with real people in places like this."

By this time, I had only a quarter of my beer remaining, and he signaled to the waitress to get me another. I didn't have the courage to tell him I was content and would rather be somewhere—*anywhere*—else, far from this table.

"Maybe I'm not being clear... Let me try again." Ernesto shook his head, as if mentally choosing a different path to go down. "War unifies the people, is what I'm getting at. It is proven that it moves humanity forward. All the great technological achievements have been made for warfare, then converted to civilian use later. We need a good war to strip us from the decline we've been on since Otto came to power. Twelve years, each one worse than the last.

"I don't blame Karl. He led us as best he could during the turbulent seventies and the American-influenced eighties, and of course that red scare in the east. I still think the Japanese were behind that, I have no proof but..." He blinked, realizing he was about to go on another tangent, and collected himself before continuing, "But we haven't had a real war since the Great One. I mean that business with Turkey was technically a war, but that was really more of a peace-keeping mission to ensure that country remained a loyal ally of the Reich as it has since forty-one."

I nodded again but recognized that my once beloved brother had become exactly as I had feared: a babbling nitwit who bowed at the altar of National Socialism. It pained me to feel this way, but as he spat out words like *history*, *war*, *bloodshed* and *weaponry*, I could no longer shake the feeling that the Ernesto I had loved as a boy was gone and replaced with this blond fanatical lunatic who believed in his blackened heart that the Third Reich was not extreme enough for him.

Ernesto ceased speaking for a moment as the server delivered the unwanted beer. He waited for her to leave before adding, "Yes, Karl should have married one of Bormann's daughters, whatever their names were."

God knew I had no love for the Führers or their vapid wives, but to ignore the history so flagrantly, I couldn't keep my mouth shut any longer. "You talk as if Bormann didn't have his hooks in Karl from the start. The man was Deputy Führer for years when Adolf was at the end." I saw my brother flinch at my flippant use of the Great Führer's name. "It would make no difference, except *maybe* Karl wouldn't have been as good of a public speaker without his father-in-law helping him with his speeches. If Bormann held that spot instead of Goebbels, he probably wouldn't have made even half the appearances did."

"Sorry, professor," Ernesto replied, rolling his eyes before his face disappeared behind his stein. "Still," he pointed at me after concluding his long sip, "I see your position, but we are debating moot points. This is merely temporary—our Reich will be on the rise again, I assure you." He slurred the last few words, and I wondered how many drinks he had partaken in before our meeting.

"Why? Because Magda is going to storm the Führer's palace? Is that what you're getting at?" I had half been joking, but my statement prompted Ernesto to nod emphatically. I added, "Well her and her spoiled kid brother should hurry up and put their money where their mouths are. Otto has been in power for over a decade."

Ernesto narrowed his eyes, the beer clinging to his lips. "It's coming." He pointed at me. "Now drink your beer."

I knew there was no salvaging Ernesto at this point. The brother I knew only existed in memories, and I no longer cared to know this fascist stranger who sat across from me. "I think I had best be going."

"Really? I haven't seen you in years and that's it?" As I stood, his tone shifted from heartfelt to the bullying ways of the Brownshirt he was now. "That's right, just run from the problems. Hide your head in the sand like the Republic of the day. You'll see, change is coming, and we will have the last laugh. Maybe it's time to finish off one of the five empires."

I exited the beer hall and moved into the overcast evening.

My face was warm with anger, which I suspected was a regular feeling for someone leaving Hindenburg's, except I hated the inhabitants of it and not the people outside of it.

I moved north, passing several intersections before concluding that it would be much safer to take a cab back to the hotel. Hailing one, I entered the backseat and told the driver where to go. Thankfully the man did not wish to engage in conversation.

As we came to an intersection and the light turned red, I watched as a portly man walked in front of us. He wore the same boots and tucked-in vintage SS camouflage pants as many of the patrons of the beer hall. The man's gut reached the far side of the crosswalk long before the rest of his mass, and he pushed the last bit of a frankfurter down his gullet.

*If this is the shape of Magda's elite freedom fighters, I don't think Otto has a thing to be worried about,* I thought as I watched the obese revolutionary waddle away as the light changed red to yellow, then green.

The driver continued toward the hotel, turning up the radio to fill the void in the absence of conversation. A nice whimsical bop filled the speakers. While I had never thought much of the song before, I enjoyed that it was about finding love, something I believed the world deeply lacked in the present day. It also helped to know Ernesto hated the band, as he told me once many years ago.

But that was back when I still had a brother.

# Chapter 6

## *The March on Germania*

I exited the hotel, my bag wheeling behind me as I headed left. I knew that I had several hours until I needed to board my train and was looking to kill some time. The sunshine was warm on my face, and it was a welcome feeling.

I walked past the Brandenburg Gate and watched as a gaggle of tourists paused to take photos, the heavy traffic of the morning rush hour flowing around its base. The drivers treated the historical landmark as nothing more than an obstacle in the way of their daily commute.

As I continued down the sidewalk, I marvelled at the *Volkshalle* in all its intimidating glory. I had to strain my neck to see the top, and even then, I could not glimpse the globe-clutching eagle that sat atop of it.

Lowering my gaze, I decided that I would take the streets that ran parallel to the Avenue of Splendors, not wanting to get caught up in the tourist crowds that would no doubt already be flocking up and down the avenue.

After several minutes of walking, I started to feel rather thirsty. I craved a coffee before the train, but felt the need to continue taking in the sun. With this in mind, I decided that a patio would do me some good. I could see a small café ahead, its umbrellas open and a small group of patrons sitting in the shade.

I walked inside, blinking to adjust my eyes to the dark interior, and made eye contact with a man I assumed to be the owner. "Table for one?" I asked.

He pointed to a ratty piece of paper taped to the front of the cash register that read: REICHSMARKS ONLY.

"Unfortunately, we don't take francs or pounds," he said.

I wasn't offended as my German, while grammatically correct, did carry a hefty accent. "I have Reichsmarks; it's no problem."

"Will you be eating?" he asked, his voice softer than his weathered face suggested it would be.

"Probably not," I replied. "Just a coffee before the train."

The man nodded and gestured to a seat toward the back of the shadowy café.

I shook my head, instead asking, "Can I have one outside, please? Beautiful weather today."

The man shrugged and moved to an open table on the patio. As I sat down, he brought me a small bread roll and I ordered my coffee. I looked at my watch and was surprised at how little time had passed for walking the number of kilometres that I had.

My coffee arrived and I paid with the change in my pocket. As I added some milk to the steaming cup, I reflected on my brother. I felt ashamed that I had missed him, and wondered if perhaps I could have tried harder to steer the conversation last night. As my spoon hit the side of the porcelain mug, I concluded that if his wife didn't have the mental strength to bear him and his crackpot theories, then what chance did I have?

I looked up and past the empty chair across from me. A police officer walked lazily down the block. He looked young, perhaps in his mid-twenties, and I detected in his features that he may have Mediterranean blood in him. As I sipped my coffee, I watched the officer greet a couple of locals with a polite nod as he continued past the café.

I could hear something in the distance but paid it little mind, my thoughts returning to my brother.

I stayed in my mental fortress until the owner of the café stepped out into the doorway. Holding onto the frame, he looked up the street, saying, "I don't know," over his shoulder to one of the patrons inside.

I heard a commotion from the opposite end of the road and craned my neck to look. The police officer was pointing at someone, his dominant hand moving down to his pistol.

Shots rang out.

The officer fell backward, dead before his skull cracked against the pavement.

Screams flooded up the street and I pushed myself up, spilling my coffee across the steel table. A group of Brownshirts marched up the boulevard, a dozen at least, rifles and pistols and several Great War stick grenades hanging from their belts.

As the group passed the café, I felt myself trembling uncontrollably and feared that coffee was not the only liquid that had spilled onto my shoes. Several members of the mob looked at me, but none raised their weapons. Instead, they continued on down the block before taking a corner and disappearing from view.

Distant gunshots and an explosion sprung from the heart of the city. Hearing this, my thoughts turned to the last thing Ernesto had said, and I realized this was not a single terrorist attack, but the start of the operation he had been alluding to.

A coup d'etat.

I knew I needed to get to the train station and out of Germania before I was caught in the resulting aftermath. I moved from the patio and ran down the street. My eyes caught a glimpse of a young woman kneeling beside the dead police officer, his blood soaking into her stockings as she wailed.

As I navigated the side roads, the once beautiful daylight shifted to a nightmare. A barrage of gunshots rang out from the Avenue of Splendors. The smells of the approaching autumn were now masked by gunpowder and smoke. The soft breeze carried the sounds of sirens and screams.

Eventually I made it to the train station and found that I had not been the only one with the inclination to leave. Thousands of people pushed their way inside.

As I entered, I heard shouting ahead. "Everything is under control! Form a single file line and we can process you quicker. This is for your safety."

I looked over the heads of the crowd and saw a police officer standing on a table, his arms gesturing this way and that. He repeated the sentence every few seconds, stopping only to answer the numerous questions people hurled his way. His answer was always the same:

"It's all under control."

In the few short moments since I had arrived, several dozen more people had pushed in behind me. The doors were now held open as everyone shoved into one another, trying desperately to get off the streets.

I looked through the tinted glass windows and saw that the police were beginning to set up barricades at the nearest intersection. They held their rifles firm, their heads swivelling up and down the block as they barked orders to one another.

After several minutes I reached the front of the line. The attendant verified my ID and valid ticket before nodding to an officer who held a panting German Shepherd, its leather leash wrapped around his fist. The dog showed no interest in me, so I was allowed past without a second glance.

I moved toward the platform I was assigned and could see several small businesses had their doors shuttered. The atmosphere of the station was tense and disturbing.

Eventually I arrived at the entrance to the platform and joined a new line. I could see that another group of police officers stood ahead and were questioning people. I handed the officer my passport as I reached the front of the queue.

"Spanish," he mumbled under his breath.

He pointed to a set of benches where a group of people sat. Two officers paced around, keeping an eye on each person. As I walked forward, I heard the officer ask questions to the next person in line. I felt angry at the prejudice I was receiving only because I had been born outside the Reich.

*They don't know the attackers are home grown. They are looking at the wrong people.*

I sat, narrowing my eyes on a man who the police had taken an interest in, two of them hurling questions at him in a rapid-fire barrage. Judging by his mannerisms and accent, I thought he may be American, possibly as far south as the fifty-second state. Eventually, he too was directed to the bench and sat beside me. His maroon-coloured polo was turning black in the underarm due to his profuse sweating. He blinked in odd intervals in a nervous tic.

Forty minutes passed, then an hour. I watched as more and more people were allowed to wait further down the platform until the train arrived. When it finally pulled into the station, it did so empty, and I assumed it was because the police patrols had removed everyone at the station prior. I watched as a slew of heavily armed policemen boarded the train and turned my head to see another group of officers speaking amongst each other at the head of the platform.

A trio of men in civilian clothing approached, pushing their way through the line. As they began to speak with the police, I gathered from their body language that they were no ordinary citizens. A moment passed and each of the men pulled out identification from their pockets. The police officers snapped to, and I realized then that these newcomers were agents of the Gestapo.

I felt an icy sensation run through my chest.

Their reputation preceded them, and I knew it was a fifty-fifty chance that I would see the light of day again if these agents decided to "interview" me.

As my hands began to tremble, I thought to myself, *You are an innocent man, you have nothing to fear. Just tell them you were here on business, and they will see that you're innocent. Even if you miss the train, you'll get on the next one. Don't worry.*

I took several deep breaths.

*That's right, keep calm. If you're shaking, they will assume you're guilty and then it's straight to the blindfolds and back alleys.*

I watched as a group of police officers led the Gestapo agents toward the train. One of the police officers raised a clip-board before gesturing to us. A Gestapo man flicked through the pages and pointed to several names. The policeman nodded, prompting the Gestapo officer's face to sour. The Gestapo agent boarded the train, followed by the police officer.

"You think they are coming back?" the man to the left of me asked, his use of English and his accent confirming he was American.

"Shut up," I replied in the best English I could muster.

The American continued, though I could only understand some of it. "It's not right for them to keep us here without asking us anything. In the States they can't do this. Detain me? Sure, but at least give me a reason."

"Oh, be quiet you Yank," an aging British man on the adjacent bench said. "You'll get us shot."

One of the patrolling police officers heard this and walked over. "Keep your mouths shut!" he snapped in German before adding in English, "No talking, anyone!" He looked between the American and the Brit as the words left his lips.

I sensed the American wanted to ask a question, but as his eyes wandered to the loaded rifle in the officer's hands, he shrank back into the bench without a sound.

Several more minutes went by before the Gestapo agents returned. Behind them were a group of two men and three women. The agents gestured toward the benches and an officer escorted the newcomers over.

I watched as one of the Gestapo members moved to the front of the train and gave a thumbs up to the conductor. My heart sank, knowing that I would be missing this train, but I forced myself to relax, reminding myself of my earlier resolution.

"You, you and you," a Gestapo officer said, looking at me and two others on the bench. As we looked between each other in confusion, he added, "Come with me."

Sandwiched between him and a police officer to our back, we followed the agent through a side door on the platform. We navigated several concrete halls before we were outside again. A group of unmarked vans sat before us with several police vehicles parked on their flanks. I looked at the road in the distance and watched as several military-looking vehicles zoomed down the boulevard.

The van closest to us opened its back doors and another Gestapo agent exited. She smiled at her counterpart and asked, "First group?"

Her coworker nodded.

The female officer gestured for us to enter the van, pulling sets of handcuffs from her jacket pocket and placing them on our wrists, saying, "Only for our safety, you understand." She sounded quite frivolous about it.

I didn't reply, figuring that silence was the best policy.

The three of us sat on the bench inside the van. The female agent entered and attached our handcuffs to a chain that came from the floor so that our arms could not leave our laps. I thought she was being rather stupid, entering the van alone with three potentially dangerous terrorists, but looking at the open back doors revealed why she was so relaxed. Standing in the doorway was the silhouette of a muscular police sergeant, his eyes scanning us. I suspected he was begging for a reason to empty the clip into the back of the van.

The female agent finished securing us before jumping out onto the pavement outside. She placed a finger against her earpiece before calling out, "Rudolf, cancel that. Put them in the second one. We have to go."

Her colleague began to reply from somewhere out of view, but the doors slammed shut before I could hear the rest of the conversation. The engine sprang to life soon after and I felt the jostle as we began down the road.

I could see that the white paint on the floor had been chipped away from hundreds of shoes that had been funneled in and out of the vehicle over the years. The dim overhead light revealed a stain of dull red that had never been washed out.

# Chapter 7

## *A Hammer Sees Everything as a Nail*

I sat in the small white interview room for an unknowable amount of time. There were no clocks or windows which one could use to monitor the time. All I knew was that I was hungry. So hungry that the fear I'd had before had moved aside, burrowed down into the recesses of my stomach.

I adjusted my hands on the table and felt the handcuffs dig into my wrists. I ground my teeth as I attempted to get more comfortable in the hard plastic chair. I recalled the American saying, "Detain me? Sure, but at least give me a reason." I agreed wholeheartedly with the statement.

*If they are going to shoot me, they should hurry up with it. At least I won't be hungry anymore.*

I recalled my exit from the van. The swastika-laden building, the red banners, the busts of a great many important party members lining the lobby. I knew from the size of the building that this wasn't any old police station, but the Gestapo Headquarters itself. While the prospect had disturbed me, I soon realized that a white room in the headquarters was no different than a white room in the recesses of Siberia. For all intents and purposes, they were the same white room.

The door to the interview room swung open with a violent crash. A single Gestapo officer entered, a ballistic vest over his civilian attire. He was sweating and his clothes looked ruffled. That and the red in his eyes told me he was having a long day.

He tossed a dossier on the table and sat down across from me. I looked at him, but as his icy blue irises met mine, my gaze darted away, instantly seeking comfort in the mirror on the left wall. I knew it was two-way glass and that one of his illustrious colleagues would be behind it, recording our interaction, but still, seeing myself in the reflection brought a slight calm over me. It was like I was out of my body, and therefore safe. Just a passive observer with no connection to the present.

"Why, Mr. Domínguez"—the officer's eyes flashed to the file before returning to my flushed face—"are you in Germania at this time?" His voice was as cold as his eyes.

I turned my attention toward him. "Business," I said as confidently as I could. "I-I— Well, I work for Volkswagen Spain, and I had meetings here ... at their world headquarters, that is."

"And what were your meetings about?"

"The *Lebensnetz*, and how it would affect our enterprise. All the Volkswagen offices from the Federation sent representatives."

"And what was the end result of those meetings?" the officer asked, his voice taking on a warmer tone. "Did you accomplish your goals?"

"The heads all agreed that the *Lebensnetz* would be a passing fad. It may speed up communication between the branches, but they've yet to see how it will change our sales strategy."

The officer looked at the dossier. Reading my name atop

the brown folder, he said, "Eduardo, tell me, what else have you been up to in Germania?" His voice was friendly now, and that scared me all the more.

"I went to the museum—the one dedicated to the World Wars—and I saw the Avenue of Splendors, and of course I spent time at my hotel. That's all."

"Nowhere else?"

I shook my head, prompting the officer to add, "You're sure now?"

I shook my head again, to which he said, "It's interesting that you left out the part where you were seen leaving a beer hall that is known to harbor those that would spread irredeemable ideologies into our midst. Anarchists and riffraff. Hindenburg's? Ring a bell?"

I felt a chill move down my sweat-coated spine.

*How long were they following me?* I thought, looking on in horror as the Gestapo officer pulled the file closer, flicking through several papers like a predator playing with its meal. *And now they've caught me in a lie.*

"It's also interesting," the officer continued, "that someone else was seen inside at the time, a man by the name of Ernesto, a known communist sympathizer." The agent was almost laughing now. "What is all the more interesting, of course, is that he happens to be your brother."

"A Communist? Ernesto is the farthest thing from—"

"So which faction are you with?" the officer asked, holding up a hand as he pointed to a series of invisible words that hung in the air in front of him. "The Worker's Liberation Union? The Siberian Free Corps? The Marxist-Leninist Popular Front, perhaps?"

"I don't know what those are, sir. I'm sorry."

The officer's face hardened. "Look, Eduardo, you can save the game. I've been doing this for quite some time now. You can dance around, deny, deny and deny some more. Deny until you are blue in the face. This is, of course, understandable." He nodded softly, and I could tell he had used these lines on many people in the past, not all of them guilty. "You feel you have to out of some sort of loyalty to a supposed resistance movement—your brothers in arms, perhaps. But here's the thing: Eventually, I'll get my information, and what would have been the point of all the pain? The missing teeth? The broken bones? Loss of blood..." He paused, allowing me to attach mental images to the words he used. "Pointless. Pointless and, frankly, stupid."

I trembled, causing the chain from the handcuffs to rattle on the steel surface of the table. "I'm sorry, sir, but I'm not with them. If I knew anything I would tell you, but I'm just a businessman from Spain. I can give you numbers to call to collaborate my story."

"I have no doubt your cover was to come here on business, and perhaps you even attended legitimate meetings." The officer nodded, his lips thinning. "I respect that. So, tell me, why were you at one of the sites where the attacks occurred then? Reconnaissance?"

"As I said, I've never been to Germania before and I—"

The officer's face shifted to a seething one. "Look, Eduardo, I'll be honest with you, which is something you are not being with me. I have in this file a typed agreement that states if you give me valuable information about these attacks and their organizers, we will deport you back to Spain. No prison time, no hanging. But you need to give me something *good.* Safe house locations, your handlers, routing, full names of the members in your cell. If I have to beat it out of you, the deal evaporates and off to a work camp in the Moscow Commissariat for you."

"Sir, I came here to conduct business, and I met my brother

for a drink. I had no idea he had become so militant. I left once he started speaking such rhetoric against the Reich. If you were spying on me, you would see I left angry."

The officer sighed, opened the dossier and began thumbing through more papers. As he flipped, I could see printed photos of me all around Germania, one showing Meriam and I speaking outside the museum. I hoped she was safe.

He pulled out a document and slid it toward me. I identified it as the deportation order he had alluded to. His voice returned to a cold growl as he said, "Last chance to see home again."

I closed my eyes, my mind envisioning all the pain that would be in my near future. I knew that I could make up information, but once they caught me in another lie, the pain would be even worse.

As I sat with my eyes clenched tight, I heard a deep thumping from somewhere inside the building. My eyes bolted open at the sound of screeching metal.

The officer was standing now. He pulled the paper out of reach and looked at the glass wall. His eyes had lost their confidence, replaced by something else.

Fear. Real and transparent.

He left in silence, but in the brief moment the door was open, I heard a series of gunshots echo up the hall. My trembling was at an all-time high, and I felt so very cold as my blood raced from my limbs and pooled in my chest. At first, I thought that the building may explode at any moment, but then I realized no one would lead an assault on a structure only to then blow it up with everyone still inside it.

I knew it had to be part of the coup, but once these fighters recognized I wasn't with them, a bullet would be sure to follow. I found it hard to breathe, but if I was being honest, I would take a single bullet over whatever these Gestapo thugs had in store for me.

The bass of the gunfire continued to grow louder and louder until the door flung open. Two men clad in identical Brownshirts and swastika armbands entered, rifles pointing frantically around the room.

The taller of the two looked at me. "Another one," he said, his eyes lighting up as he pulled a key ring from his chest pocket and fumbled to find a handcuff key. Doing so, he inserted it into the lock and pulled the cuffs from my tattered wrists.

"Long live the true Reich," he said as I stood. "You know how to shoot, brother?" he asked, and I nodded. He looked over his shoulder, more gunshots coming from the hallway behind. "Otis, give this guy the gun from the dead one."

The second Brownshirt spun around, his back now to the doorway, and handed me a pistol that was tucked into his belt. It felt warm in my hand.

"Come on, we've got to leave. The SS will be here any second. We can't match them, not until the *Wehrmacht* loyalists arrive," the first Brownshirt said.

We moved into the hall, and I heard the gunshots continue behind me. I looked to my feet as we passed several dead bodies, some Gestapo, others a mix of Brownshirts and those in various camouflage-patterned clothing. We exited the building and descended the steps as an explosion in the distance drowned out the sound of sirens.

"Come on, left, in the back," the Brownshirt said, pointing at a military truck down the road.

On instinct, my feet followed, but the voice of reason in my head took over. I knew following these men would end in death. Either from the police or from these guys once they determined that I was not seeping with their same nationalistic pride. No doubt they would think I was a spy.

I changed my direction and headed across the block.

"No, this way!" the Brownshirt yelled.

I half expected a bullet in the back, but I continued to run.

As I was about to enter the alley, I heard another explosion, this one much closer. Then the screams followed. I looked over my shoulder and saw a tank approaching from several blocks away, a complement of infantry scurrying alongside it. My eyes widened as I recognized their uniforms.

The SS had arrived.

I ducked into the alley and let my feet carry me the rest of the way.

The streets became a blur, and the distant sound of gunfire was muffled behind the concrete of the buildings. I ran, my mouth tasting of copper. At each intersection I stopped to check if the coast was clear before I emerged into the open. No Brownshirts, no SS, and most importantly, no tanks.

The sun was quickly disappearing behind the Germania skyline as I neared the river. The memory of the advancing tank moving methodically down the road replayed in my mind on a loop.

I moved down to the riverbank ahead and felt the rocks shift under my weight. I walked toward an overpass that crossed the river above and took shelter under it. My eyes fixed on the graffiti that covered the underbelly. Caricatures of Mussolini and Hitler spewing speech bubbles of rhetoric, standing beside a voluptuous blonde wearing nothing but a Red Army field cap.

I sat down and looked at the water bobbing against the rocky embankment. I felt completely lost and exhausted. I knew there was no use running blind through the city at night, not when I could still hear the frequent sounds of battle in the distance. With my luck, I would run into a squad of Brownshirts. If I didn't like the way they looked in the daytime, I could hardly imagine them at night.

I lay my head against the stone of the overpass and felt the last bit of adrenaline slip away.

I became unbelievably tired, my legs aching from the sprinting of the day. As my eyelids grew heavy and I slipped into unconsciousness, I could hear the sounds of gunfire advance slowly but surely into the heart of the city.

# A Change in Perspective:
## The Nurse

Head Nurse Caroline Adler peered through the glass window overlooking the nursery. She admired the rows of babies and the little tufts of blond hair on their pale scalps. She felt the same level of pride every time a new litter entered the ward. But the happiness was not without its touch of sorrow, for these children would never meet their parents, as their names were to be redacted as part of the Aryan Breeding Program.

Adler took pride in playing a part in keeping the Great Führer's dream of *Lebensraum* alive and populated by the peak of humanity. These children would go on to work and thrive in the breadbasket of the Reich. Then, someday, they would marry other Aryans and have their own pure blood children, continuing the process for a millennium—or so she hoped.

Adler watched the nurse who moved softly through the nursery, clipboard in hand as she observed each sleeping child. As the nurse looked up toward the glass, Adler nodded at her. The nurse jotted down a note before moving toward the door and entering the observation room where Adler stood.

"All healthy?" Adler asked, watching as the nurse placed her clipboard down on the nearby desk.

"Doctor Reinhard wanted baby twenty-two cleared for evidence of brain damage." She paused, her hand moving toward a mug of coffee that had long gone cold. "But nothing that can't wait until morning."

"Another birth defect?" Adler asked, scowling. She couldn't bear to see what happened to the babies the doctors deemed unfit for the Reich. "Did you check the parents? Has the mother had too many children as part of the program?"

"I checked, the mother has been a long-term member, on the higher end for sure, but nothing we haven't seen before. The father..." Her eyes flashed toward the clipboard as she read off it, "Second-generation colonist, hailing from SS lineage. Third child on record, no prior issues."

"I trust you'll keep me informed of any changes," Adler said.

The nurse gave a thoughtful nod as she sipped her coffee, prompting Adler to pivot and exit the nursery. She moved down the hall and out of the maternity ward, humming an old victory song that had played on the radio earlier in the evening. She pushed open the double doors that connected to the recovery wing. Two *Wehrmacht* soldiers stood guard outside a room on the right, their eyes suspicious of everyone who passed.

*No doubt feeling shame for allowing their general to be shot by those Slav terrorists,* she thought as she walked on, not bothering to make eye contact. She was a busy woman, after all. Still, her mind lingered on the topic. She felt her face harden, annoyed by the very existence of so-called "resistance movements."

*The Marxist-Leninist Siberian Corps or the Soviet Popular*

*Front—how can these factions thrive out there past the Urals? How can they cause so much destruction to our beloved Reich?*

Adler moved behind the counter of the nurse's station and picked up a clipboard, checking over the stock of painkillers and patient rosters.

Her mind continued to spin. *The Japanese! They don't police the zones like we do. Our supposed allies have allowed our enemies to fester; they've always been too tolerant of the Slavs.*

She recalled the news reports she had heard over the last few years of the Manchuria Revolution and the guerrilla war in south-east China that Japan had been fighting for decades now. It was clear that Imperial Japan had its own fair share of problems.

Nurse Adler moved on from the station and looked into several rooms to ensure no patients had been moved or discharged without her knowing. The day staff had been too relaxed over the last few months.

*That new girl—the transfer from Norway—she never fills in anything correctly. No wonder Trondheim was eager to get rid of her.*

As the thought left her mind, she rounded another corner and saw the elevator at the end of the hall open. An elderly man in a Great War-era SS uniform exited. A woman, perhaps thirty years his junior, trailed behind him, along with twin girls and a boy. All the children were blond, just like their mother, with none being over the age of twelve.

Doctor Schmitt walked into view. He extended a heil as the family approached him before gesturing down the hallway and leading the group out of Adler's sight.

A young nurse could see Adler had been watching and approached, her small heels clicking on the linoleum floor.

"Doctor Schmitt approved it, last minute. I didn't have time to add it to the list," Nurse Ella said, her voice hardly more than a whisper.

Adler held up a hand to silence the girl. "Veteran?" she asked, and at the nurse's nod, she added, "Self-admittance?"

"Doctor Schmitt said it's third-stage cancer. The man is tired of being a drain on the system."

Adler shook her head at the simple mindedness of the veteran. "War heroes are never a burden. He paid for these years in advance when he fought for the Reich. He should spend every moment he can with his grandbabies." Adler moved forward, and Nurse Ella followed. "Still," Adler continued, "we should keep him company and honour his service."

The two nurses rounded the corner in silence, heading in the direction the group had gone. They saw the mother was kneeling down, talking to the children and removing the tears of her son, who was the youngest.

*Never an easy thing to see,* Adler thought, suddenly aware that she still held her clipboard. Wanting to keep her hands free, she placed the object on the ledge of the nurse's station.

Adler smiled politely at the mother, who continued to sooth her children before entering the room. The veteran was speaking to the doctor, who stood beside him, listening intently as the man sat on the bed. The veteran had removed his jacket and was in the process of rolling up his sleeves.

"Signed up at seventeen," he said. His voice was crisp, and Adler was surprised by how articulate the man was. "I couldn't wait to do my duty. I was sent to the Eastern Front at the time, and I'm happy to report I fought valiantly."

"Did you serve at the battle of Moscow, Ernhard?" Doctor Schmitt asked as he kept his eyes fixed on the retired soldier.

"No, the second one ended a month before I shipped out. But I was in the battle for the Urals." Ernhard gestured to his coat that hung on the hanger. "That's where I got my first Iron Cross."

Adler looked over to the jacket and marveled at how many medals the man possessed. An Infantry Assault Badge, Eastern Front Medallion, SS Long Service Award, a Wound Badge and a cuff title on the left wrist of the jacket showing he had taken part in the Archangel Offensive as well. Those were just the ones she recognized from her limited memory of the classes she had been forced to take in the tenth grade. A dozen additional pins, merits and citations were clasped to the jacket as well, and she wished she could remember what they all meant.

Her eyes met the veteran as he added, "The Eastern Front commemoration was handed out by the Führer himself. I met the man that day."

Hearing this, Ella gasped, seemingly shocked that someone could have been alive—let alone remember meeting—the Great Führer.

Ernhard looked over to her pale face. "Oh, yes; I was maybe a little younger than you are now. He shook my hand and noticed my Golden Tank Destruction Badge. I still remember what he said to me: 'Soldiers like you are the future of the Reich.' He was a kind man." The veteran paused, his eyes moving toward his daughter and grandchildren. "That was the second most important day of my life. The most important was your birth, Klara."

The woman held back tears as she struggled to talk. She wanted to stay strong for her children, and most importantly, her father. All she managed to get out was, "I'm sorry Werner couldn't be here. I called, but—"

Ernhard gave a soft smile and replied, "Let him work. I can appreciate his commander not releasing him. Those joint training courses with the Americans are few and far between. Besides, America is a beautiful place. I went there in my thirties with your mother." He paused, taking a deep breath. "That's why I'm doing this; I'm tired of being a burden."

The daughter could hardly take it. "You're not a burden, Dad. Stop. It's not too late—"

"I can't be mended, Klara. The Reich has been good to me. I swore to protect her, and this is my final way to do so. I wish to go out on my terms, not as a skeleton, unable to remember my own accomplishments or my grandchildren's names all because of this incessant disease. I will die a man of Hitler's SS. The Russians couldn't kill me, neither could those Ukrainian guerrillas. I'm going out with my own actions." He lay back and nodded at the doctor. "I'm ready to do my duty, sir."

The children began to cry, and their mother tried to console them, but tears stung her eyes as well. As the doctor pulled the syringe of poison from the tray, he wiped the injection site with an alcohol-soaked cotton swab. Holding the needle to the side, he looked into the man's eyes, giving him one last chance to reconsider.

The veteran did not waver.

Doctor Schmitt cleared his throat, and Adler could see how much it bothered him, but like the veteran, he too had a duty to perform. Schmitt inserted the syringe, and the clear contents moved into Erhard's veins. Soon it would work its way through his Aryan blood stream and the world would lose another veteran of the Great War.

Erhard looked down at his grandchildren and said, "Eva, Sophia, Albert take care of your mother and remember me for what I was, not what I am now." His eyes went to his daughter, and he said, "Klara, I'm so proud of the woman you've become." He paused, his voice becoming strained. "I'm off to see your mother now."

The wailing was nearly deafening, and Adler could feel the tears rushing to her own eyes. As the war hero drifted off to his next conquest, the staff stood over him, right hand extended in the air, feet together.

"Heil Erhard," Schmitt said, prompting the others in the room to reply in unison through broken voices.

"Heil Erhard."

# Act II

## The Battle for the Twisted Cross

"We only have to kick in the door, and the whole rotten structure will come crashing down."

— Adolf Hitler on the invasion of the U.S.S.R.

# Chapter 8

## *A Post Not Abandoned*

I awoke to the pleasant sound of the tide sweeping across the rocks of the embankment, a soft light resting against my eyelids. I opened my eyes and looked around, trying to remember how I had gotten here.

I began to stand but stopped myself as the memory of the day prior came back all at once. *I need to get out of the city,* I thought. *I need to get home.*

I checked my pants pocket for my wallet and felt a surge of adrenaline upon realizing it wasn't there. I patted my shirt for my passport and swore as I remembered the Gestapo agents had taken both items before confining me to the interview room. I felt my heart begin to thunder in my ears as the terrible reality of being stranded in a strange, hostile city with no identification and no money became a reality. I stood and kicked a fair-sized stone into the river beyond, scuffing my dress shoe as I did so.

I let out a deep, agonizing breath and looked to the skyline. The sun was coming up and I estimated it to be somewhere in the vicinity of seven in the morning. I regretted keeping my watch in my suitcase, which was likely still at the café I had stopped at before everything had flown apart.

I clicked my teeth together several times as a nervous tic, contemplating what to do. I knew that I would get nowhere in the Reich without my identity documents, and without money I couldn't even pay someone to smuggle me away.

Envisioning my passport and wallet locked away in a safe in the basement of the Gestapo building, I clenched my jaw, the wheels in my brain churning, searching for a solution. I paced the river, the sound of the water keeping me grounded. Several minutes passed before I came to the realization.

*I need to go back to the Gestapo headquarters.*

I stopped in my tracks, my heart sinking, knowing the mostly likely outcome if I went along with that plan.

As I resumed pacing, I tried to think of a better plan. None came.

I ran a hand through my hair and reasoned, *After all, I'm innocent. I'll go in and explain that I was wrongfully detained, tell them that I was forced out of the interview room and ran because of the gunshots. They are people, after all; they must understand. If I was guilty, why would I come back?*

My hand left my scalp and reached for the gun tucked into my pants. I thought of tossing it in the river, but I suspected I would need it before the day was over. Plus, if I turned it into the Gestapo I may gain more favor with them. I felt my hand retreat from the grip.

I moved out from under the bridge and up toward the road. It was then I realized I had heard no gunshots since waking. Buoyed by this knowledge, I picked up my pace and headed in the direction of the headquarters. The cold morning breeze felt nice on my back.

---

By the time I arrived at the headquarters, the crisp air had turned to the heat of the day. Sweat dripped from my brow, and I would have traded a great deal of Reichsmarks to be dressed in something more comfortable than the business outfit I had been forced to wear for the past twenty-four hours.

As I neared the end of the alley, I listened to the road for several moments. All was still.

I stuck my head out and looked right. In front of the entrance to the building was the same tank I had seen before, but the smoke billowing out of the open hatch told me no one was alive inside.

*How did they take out a tank?* I thought as my eyes returned to the quiet headquarters. Only my objective remained.

I moved from the cover of the alley, but as I reached the stairs to enter the headquarters, I froze. In all my imagining of how this would go, I never imagined the building to be empty. I had envisioned the government retaking the facility shortly after I fled, the entire coup mopped up in a few hours. I began to tremble as I ascended the steps. If I had to search an entire government building, full of rooms and safes I didn't have access to ... well, the chances of me finding my documents were slim to none.

I entered the front door and could see several bodies lying on the beige tiled floor of the foyer. I struggled to remember if they had been there when I had made my exit. The glassed-off desk ahead was littered with bullet holes and I could see the blonde hair of a female officer dead on the ground behind it, her weapon gripped in a chubby hand.

I looked to the right and saw the entrance to the secure area had been blown open, the heavy door hanging from a struggling hinge. I gulped as I entered. The entire building felt like a mausoleum.

I stepped over additional bodies and took a left, attempting to remember the way I had been brought in. I walked several paces up a large hallway, my eyes darting into the passing offices, the only commonality between them being the spent bullet casings that littered the floor.

I was stopped in my tracks as a figure exited an office at the far end of the hallway. The man turned and looked at me. His ballistic vest over his business casual appearance marked him as Gestapo. My eyes wandered to his hands, and I could see in his left he clutched a bottle of alcohol. I stepped forward, wondering if perhaps he was an imposter that had put on the vest for its protection and not for its mark of affiliation.

The intruder turned and raised a pistol.

I threw my hands above my head saying, "I'm a civilian, I'm not with them."

After several moments and no gunshot, I watched as the man lowered his weapon. "If you've come to loot, I'm afraid there's nothing left."

He slurred his words, putting the situation I found myself in all the more precarious. Alcohol and loaded firearms never mix, least of all when surrounded by dead comrades.

"I'm not here to steal. I'm here to see an officer," I replied, my trembling hands returning to my side.

"You've found one," the man replied before moving into the office across from where he stood.

I looked around the hall as if this was some sort of joke, but as my eyes landed on a blood-encrusted Brownshirt, I knew that humor had taken the express train out of Germania long ago.

Moving down the hall and looking into the room the officer had entered, I found him sitting in a semi-relaxed position, his scuffed boots on the desk. An overflowing ashtray lay close to his feet.

"I shall let you know that I am armed, sir," I said in an attempt to diffuse a situation before it arose.

"That makes two of us," the agent said, lifting his right hand lazily to show me that he was keeping the weapon close. He took a swig from the bottle, and with his index finger, pointed to the chair across from him. "Sit."

I took three steps forward and did as I was instructed. As I made contact with the seat, the officer spoke again. "So, tell me, what do you need to see an officer for? Come to tattle on a neighbor, someone reading an outlawed book, perhaps?"

"No sir..." I began to say, but trailed off, my mind turning to Ernesto, wondering if he was still alive. I cleared my throat and concentrated on my initial goal. "I was questioned here yesterday and your ... well, your colleagues took my IDs and wallet. I've come to get them back."

The officer nodded, a curious expression clinging to his face. "And why would officers bring you in for questioning?"

"I was boarding a train to go home to Madrid—this was just after the attack. I think they wanted to interview anyone from outside the Reich."

I stopped speaking as the man reached into the desk drawer and produced a mug. He looked at it, shrugged and poured a healthy dose of the alcohol into it. As he slid it over to me, a toothy grin appeared. "Spaniard, huh?" I nodded, and he added, "I'm a third Spanish myself. So, tell me, stranger from Madrid, what are you doing so far from home?"

I explained the business trip and my brother being a permanent resident of the Reich. The officer nodded once before sipping the bottle. He appeared to go into deep thought before removing his boots from the desk and sitting forward. He placed the handgun on the table and extended his hand. "If we are going to be drinking together, I should know your name."

"Eduardo," I said, quickly shaking the officer's hand. His grip was firm, and I could see his eyes were glossy.

"Kurt," he replied, before leaning back into his chair, his feet staying on the ground. "You know, I used to hate my Spanish blood," he said after a moment. "I had tried in my late teens to join the SS, and they rejected me because of my Spanish third. If I had been a quarter Spanish, I could have gotten in, but as it was my bloodline was considered, 'too impure.' It took me years to get over that."

I sat there in silence, not knowing what to say, but Kurt continued all the same. "In a moment of clarity right around when I hit twenty-five, I decided to join the Gestapo. I wanted to show my mother she had raised a good National Socialist and I knew of the shared bond the SS and the Gestapo had during the Great War." He chuckled to himself. "Of course, if this had been fifty years ago when the SS and the police were one in the same, I wouldn't have even bothered, but fortunately for me they became separate entities again after ... well, after a lot of things."

He returned his vision to the present, clicking his tongue. "And to think I joined with so many delusions of grandeur running through my head. In my years I've uncovered things... Things you wouldn't even dare to think. Our Reich has done heinous acts; things we will all have to answer for. Not just against undesirables either; some of them high ranking, some of them SS. An 'accident' here, an 'aneurysm' there, and then, just like that, they are erased from history. And don't think for a second that it ended with the Great Führer. No, it continued on through his son and so on..." He waved a hand close to his face in an attempt to rid his mind of what he was thinking.

"Sir— Kurt, I mean. Why are you here?" I asked.

"It's my post, isn't it?" he said, cocking his head. "The government is paying me to be here, so here I am. Besides, I'm sure there will be a great need for Gestapo officers under the new leadership. The past two Führers loved the information we poured into their ears and I'm sure there will be a great deal of talking in the days to come."

"New government?" I asked, before taking a drink from the mug to cover up my surprise.

"Oh yeah, didn't you hear? Führer Magda Hitler announced this morning that she has taken the position. Her brother was captured and forced to abdicate. His own SS guard division turned on him, seeing him as the traitor to the Reich that he is. He wasn't a true believer, you know." He shook his head. "But who is a true believer anymore? It's a sentiment that has lost all its meaning."

"The Führer's been captured? So, the coup is over?" I began to stand. I needed to get my documents before the new regime swept in and ensnared us all in its iron fist.

Kurt laughed as he poured more of the booze into my still full mug. He gestured with his chin for me to drink. I returned to my seat slowly and complied with the unspoken order, savoring the sweet taste of the schnapps. Upon hearing the government was in such shambles, I needed a drink.

"Trains have been closed. Magda ordered that no one leaves Germania. All must stay and fight for the survival of the Third Reich. Against the 'pathetic and weak-minded that are still standing in the way of progress and the National Socialist dream,' as she put it so bluntly. Elegance has never been at the forefront of her abilities. But hatefulness, she has that."

"I guess she wasn't hugged enough as a child," I said after another gulp of the alcohol.

"She'll have no shortage of that now. All those lickspittles will come out of the woodwork to swear allegiance, I'm sure. Many being the same who took the oath to her brother just twelve years ago. Loyalty is like the wind." He paused. Seeing the distress in my eyes, he added, "But if you are serious about leaving Germania, you should go south. Get to Hartmann Airport. Last I heard there is a strong SS presence there getting refugees out on planes. If there is anything left with wings and an engine, that would be your best bet."

"The SS," I said as a chill ran down my spine. I was well aware of their track record in Turkey.

Kurt seemed to read the contempt on my face as he said, "You'll have to pick a side eventually; it's the only way you'll get out. You'll need friends. Regardless of what form of Swastika you fight under, you can't get out alone."

"I could lie low for a few weeks, until it settles down. Assuming I get my money and ID back."

I thought I had been subtle in my asking, but Kurt gave a slight smile. "Sure, let's get that." He stood and walked by the desk, placing his bottle on the table but bringing the gun. He grabbed my mug and handed it to me. "Lie low, huh?" he said over his shoulder as he exited the office and turned down the hall. As I followed, he added, "When have you ever known a civil war to be short?"

We arrived at another office and Kurt pulled a keyring from his pocket as he said, "No, I'm sure this will go on in some form or another for several years." He sounded exhausted.

Kurt pushed the door open, and I saw a series of file cabinets behind a chain-link fence. He flipped through several keys before arriving at the correct one and inserting it into the lock of the cage. He pulled open the squeaking gate and moved to the far right of the fenced-off area.

"New arrivals should be kept here, assuming they logged it." He paused, watching me approach the cabinet in question. "If it's not here that means the officer who seized them still has it on them. I'd help you search the bodies, but..." He trailed off, and I heard the sadness in his voice.

I pulled open the drawer and pushed aside several file folders. Inside each I could see money, wallets, keys and documents from all across the National Socialist Federation. I saw a file with my name written on it and opened it. Staring up at me was the red of the Spanish passport and the black leather of my wallet.

I lifted them out of the drawer and after verifying they were in fact mine, began to pocket them before hesitating. I extended them toward Kurt for him to inspect, figuring he would want to ensure I took the correct ones.

He held up his hand. "I trust you took whichever one you thought would help you most."

"I think staying honest is the best course of action," I replied, stuffing the items into my pockets. "It's worked for me so far."

"Honesty is the best policy," Kurt said with a quick grin. He closed the gate behind me and turned the key to lock it.

"I would ask you to come with me, but I'm sure you have a family and your reasons for staying," I said as we moved out into the hallway.

"The new regime can call me a lot of things, but they can't say I abandoned my post." He pulled the office door closed and gestured forward.

I couldn't imagine why he held firm to the mundane tasks of a regime that had sent kill squads to eliminate his coworkers. I supposed clinging to a certain order of things kept Kurt sane, and in an insane time that spoke to his character.

As we returned to his office I took a final swig of the booze and placed the mug on the desk, unsure when I would be able to have a drink again.

Kurt extended his hand. "Good luck, Eduardo. I mean that."

"Thank you for helping me today. I know you didn't have to—"

"Have a drink for me in Madrid. That will be thanks enough." He let go of my hand and sat down in the chair. "I guess I should start cleaning up. Sooner or later someone in authority will want this building used again." He shrugged and lifted the bottle to his mouth. "But I don't think that day will be today."

I left without saying anything further. Kurt and I were very different people and while I respected his choices, I knew I would not be doing the same if I were in his situation.

I exited the building, and the sunlight of the warm day surrounded me. I took a moment to become accustomed to the light and looked up and down the street. I knew approximately where in the city I was and thought back to the maps I had studied in the train station at my stopover in Paris. I knew I was north-west of the airport and that I had quite a walk ahead of me.

I decided I would head to my right as the next intersection was closer and less bodies populated the pavement.

# Chapter 9

## *A Spaniard, the SS and the French Foreign Legion*

For a city that was hellbent on tearing itself apart, the streets on the way to the airport were bustling with activity. While I had been expecting to see abandoned avenues, broken up by roving patrols of SS or Brownshirts, I was surprised to see so many civilians. Everywhere I looked, there were cars full of people dressed for work or groups huddled on the stairways of their apartments, conversing quietly. I sensed these people knew they were living history and wanted to see it unfold in front of their eyes, as opposed to on the TV screen. Perhaps they felt they had more control that way.

As I became accustomed to the number of pedestrians again, I eventually reached an east-west cross street that appeared to be acting as a dividing line. On one side of the street, shop owners stood smoking outside their businesses. On the other side, not a soul.

One of the shopkeepers to my right tossed his cigarette butt onto the road and said, "If you're thinking of going up that way, don't." My face must have given me away, as he added, "Unless you've got a girl begging for you, whatever it is, it isn't worth it."

"What group is waiting down there? SS or true believers?" I asked, my voice cracking partway through.

"Hell if I know, but the amount of ordnance they shot at each other last night ... you go a few more blocks and I'm sure the river of blood will be up to your ankles." He cleaned his hands on his apron before saying, "Come inside, have a drink with me."

"I'm going to get a bit closer. If it's as bad as you say, I'll come back. Okay?"

The man made a noncommittal face before saying, "I'll keep a chair open for you." He retreated into his shop, an air of disappointment about him.

I could feel the eyes of the other owners watching me, and I became aware of how silent the street had become. It was as if by moving forward, I would be penetrating the delicate membrane of a world these people dared not venture into. The road, which couldn't have been more than ten metres wide, had become a trench so insurmountable in the eyes of the locals that it rivaled the Grand Canyon in scope. With a deep breath in my lungs, I built up the courage to shove off from the mainland and venture into the open waters of the unknown.

I moved across the street, my shoes clicking on the cobblestone roadway. I found myself trying to ignore the odd feeling that this journey to the airport would be a one-way trip. As I continued down the road, my eyes drifted between the closed-up shops and newspaper pages that blew frantically in the wind.

I followed the twisting road for several blocks before my path was blocked by rubble. The west facing wall of a building had been stripped away, revealing the steel skeleton and burned furniture of several rooms.

I ducked into an alley that connected to the next street. As I emerged, I looked ahead and could see a green field, and beyond it the brown-grey walls of the airport in the distance. My feeling of euphoria evaporated soon after, as my eyes met the carnage on the dividing road.

Dozens of blackened trucks were surrounded by heaps of gore that littered the street up to the decimated perimeter fence. Further down the block, I could see the twisted remains of a mobile anti-aircraft battery and what looked like a pair of armoured personnel carriers, their wheels sitting upon the torn-up remnants of the pavement.

I moved to the far side of the road, careful not to fall into any craters. I hopped over the guardrail and stepped across the mangled remains of the chain-link fence before moving onto the grass. I looked to the small windows of the terminal in the distance, my feet propelling me forward as I saw no movement.

A few metres before I came to the tarmac, I was stopped in my tracks by the amount of *Wehrmacht* bodies I saw crumpled before me. Their positioning told me they had been on the offensive. My eyes gravitated to the abandoned machine gun emplacement that lay ahead.

*If they attacked at night, they wouldn't have seen it until it opened up on them.*

I looked away as I saw several of the bodies had been disemboweled. None of them wore night vision.

I moved around the machine gun nest and stepped onto the runway. A row of shot-up trucks lay in the grass on the far side, and an SS soldier's body hung from an open door of the farthest truck. I walked around the destroyed convoy and approached the airport apron. I scanned the gates, looking for the plane that would serve as a source of escape, but my heart broke a little more with each empty spot.

I approached the terminal, hoping that the far side of the building would offer me solace. I didn't make it far before I heard a sound to my left.

I turned just as six SS members fanned out from behind a set of baggage carts. Their rifles aimed at me.

"Hands up," the nearest soldier said.

I complied immediately, feeling the surge of adrenaline.

"Down on your knees," the voice called out, and again I complied. "Face on the pavement."

I felt my cheek burn as it met the tarmac.

"Gun, in his waistband *Unterscharführer*," a different voice said, this one female.

"I see it," the original man said, his gruff voice remaining steady. There was a pause. "How many are waiting for you back there?" I couldn't see where he was looking.

"I'm alone," I replied. "I heard you were evacuating refugees."

I felt a knee depress into my back, followed by the pistol being removed from my possession.

"You took your sweet time getting here. Our snipers clocked you as you exited the alley." I felt the knee lift slightly before the sergeant added, "Hands to the sound of my voice."

A pair of flexicuffs found my wrists and I let out a grunt as they cinched up, tight. The soldiers rolled me onto my side before hoisting me up. I stood there looking at my captors. None of them could have been over the age of twenty-three.

"So, you're a refugee?" the sergeant asked, his brow moving under his caked-on camouflage paint. "Explain the weapon." I felt the two holding me up tighten their grip as the question was asked.

"What? Refugees can't be armed?" I replied in disbelief. "We are in a warzone, it's—"

Before the sergeant could answer, the female soldier on my left said, "Didn't you hear the broadcast from Doctor Fertig? There are no refugees; everyone must fight."

"Doctor...?" I began to ask, looking between her and the sergeant in confusion.

"Doctor Fertig, the acting Führer during this crisis," the woman said. "Our Führer is..." She paused, her lip quivering for a moment before she added, "The *Wehrmacht* shot him." Her grip tightened again. "But how can you not know that?"

The sergeant looked over his shoulder toward the edge of the airport. The destroyed buildings stood misshapen in the distance, their windows long shattered and cast to the street below. He returned his gaze to my sweat-soaked face before saying, "Frisk him for more weapons. Then we'll take him to Vogel."

As I felt the soldiers tugging at my clothing in their pat down, I contemplated asking questions about the evacuation or if there was a rendezvous point for civilians. I wanted to speak to someone higher up in the chain of command, not some lowly sergeant and his band who were pretending to be judge, jury and—if I dared say the wrong thing—executioner.

As the frisk was completed, I saw the soldier on my right pass my passport and wallet to the sergeant before shaking his head. It pained me to lose the two items I had spent the morning retrieving, but I tried to keep my focus on the events at hand.

The sergeant nodded before guiding us past the baggage carts and toward a restricted access door embedded in the wall of the terminal.

He grabbed the radio that hung from the webbing of his combat vest and said, "One in custody at the northern entrance, coming in." He waited for several moments, and I could see the clear wire of a speaker lodged in his ear.

He pressed a code into the keypad and pulled the door open. We stepped into a dimly lit roadway-looking area. I blinked to get used to the different lighting and saw baggage carts parked beside the belt systems that connected into the bowels of the terminal. Several military trucks were farther down this interior roadway. One SS soldier sat on a collection of crates, her legs swinging as a cigarette hung from her mouth, while another took stock of their armaments.

The soldiers guided me through another door which led into a short hallway. The sergeant typed in the same code and pulled open the door, escorting us into the baggage hall of the terminal itself. I looked at the overhead television that had broadcasted the arrivals and belt numbers. Beside each flight number was the word: DELAYED.

*Understatement of the century,* I thought to myself in annoyance.

I pulled my eyes from the screen as my captors forced me to take a sharp right and head up an escalator. As we ascended, I remembered the business owner who had invited me in for a drink. I should have listened to him.

Another code was entered, and we arrived at a room that looked like it was meant to be an employee lounge. Sofas, tables and a small fridge sat in the corner. As we entered, an officer looked up from a series of handwritten notes and a map he had laid across the table.

"*Hauptsturmführer*, sorry to disturb you, sir, but we've got another one," the sergeant said. He clicked his heels together before approaching the officer who looked annoyed by the disruption. "He had a firearm on him, sir, but nothing else other than identification." The sergeant placed the gun and my belongings on the table.

The captain looked at the items before his eyes flashed with intrigue. "If you have a weapon, you must have some knowledge on how to use it, no?"

"Yes, sir. I completed my military course as required."

The officer tilted his head, noting my accent. "French?" he asked, his eyes appearing to light up.

"No, sir, in Spain. It was a one-year commitment."

The captain looked at the sergeant, a pleased expression on his face. "Good. Sounds like you'll be perfect for use around here."

"No, sir, you misunderstand. I'm not here to fight; I came here because I was told you were evacuating people—"

The officer let out a humorless chuckle. "That stopped the moment Doctor Fertig announced the Führer's death. His broadcasts have shown us Magda's lies. She says they captured the Führer alive, but as I already said, that is not true. Now every citizen of the Reich must do their duty."

I opened my mouth to correct the officer on my citizenship, but he continued before I got a chance. "And those countries that sponge off the Reich and its ideals must work doubly hard to fight for it."

He stood tall then, moved over to me and grabbed my chin, turning my head to study my features. I could see a pair of dueling scars displayed proudly on his left cheek and I recalled hearing the fencing practice had received newfound fervour in the upper-class universities of the Reich.

The officer clicked his tongue. "Not good enough for the SS..." He trailed off, his hand dropping to his side before he looked to the sergeant. "Take him to the French. They'll find a place for him."

"But I don't speak French. I won't be able to understand them," I lied in an attempt to get out of this situation.

"Spanish, French? Close enough." A cold smile appeared on the captain's face as he said, "Or speak in German; you're doing it now, they'll understand enough. It is the superior language, after all." As my captors began to direct me to the door, the officer added, "Oh and cut those cuffs off him. He can't kill traitors in those."

I felt my hands being manipulated before hearing a sawing motion from behind. My wrists were soon freed. As I brought my hands forward, I said, "Is it true the Führer's own bodyguards turned on him?"

"Pure propaganda," the captain said. "It was paratroopers that attacked the *Burghof*. Those members of Hitler's SS that defended him until the end will be given warrior funerals and iron crosses with oak leaves for their valiant sacrifice."

The captain grabbed my wallet and passport from his table and took a step forward, thrusting them into my hand as he said, "Now do your duty just as they did!"

As I was shoved out of the room I thought, *He thinks he knows so much about it. He wasn't there—he has no idea if the guards fought valiantly or ran off into the woods.*

As we moved out of the office and passed the empty arrival hall, I made peace with myself that I would not be boarding a plane home anytime soon. For a split second I thought of running, but that notion dissipated with the imagined sounds of gunfire echoing through my mind.

As we walked through a set of doors I asked, "Why are there French forces here? Are they volunteers or—"

The sergeant spoke without looking back at me. "A company of the Foreign Legion came in this morning. They said they heard the reports and asked permission to render aid." I opened my mouth to reply, but was cut off when the sergeant said, "Here we are."

We walked into a long room with counters to the right and a set of cubicles and offices tucked toward the back. Hundreds of troops in French uniforms stood around chatting amongst each other. The ones that weren't standing were sitting on the few chairs they had managed to find or were balancing their weight on their rucksacks. Several turned to look at us, many of them eying me with contempt.

My gaze drifted to the golden letters emblazoned on the wall behind the counter. The word IMMIGRATION was sandwiched between two swastika flags that hung from the wall. I detected the irony of a foreign force having their assembly point in this particular section of the airport, but kept the thought to myself.

A French sergeant moved forward from the group and spoke in the most heinous German I had ever heard, saying, "Volunteer this one? Front line?"

"Orders from *Hauptsturmführer* Vogel, he's a Spaniard so he is going to be placed with your group." The SS member paused, looking between the two of us before adding, "Can we leave him with you?"

My captors appeared impatient, no doubt eager to return to their patrol and cease babysitting someone who had been attempting to flee.

"Yeah," the French sergeant said. As his eyes met mine, I could see that he only understood some of what the SS member had said. "Come, Spanish."

My SS escorts turned and departed the immigration room, leaving me to follow my new commander as he guided me through the ranks of the French Foreign Legion. The soldiers gave disgusted looks as they marvelled at my appearance—no doubt they could smell my lack of fighting spirit and my unwillingness to be there.

"No French?" the sergeant asked, still in German.

"Oh, I speak it quite well, I just didn't tell them that," I replied in his native language before stepping around a soldier.

"Good, it will make all of this much easier," he replied, his tone softening. He gestured vaguely toward the back of the room. "I'll be over there. I'll check to see if you can stay in my squad. The others have already taken in several civilians. We have one too, she's over there." He pointed to the left before walking off.

I looked in the direction he had pointed and saw a brunette examining the helmet in her hands. I felt my heart stop for a moment as I recognized Meriam. I moved past a group of legionnaires and headed toward her. She looked up just before I reached her, a wide smile appearing on her face as she stood. I opened my mouth to speak, but stopped as she hugged me.

"Did they conscript you too?" she asked.

"It would seem so," I replied, releasing her from the hug. I was taken aback by the embrace but felt grateful to see someone I knew. "What are you doing here?"

"Same thing as you, I'm guessing. Trying to get out. I got here for my flight just before they announced everything was cancelled. We— Well, there was a group of us for the same flight. We waited, but after a while so many of them left, trying to get trains or a ride with someone out of the city..."

"I know how the train route worked," I muttered to myself before adding, "Did they ever get any flights of refugees out?"

"Not that I know of, but I did see a plane or two take off even after everything was cancelled, so maybe... But I don't know where they were going."

"So, what's the plan now?" I asked, looking at the legionnaires as they conversed with each other, growing restless as they did so. "Surely someone is in charge and knows what they are doing?"

"The SS guys were in here a little bit ago, took all our officers including the commandant. I think they are talking strategy. But I'll tell you, I'm good with staying put. I did my service for France already." She paused, searching my face for a moment before adding, "I'm surprised they put you with us, but then again, there's no way you would pass the SS entrance test."

"Hey!" I said with a laugh. "I'm strong enough, fast enough. Well, I was two, three years ago."

"No, I meant racially. But that's fine, they all look the same to me anyway. Big, blond, and stupid."

"Shh," I said, looking over my shoulder to ensure no one had overheard. "You can't say stuff like that here."

"Why? Everyone here has loyalty to France first, the Reich second. Besides, a girl can't have her own opinions?"

"Well..." I paused, deciding on the best route to steer the conversation toward one that might prevent us from being shot. "But hey, you look good." I gestured to her uniform.

"Thank you. The pants are a little big, but I guess that will mean they are air conditioned." She paused, looking at my muddy clothing. "You look like you've been through a lot."

"I slept under a bridge last night," I said, prompting Meriam to laugh.

"Spaniard," someone said from behind me, causing me to turn around. It was the French sergeant from before. "Come with me. Time to get you in uniform."

"Good luck," Meriam said with a grin before sitting back down on one of the office chairs, pulling on her braid.

I followed the sergeant to the back of the immigration room, and we took a left. He typed a code into the keypad and pushed the door open. I could see this was once a storeroom for stationary and other office supplies, but in the middle of the floor were open duffle bags of clothing and gear.

"The Foreign Legion always brings spares," he said, a sense of pride in his voice. He turned, his eyes intense as he added, "I don't agree with them tossing their unwanted civilians into our unit. We are not here for tourists."

"I hardly want to be here either," I replied, and the sergeant's back stiffened, brown eyes narrowing. Despite this, I added, "But if serving with you for a few weeks gets me home to Spain then I'll gladly do it."

"I can accept that," he replied, appearing to relax. "But tell me, the others they gave us all had military training. One of them was police in Belgium. What do you offer?"

"I did my one-year service as required. Mostly weekends, never deployed," I said, prompting the sergeant to nod. "But I can march with the best of them, and most importantly, fire a gun."

"Good enough," he said before looking at the open duffel bags and pointing to the closest one. "Grab a uniform shirt, a helmet and pants. I'll get you a carrier that's already set up with magazine pouches from the other room." He turned to leave before stopping and saying over his shoulder, "And be quick about it."

With that, he left, shutting the door behind him.

I was surprised that he was leaving me unsupervised with all the French uniforms, but as the thought occurred to me, I realized that I wasn't going anywhere. And even if I was, what would I steal? A helmet?

I picked up several shirts before finally settling on one that fit me well enough. The pants were much easier, picking a pair that fit on the first try. As for the helmet, none of them fit particularly well, but I made do.

I looked at the camouflage pattern of the clothing, noticing the differences between the SS and *Wehrmacht* patterns I had seen and noting the similarities it shared with the Spanish patterns I had worn some eleven years earlier. I recalled a photo taken of me when I was at basic training and how my mother had framed it in the entranceway of our home. I wondered what box the picture was collecting dust in after the house had been sold.

The door opened and the sergeant entered, a carrier in his hands. "I figured this one would fit." He held it out for me to grab.

I accepted it and said, "I have everything but boots. Where do you keep them?"

"We have a few pairs but..." He tilted his head. "Whoever packed the plane sent us with the women's shipment." He laughed, looking down at my dress shoes. "You're welcome to try but I think you'll be better off in those. We can always get you some later if they send us into the city."

"And what do you think the chances of that are?" I asked.

He shrugged. "Either they do, or they don't." He gestured toward me with his chin. "Finish getting ready. I'm sure the officers will be back soon; we will know more then."

As the door shut, I put on the carrier and felt the air leave my lungs by the weight of the plates and loaded magazines. I clipped everything together and adjusted the straps to my desired tightness. It took several breaths before I was able to get used to the weight. As I gathered my civilian clothes from the ground, I wondered when I would next wear something that wasn't a military uniform.

I exited the room and returned to the area where Meriam was sitting. I saw the sergeant speaking to several soldiers who I assumed were part of his squad. As I approached, they ceased their conversation. I gave a polite nod toward the other team members and said, "I think I'm just missing a rifle and that's it."

The sergeant smirked. "Not missing—I know where it is. But you aren't getting one yet."

I looked at Meriam, and she gave me a look that told me she lacked a weapon as well.

As I turned to face the sergeant, he added, "Not until we

trust you." My eyes met a pair of legionnaires, sleeves rolled up, scowling. I returned my gaze to the sergeant, who gave an exasperated sigh. "Anything else?"

I bit my tongue and sat down on the carpeted floor beside Meriam. The sergeant returned to conversing with his squad, but their voices were mumbled and curt.

"What's his problem?" I asked Meriam in Spanish.

She grinned, her eyebrow raised. "Who, Belmont? He's getting heat from everyone: SS, French officers, his subordinates. He was nice to me though."

"I don't doubt that," I replied, giving her another once over.

"He'll warm up to you. You just need to... What's the word? Prove yourself. Then it will be fine. But don't look so down. You have to ask yourself, 'Does it make a good story?' and if the answer is yes, then at least that's something. What's a better story than fighting with the Foreign Legion while the National Socialists battle it out?" She adjusted her posture in the chair before looking down at my dress shoes. She held a peculiar expression on her face before returning to her native language to ask, "Where are your boots?"

"Somewhere in France," I said before gesturing to her fresh pair. "You're lucky you got some, he said they only shipped women's sizes."

She found this particularly amusing and let out a laugh before saying, "A win for me, I suppose." She chuckled again. "I think I've only seen a dozen or so women here. Good thing they brought enough extra pairs for us. You know, I might need a set for hiking, another for the mall, one for the clubs..."

I waved my hand to dismiss her playful teasing. "Yeah, yeah. So, what's the plan? Any updates?"

"The officers still aren't back yet so it's the same as it always is: 'Hurry up and wait.' It was like that when I served too."

"I guess that's something the French and the Spanish

armies have in common. They love the 'hurry up and wait' approach."

The conversation faded as we both looked forward, watching the hundreds of legionnaires continue to mill about in boredom.

I had a feeling that it wouldn't last.

# Chapter 10

## *Patriots in One Hand, Traitors in the Other*

I stood on the roof of the terminal, facing the runways, a cigarette affixed to my mouth. I had not smoked since high school graduation, but judging by the situation that I found myself in, I decided it was an appropriate time to break the streak.

In the three days since I had been amalgamated into the Foreign Legion, the only thing of note to occur was Sergeant Belmont supplying me with a sleeping bag and thin mat from the French surplus.

We continuously prepared for a counterattack that never came. There were rumors that battles were being fought across the southern outskirts of the capital as Magda's so called "loyalist" forces tried to open up a new front, but I hadn't heard anything about that since the day prior. No, most of the fighting was out in Munich, Vienna and some big tank battle in Ludendorff and the surrounding countryside, all of which the radio reported as SS victories. It looked for now like our war was over before it had even started.

I watched a few dozen French soldiers move toward the

smaller satellite terminal of the airport, crossing the tarmac in a slow parade. It was our most exposed position and command believed that was the likeliest strike location.

I felt my stomach rumble and tried to remember the last good meal I had eaten. The preceding seventy-two hours had been relatively small in nutritional value but high in calorie count. Snacks and precooked meals from storerooms of the various shops around the airport had been in abundance. I knew for a fact that there were several upscale restaurants in this terminal, but so far the best I had eaten were two frankfurters with enough sauerkraut to kill a small mammal. Meriam and I figured the SS were hoarding the best food for their people and the senior staff.

I felt a tap on my shoulder. "Guess who?" Meriam said.

I turned, a smile on my face. "I was just thinking about—" I looked down as she extended a hamburger wrapped in foil.

"That SS captain or however you say his rank had someone break open the gate on that American food stand," she said as she unwrapped a burger of her own, a thick layer of mustard clinging to the side of the foil.

With haste, I plucked the cigarette from my mouth and tossed it aside before removing the wrapper and watching as some shredded lettuce hit the roof panel beside my shoe. I bit into the beef patty and tasted the sweetness of the pickles.

"Armies travel on their stomachs," I said after the first bite.

"It's not bad," she replied, looking at the burger in her hands. "They must be expecting us to move out soon."

I took another bite and chewed for a moment, savoring the taste before replying, "What makes you think that?"

"They are feeding us something real and we've been sitting around for too many days now."

I had hardly heard her. "This is great. This might be the best hamburger I've ever had."

She looked at her burger again, appearing to come around to my assessment that this burger should be nominated for the Peace Prize. She took her eyes off her food and looked at the cigarette I had snuffed out on the roof, saying, "You think we will move to defend the chancellery? Or the *Volkshalle*?" She sounded almost excited. As I raised a quizzical eyebrow, she quickly countered, "What? Nothing is happening here, and if I was Magda, I would try to capture those buildings. They're symbols; holding them would prove her legitimacy."

"You just want to explore them, don't you?"

"Is it that obvious?" She kicked a pebble, causing it to bounce off some of the pipework. "I've never seen the inside of them, and can you imagine—going into all the rooms that are normally blocked off, but now we would have a reason to be there. The history in those buildings" She looked to the horizon, visualizing her journey through the structures. "I've seen enough paintings of them in my art books. It would be interesting to say I had been inside."

I swallowed a large bite of food before saying, "You're an odd one, you know?"

"Me? Why, what did I say?"

I took my time responding. I had felt like Meriam and I were really getting along the past few days, but I wasn't sure how she would respond. With caution, I continued, "You are really excited to see the buildings but ... well, at the museum I got the impression you hated the Reich."

She thinned her lips, shaking her head as a response before saying, "Can't hate the greatest empire that ever was, right?"

Her sarcasm could be heard from the other end of Germania.

She paused before adding, "Buildings of power, even if constructed by ... people I don't agree with, someone still made them, plans were created, material brought in. They are still great feats of human ambition." She paused again, this time her eyes appearing to look through me. "I just wish they hadn't been built on the backs of slave labour."

As we continued to eat, we watched as a formation of SS troops exited out onto the tarmac below us. I felt that Meriam's hunch had been correct—an advance was coming, and I wasn't feeling optimistic about it.

The order came no more than thirty minutes later. Two thirds of the French forces had been instructed to report in full kit by the entrance to the airport, our squad being one of those on the list. As we headed to the immigration hall, I could see Sergeant Belmont approaching us. He was gripping two unloaded rifles, one in either hand, his face red.

"I've been looking for you two," he said. Not waiting for us to reply, he shoved the weapons toward us. I noticed the hesitation as he released his grip on them. "Don't make me regret this."

"Where are we going?" Meriam asked as we began to follow him toward the assembly area.

Belmont side-stepped around a group of legionnaires who were hunched over a map, a lieutenant pointing to various locations. Leading us on, he said, "If you had been at my briefing ..." He trailed off, his hand wiping his face. I sensed that he wasn't so much upset with us as unaccustomed to the lack of discipline. He continued after a deep breath. "Orders are to set up machine gun positions on the flanks of the assault. The bulk of the force will move around to encircle a company-sized garrison of *Wehrmacht*."

My back stiffened upon hearing the word. I envisioned hundreds of battle-hardened troops marching down a bombed-out road, their blue eyes beaming forward as they descended upon me, the steel of their rifles catching the sun.

Belmont raised his voice as we neared the departure hall, nearly being drowned out by the sounds of legionnaires shouting instructions at each other. "We shouldn't see any contact unless they send out some probes to check for weak spots in our lines. But if they do, they'll be walking into a perfect kill zone."

We exited the terminal and lined up along the sidewalk. The remainder of Belmont's squad appeared to have beaten us there and stood under a sign advising the parking location of taxis. They stood in formation, arms to their side, heads forward. A group of SS soldiers moved along the far side of the road, cigarettes hanging from their mouths as they headed to their patrol point.

We stood beside our squad mates and waited for orders.

Farther down from us I could see a collection of French officers huddled around one man in particular. He was the oldest of the group, but was still a relatively young man. I recognized the rank insignia of a major on his uniform. He ceased speaking after a moment and the collection of officers dispersed, one of them heading toward Belmont.

The orders were given with haste, and before I knew it our formation of nearly two hundred legionnaires was marching down the autobahn toward the city. A traffic jam of abandoned cars snaked off toward the distant horizon. A few dozen bodies of civilians were scattered about at random intervals. Judging by their appearance, they had been nothing but normal people who had dared to venture too close to the airport at night.

Meriam looked at the pale body of a young woman as we passed by. "Do you think these SS animals feel anything for gunning down innocents?" Her face held a look of disgust.

Sergeant Belmont looked over his shoulder. "They aren't

taking any chances; it was dark, we have an entire hostile city around us and we know a counterattack is coming. They could have been enemy scouts."

"So, you don't blame them?" Meriam asked. Rage sat on the cusp of her voice.

"Didn't say that. Just saying that once the sun comes up, then you can see what you've done." Belmont's voice hardened. "Besides, this whole thing started when those Brownshirts and want-to-be soldiers started shooting up cities. They looked like anyone. Hell, the day before they *were* anyone. All it takes is for one of them to remove their colours and they could attempt to infiltrate our stronghold here. The snipers might have seen indicators of weapons or a radio and had to make a split-second decision."

Both Meriam and I looked at the body of a man in a suit. Neither of us saw weapons or communication equipment, just the dried blood around the hole in his skull and the culmination of his life experience caked upon the pavement.

---

If this is what war was like, I had no reason to be nervous.

We had set up our position inside an aging bookstore. Two men next to me manned a machine gun while Belmont and several others were up on the second floor. Meriam was to my right, leaning against a shelf, tossing stones into her helmet. Hours had gone by, and I could tell even those manning the machine gun were growing restless.

If the *Wehrmacht* group had wanted to fight their way out, we would have heard gunshots by now, possibly mortars depending on their armaments. But instead, it was calm, the sound of a breeze moving past the shattered storefront window.

"If this coup stays like this, I might have to join a different unit to get a story to tell," Meriam said, her eyes dull with boredom. She tossed a pebble and frowned when it hit the side of the helmet before skidding off under a rack of magazines.

"Of all the stores we set up in, it couldn't have been a boot store," I muttered, looking at my worn dress shoes. I settled against the wall and adjusted my grip on my weapon.

There was movement on the floor above us.

"Belmont's on the move," Meriam said, her eyes following the footsteps drifting toward the stairs that lay at the back of the store.

Several seconds passed before I heard a door open and saw Belmont marching toward us, rifle in hand, a poised expression on his face. "Spaniard, with me," he said, before looking to his fellow soldiers and giving them an order to hold position.

"What's going on?" I asked, scrambling to my feet.

Belmont looked to Meriam before returning his gaze to me. "Our spotters have eyes on an enemy scout with a white flag. We are going to snatch him, make sure it's not a trap." With that, he stepped around the machine gun and was out on the street. I followed suit.

As we moved down the road, I felt the blood rushing to my head as the adrenaline kicked in. I was aware that Belmont was bringing me because of my proficiency in German. The other reason being that I was expendable, and if I died, at least it wasn't one of his own people.

We turned down an alley and Belmont motioned for me to stay still as we took cover behind a dumpster. He gestured to the edge of the alley only a few metres ahead before saying, "When he's here, we signal him over."

I nodded that I understood, but I had only been half listening for a thought came to me, stealing my focus. My weapon was still unloaded. I gritted my teeth, thinking back to my drill sergeants and the absolute verbal thrashing they would have given me if they knew I had walked into a combat situation with an unloaded weapon.

As Belmont turned his attention to the street beyond, I grabbed a magazine from my webbing and inserted it into the rifle. Belmont snapped his head back at the sound of me pulling the bolt back to chamber a round. He mumbled something under his breath and shook his head before returning his gaze forward.

I took a deep breath to calm myself. I needed to focus. This soldier may be able to give me some information and it would come down to me being able to interpret him correctly.

A few seconds passed before I heard a disturbance in the rubble outside. A man in a *Wehrmacht* uniform moved by.

"Come here," Belmont said in German, putting the emphasis on the wrong syllables.

The soldier understood all the same and flinched as he approached, raising the white flag, his free hand high above his head. The soldier moved into the alleyway, saying, "I am unarmed."

I repeated what the man said in French, lowering my rifle as I did so.

Either not caring or flat-out ignoring what I had translated, Belmont snapped, "Keep your weapon on him."

Belmont grabbed the soldier and pushed him against the wall, letting his rifle fall to its sling as he performed a frisk on the trembling man. Satisfied there was nothing on the soldier, Belmont released him and spun him around to face us.

"Why alone?" Belmont asked, his poor German shining through again.

The man looked between us before asking him to repeat.

"Why are you alone? Where is your unit?" I asked in German.

Hearing that I was able to speak his native tongue with

ease, the man perked up. "We are on the same side," he replied, pointing to the *Wehrmacht* emblem on his collar. "We both fight for the Führer ... the *true* Führer."

"How do you know we aren't with the terrorists?" I asked.

"My commander heard over the radio that there were reports of French forces landing at Hartmann, working with the SS. That was before our battalion broke contact with the rest of our regiment. We saw our chance to link up with true patriots and took it. They sent me to find you and report that we are allies. We know you have other units moving to attack our garrison."

"Couldn't you have radioed us?" I asked. "Why resort to risking yourself?"

"No one can be trusted. Not with words, only action." The soldier paused, pointing in the direction of the airport. "We heard so much gunfire from there, we didn't know who owned it. That's why we stopped our advance. Couldn't risk running into *Wehrmacht* forces loyal to Magda." He sized me up, looking at my helmet before his eyes lingered on my dress shoes. "Are you Gestapo?" he asked, appearing to think that was the only likely reason for my mismatched appearance.

"No. Conscripted."

"What are you two talking about?" Belmont snapped, his hand still pressing the man to the wall. "How many are with him?"

I explained the situation and that the unit this soldier was with wished to defect to our side, or in more correct verbiage, remain on the side of the sitting government.

Belmont licked his lips before grabbing his radio and beginning to speak quickly into it, releasing the man as he did so.

As the soldier adjusted himself, he gave a hateful glance toward Belmont. Seeing this, I said, "Sorry about him, but like you said, no one can be trusted. We can't be too careful."

"Terrible times these siblings put us through. To turn on their own brother for something as trivial as politics. Entitled and spoiled children, Magda and Wolfgang, the pair of them."

Belmont took a step down the alley, a gloved finger blocking his exposed ear. I could tell our conversation was distracting him from the orders he was receiving via his earpiece.

"Why are so many *Wehrmacht* forces in leagues with them?" I asked after a moment. "I have passed so many bodies."

The soldier gave me a quizzical look before replying, "We aren't in leagues with them; a rogue general here and there, but the *Wehrmacht* have always been loyal to the Führer."

Belmont pushed his radio toward me before unclipping his earpiece from the speaker so I could hear it. He gestured with his hand for me to hurry up. I pushed the button on the side and said in French, "Hello?"

"Hello? This is Commandant Delacroix. My sergeant doesn't speak enough German to tell the surrendering soldier what I need him to do. Tell this man to return to his commanding officer with the instructions that they are to move south along the main road toward our lines. Weapons are to be unloaded and slung. We will brief them once they are secured behind our forces."

I handed the radio back to Belmont before translating the orders from the French officer to the German soldier. The man nodded after each sentence, determination in his eyes.

"Yes, sir," he replied, his gaze fixed on the radio in Belmont's hands. He pivoted and moved up the alley with a cautious step before breaking into a slow jog and disappearing around the corner.

"What's the plan now, sergeant?"

"We go back to our position," Belmont replied, sticking his head out of the alley, watching the *Wehrmacht* soldier to ensure he was still heading in the proper direction. After a moment,

Belmont stepped back, and we moved out of the alley and toward the French lines in the distance. "And then we wait."

---

And wait we did.

For hours we sat in silence, listening as the wind continued up the street. Belmont leaned against the machine gun, eyes glazed over, a cigarette slowly burning its way toward his gloved fingers.

Meriam and another member of the squad, a Legionnaire named Henri, had been tasked with covering our flank by watching the back alley. I will admit I was jealous that Belmont had tasked Meriam to go with someone else, especially the tallest and most chiselled of the group. I told myself to keep the thoughts buried. I knew I couldn't be with her all the time, nor would that be healthy. But as the other members of the squad sat in various positions around the storefront, I found I could think of nothing else.

Standing, I said, "Sergeant, I'm going to go out back to stretch a little."

Without taking his eyes from the street, he replied, "Don't be long."

I moved out toward the back of the store. One of the legionnaires sat on a chair, his fingers running along the top of a loaded magazine. He watched me with an accusatory look and I could tell he thought I was deserting, yet he said nothing.

I moved around him and through a small office where a wilted plant sat on a cluttered desk. I pushed open the door leading to the alley and was surprised to see that neither Meriam nor Henri were present.

I looked both ways, ignoring the smell of rotting food from the various garbage cans and took a step westward. My mind filled with intrusive, envious, ugly thoughts. The two of them naked, camouflaged pants strewn around a backroom as the pair came together in a sweaty embrace. Meriam's hair hanging down, covering her exposed breasts—

I felt sick, a heat in my stomach billowing up, forcing me to pick up the pace. I knew I was being irrational, but realizing you had feelings for someone was never a rational thing.

As I moved down the alley, the sound of a crow cawing from a rooftop above me forced my eyes skyward. It was mocking me.

A door flung open further down the alley. Meriam emerged, laughing, Henri soon after her, a smile across his face. The jealousy reared its ugly head inside my skull.

Upon seeing me, Meriam pointed and said, "Speak of the devil."

I looked between them, attempting to deduce if anything romantic had gone on. I stared at their clothing as if that would reveal the secret of their affair.

"We were just coming to get you," she said. "Don't tell Belmont but we investigated some of the buildings, looking for food."

"Most are locked, no?" I asked, pulling on a door beside me to prove my point. It did not budge.

"They all are, but Henri can pick them."

"That I can," he said. His French was as smooth as silk, making me painfully aware of my accent whenever I spoke.

"And did you find anything?" I asked, my voice sounding more intense than I would have liked. I was not keen on hearing about Henri's skilled fingers.

"Nothing but snacks and condiments. But ... there is a shoe store," Meriam said, gesturing toward the door they had just emerged from. "We... I was coming to get you to show you.

They have lots of boots. Nothing military, but good enough that you won't stick out as much."

I appreciated that she had thought of me while she had been off gallivanting with this absolute specimen of a man. I took my eyes off Henri and approached the door as Meriam held it open.

As the two of us entered, Henri said, "I'll wait down the alley, in case Belmont comes looking for us."

I thought of the sergeant and the burning cigarette. The chances of him moving from his spot were unlikely.

Meriam and I moved past the storage room and into the main store. She ran her hands across several pairs of heels.

"If only there wasn't a war on..." she muttered to herself, but I moved out of earshot, looking at the men's boot section.

I tried on several pairs, all the while Meriam milled about the store, rifle in hand. It was as if she was my personal bodyguard, and I found myself watching her more than looking at the boots.

After the third pair, I found a style that fit well and looked relatively similar to those worn by the French. I stood and walked around the storefront in them to ensure they would not blister my feet. Meriam whistled at me as I moved down an aisle that she had taken up residency in.

"Looking good. Not as good as me in a pair of these of course," she said, a finger running up the side of a pair of thick heeled black boots. Then her hand froze. "Listen..."

We both paused, tilting our ears.

The sound of marching.

I took a few cautious steps toward the window and looked out. A formation of *Wehrmacht* troops moved up the street, unloaded rifles slung behind their shoulders.

"We should head back," I said, prompting Meriam to nod slowly, her eyes fixed on the column of Germans.

We retreated from the store and out into the back alley. We rounded the corner, and I could see that Henri was not at his post. This caused me to worry, but as Meriam pulled open the door and we moved into the back of the store, I realized my worry was for nothing.

"We thought you ran off," Belmont said, before his attention moved forward again.

I looked over to Henri to gauge his reaction. He was leaning against a bookshelf, arms folded, watching the *Wehrmacht* troops approach. He couldn't have cared less if we had deserted, making me feel foolish for thinking that there had been anything going on between him and Meriam.

"Thought about it," Meriam replied, sounding aloof, as if the comment stood in the way of what she really wanted to say. "Are these our defectors?"

"It would be a hell of a coincidence if they weren't," Belmont replied.

Meriam paced toward our comrades, her eyes watching as the Germans turned right and moved up the road. "I thought they were going to approach from somewhere else. Isn't this out of the way for them?"

Belmont did not reply. Instead, he moved away from his position and began speaking into his radio. I didn't care to follow the conversation, as I could guess what it entailed.

By the time the last dozen members of the *Wehrmacht* infantry were past us, Belmont said, "Our SS counterparts have intercepted them and are escorting them to the airport, they are hoping the officers can give us intel on enemy positions."

"But we aren't going with them," Meriam said, prompting Belmont to shoot her a glance before his eyes returned to the other members of the squad.

"No, we aren't. We have a different mission. We are to

report to a building on Kleps Platz. It's near Speer *Straße*. Our next assignment is there."

"Is that far?" I asked.

"It isn't close," Belmont replied, his voice sounding tired. "Lieutenant Boucher will be by in a few minutes to collect us and amalgamate us with other members of the company. But remember, this city is still hostile. Just because these *Wehrmacht* ended up being the good guys doesn't mean the rest will go quietly."

Meriam pulled out a cigarette, and as she plopped it in her mouth she mumbled, "I think the word 'good guys' is a stretch." The hate in her voice was plain.

I didn't hear the rest of what Belmont said as I handed her my lighter. She pivoted and moved to the rear of the store. I followed her into the back room and saw she stood trembling, the lit cigarette grasped unsteadily between her fingers.

"What's wrong?" I asked.

"This whole thing." She took a drag before blowing the smoke into the air. "One minute we are sent to kill these soldiers, then they defect and now we are best friends. I just... I can't wrap my head around it." She bit her lip before adding, "I guess I should just stuff it into a mental box like all you guys but ... there is no clear side here. It's messy and I want no part of it."

I moved beside her, pressing my back to the wall and slowly sliding down.

A long moment passed before she added, "It's never clean. Lord knows I knew that. My instructors beat that into me when I served, but I never thought I would be living through a civil war."

"I don't think anyone expected they would be living through a civil war, but I try to think that God put us on this earth at certain points in history because he knew we could handle it."

"That's a nice sentiment," Meriam replied, the end of her cigarette turning bright as she puffed again. "But I think it's all random. Men kill men, which leads to more killing. I don't think God has anything to do with it."

I shrugged. "I get that. But sometimes the killings stop, and life can be beautiful again. I like to think God exists in beauty."

She flicked her ash to the hardwood floor. "I think God exists in this cigarette." A soft laugh escaped her lips. "It's the only peace I have in my life right now."

"It's the little victories."

# Chapter 11

## *Partisans For a Lost Cause*

I could smell the storm long before it arrived. The sky was grey by the time our march was ordered to a halt. Belmont pressed his earpiece further into his ear canal, tilting his head. He nodded to himself as he took in the orders, his eyes locked on the pavement. As I turned, I caught Meriam looking at me before her gaze darted to the surrounding rooftops.

The legionnaires behind me began to fan out as they set up a defensive position. Looking over my shoulder, I could see the other squad leaders all shared a similar expression as our own.

A moment passed before Belmont lowered his hand and gestured for his subordinates to form up around him. "The commandant wants us to link up with an SS platoon a few blocks away," Belmont said, looking at each of us.

"Any particular reason?" Meriam asked, sounding less than enthused by the order.

"They are being harassed by snipers. Their advance has stalled. We are being tasked to offer them support if we can."

"Great," Meriam said. She bit her lip, her eyes gravitating to her boots.

I fully understood her hesitation. I too had no desire to go out and be target practice for sharpshooters. If the SS had been hit hard—hard enough to stop an advance in its tracks—I wasn't hopeful of our chances.

But the order had been given and we were on the move again, gradually and without fanfare.

After several blocks we came to an open avenue surrounded by three-story buildings. A blinking light in one of the windows ahead caught our eye. The officer at the front of the formation spoke to a pair of sergeants before coming to the conclusion that the light must be a signal from the SS unit we were sent to link up with.

We crossed the road, our squad covering the southern flank where the various streets joined the avenue. Our officers entered the building, leaving the vast majority of us on defensive duty. As the minutes passed the road stayed peaceful, which prompted my eyes to wander.

At the centre of the avenue, I saw a dozen pillars in a Roman design. The statue that had laid atop it had been pulled down, the nude figure shattered into several large chunks of marble. A trio of chains were still wrapped around its fragments, as if whoever had toppled it had abandoned them in haste.

I was unaware of the significance of the statue, but I knew it was old, most likely from the time of the Great Führer. I found my mind running through all sorts of scenarios as to why a group would want to desecrate a piece of history such as this, but all my speculations failed to provide me with a reasonable answer.

We stood outside for some time, long enough to allow the overcast skies to bear fruit, engulfing us in a heavy downpour. It was a dreadful rain; the kind that offered no hydration as the humidity was murder and made me feel like every pore on my face was suffocating. The incessant clicking sound of the droplets on our helmets kept me tethered to the wet streets, making it impossible for me to detach to inward thought.

The French officers exited the building sometime later with several squads of SS soldiers behind them.

"We are splitting up," one of the French lieutenants said. "Four teams, and an SS squad in each." He looked at the French sergeant beside him. "Cross, you and your squad stay back here with *Untersturmführer* Gertz and cover this block. Keep their wounded secure." He then looked to Belmont. "Sergeant, you and your amalgamated squad are going to be placed with *Scharführer* um"

The lieutenant looked over his shoulder as a man with bright blue eyes approached. His helmet was scuffed, and a blackened bruise marked his cheek.

"Müller," the SS sergeant said as he stepped beside the officer.

"Yes, *Scharführer* Müller," the lieutenant said. "You'll go with his people and explore the northern blocks up to Heydrich *Straße*. If these terrorists have retreated past that we are not to pursue. SS command has reports of a *Wehrmacht* tank column spotted north of there." Belmont nodded, prompting the officer to add, "Happy hunting, I'm counting on you."

Belmont rounded up his people and ordered us to move. We headed off, SS squad in tow, leaving the lieutenant to divvy up the remaining teams as he saw fit.

The rain was hammering us now and the once pleasant walk around the world capital had become a grueling march. My pace began to slow, the weight of my gear and carrier wearing me down.

Sergeant Müller matched my pace. He held out a pack of cigarettes, the rain quickly getting to them.

"A head rush is good for a march. Takes your mind off the rain," he said, a friendly smile on his face.

I accepted the cigarette, and the sergeant immediately grabbed one for himself, placing it between his lips. Müller lit mine first with a lighter he produced from a jacket pocket before lighting his own.

"You know, you Frenchmen might not hear it, but all of us appreciate you being here—France sending aid to the Reich to eliminate these traitors, I mean." He let the smoke exit his nose. "The only one of our so-called 'allies' to do so." He shook his head. "If the Führer was still alive, I know he would be treating the other nations and their transgressions harshly."

The cigarette was helping, and I appreciated the sergeant bridging the gap between the SS and our squad.

Meriam moved up beside us and Müller offered her a cigarette, but she shook her head no with a soft smile.

There was something about this sergeant that made me feel comfortable, despite the SS lightning bolts on the collar of his uniform. To fill the lull in conversation I decided to say, "I'm not a Frenchman, you know. I'm Spanish."

"Oh, *conquistador*, eh?" Müller took another drag. "It's a shame our ancestors never fought. The Imperial Spanish legions against the Nordic hoards and our berserkers would have been a battle for the ages," he said, smirking like a cat that had just finished a bowl of warm milk.

Belmont looked over his shoulder, his pace slowing to meet ours. He used the opportunity to break out his clumsy German, asking, "Where do we go?"

Müller moved up beside Belmont, saying, "We are just to patrol the sector. We keep moving north and stop at Heydrich *Straße* as ordered." He sniffed the air, his eyes bouncing between the shuttered shops, adding, "I don't expect us to run into anyone. The last report of contact was west. Holzmann's team will likely engage them. I expect we will be sufficiently bored by the time the day is out."

Belmont looked between Müller and I, clearly not understanding. I took a drag of my cigarette before translating. Belmont's face soured and he gestured us forward. I could tell by his expression that he wasn't pleased with Müller's nonchalant attitude toward the operation, but there was nothing he could say; the SS had authority over us.

A few steps on and Meriam asked, "These sharpshooters that have been harassing your people..." Müller raised a quizzical eyebrow prompting her to add, "are these Brownshirts or *Wehrmacht*?"

"We haven't been able to identify them yet, but they are unorganized as far as we can tell, so no, not *Wehrmacht*. I would say SA hoodlums and unemployables who didn't read the history books enough to realize what happened the last time the Brownshirts went against the SS."

"Some people idolize an underdog," Meriam said, her tone biting.

This caused Müller's face to harden. "A defeated opponent should not be studied," he said before flicking his cigarette to the gutter and walking ahead.

---

An hour passed before Müller finally stopped our incessant march as we reached a north-south road. The rain had ceased, and the rumble of artillery could be heard in the distance.

"I know this street," Müller said, his fist lowering.

Judging by Meriam's face, she was thinking something along the lines of, *No shit.* I found myself thinking that she should take better care to hide her emotions. Lord knows I had no great love for the SS or the Reich, but she was asking for trouble if she kept it up.

Müller turned around, looking for me to translate as he said, "Near the northern end of this road is an open plaza with an office building on the corner that has a perfect line of sight down several blocks. If I was a sniper, I would be in there. We should cross quickly and flank the building via the side streets" —he gestured over his shoulder—"and come out farther west. More of an awkward angle for sharpshooters."

As I ceased interpreting what had been said, Belmont looked pleased that Müller was giving direction for once.

"Where they won't expect us," Belmont replied in German. It was his best sentence yet.

We headed across the road and down the side streets at Müller's suggestion. I found myself thinking about what it meant that Müller recognized the street and how these SS troops called Germania their home. Many of them were probably born here. I thought back to my grandfather, imagining what he must have felt as he fought against the Nationalists in the eastern reaches of Spain. The images that flashed before my mind brought on a feeling of melancholy. It pained me to think about having to fight one's own countrymen on the same streets they had grown up on. Sticks replaced with rifles, cars with tanks, footballs with grenades.

I was brought back to the present as we came out onto the main street, some four hundred metres from the building in question. Our team took cover behind a line of cars that had been involved in a collision. A bullet-ridden police car sat in the centre of the next intersection. Images filled my mind of Brownshirt gangs coming out of the surrounding alleyways and ambushing the police who attempted to direct traffic.

"People just trying to get to work," Meriam said as she looked over the hood of the car at the crumpled Japanese import ahead. She had clearly been thinking the same thing. After a moment of silence, she gestured to the multi-story building in the distance. "You think we are going to investigate it?" Her eyes went to Belmont and Müller, who had taken position behind a car ahead. Their backs were to us as they appeared to be studying the building.

"He was worried enough to mention it," I replied.

I watched as Müller grabbed his radio and tucked his head down behind cover. Before I could wonder who he was talking to, an SS corporal with two others behind him came up and stood over us. The corporal's helmet was above the roof of the car, clearly unbothered by the fact that the building was not yet secure.

"The *Scharführer* has us on point; he singled you out," the corporal said as he pointed a crooked finger at me. I wondered how many times it had been broken.

I shook my head. "I'm the last person you should pick—" I began to say.

The corporal stood a little taller now, his disfigured mitt raised in the direction of the building. He turned so his full body faced me. "Müller wants that building investigated. Us four are going, so let's go—"

The bullet entered his helmet, slicing through his skull and exiting through the back of his head, leaving what was left of his face a shattered mess of gore and teeth.

I tensed up, my eyes still locked on the spot the corporal had been.

Meriam gasped.

"Sharpshooter!" one of the SS men yelled.

A bullet whizzed overhead, immediately followed by a crack in the distance. I thought the sniper must have missed but I looked over and saw one of the SS riflemen clutching his throat and writhing on the ground, a series of gurgling noises emanating from him as his blood flowed out onto the cobblestone streets.

Belmont was on the radio, and I could hear Müller in the background shouting orders to his men. They scrambled to better cover before returning fire.

Belmont yelled over the barrage of bullets, "Gibault, Lemann, throw smoke grenades up the road to cover us!"

I saw Henri and another man throw a pair of smoke grenades up the block and we waited for the clouds to conceal us enough so that we lost sight of the building.

Belmont ran by us, gesturing to the group of legionnaires in our vicinity, "Let's go! The smoke is covering us." He paused, making a gesturing motion to the ground as we began to move. He crouched beside Meriam, his hand flying to his earpiece. "Command wants us to—" He stopped speaking, his eyes studying Meriam's face for answers she didn't have. "Command wants us to hold position. No—" He broke off again.

The sound of machine gun fire echoed farther up the block. I could tell it wasn't aimed at us.

"We are to stay at this flank and push up. Another squad is engaging them from the east," Belmont finished, pivoting on his heels, his eyes looking at the line of cars ahead.

Müller gestured for his squad to get down as they were becoming uneasy while waiting for orders.

Belmont looked back at us. "Four plus targets exiting the building trying to better engage the second squad." He paused, swore and said, "I wish this smoke wasn't in the way so I could see what we are walking into..."

Müller moved from around a car, crouching beside Belmont. "They want us to assist," he said, slapping Belmont's back. "Let's get you into the war. Take the rest of your squad and provide a base of fire. Stick to the right side of the street."

Belmont nodded and I hoped he understood the majority of

what was said. Müller fired a burst of rounds toward the concealed building before moving across the street to join his comrades.

We pushed forward, stopping often to let off rounds whenever Müller signaled us to do so. My shorts were hardly aimed, just lighting up the structure in my best estimate of where it was as the smoke billowed around us.

After several minutes of the same drill, we had long cleared the smoke, and the enemy fire was becoming more accurate. As my gun clicked dry for the second time, I pulled a magazine from my carrier and inserted it into the magazine well just in time to see two figures retreat from the road and head into the building. A round rushed past my head and shattered the windshield of the car behind me. I crouched low, swearing to myself, unsure if the bullet had come from the enemy or our friendly unit.

Eventually we pushed close enough that Müller tossed a fragmentation grenade into the remains of what had once been the lobby. We waited for the explosion before I heard Belmont yell from ahead of me, "The SS are pushing in—cover them!"

I did as I was instructed, firing upward of the third floor. Henri moved beside me, bumping me in the process, which caused one of my shots to go wide. He fired several rounds, sending hot casings bouncing off my cheek before he got up and scurried to another piece of cover.

"Müller's inside," Belmont yelled over the roar of gunfire. I could then hear him speaking into his radio, telling the eastern force to cover us. He looked back at Meriam and yelled, "Let's move!"

We charged forward, and to my surprise no gunshots came from above, though I knew I would be a fool to assume all the hostiles were dead. Our squad pushed into the lobby, and I could see Müller and his people had taken cover behind several pillars, watching the various doorways that lay at the end of the connecting hallways.

Müller wiped the sweat from his face as he said to the soldier beside him, "It's time to clear the rats out of the attic."

I grabbed Belmont's shoulder and translated. He nodded, then said, "Tell the SS we will take the eastern stairwell. They will take the west one."

Müller hardly waited for me to finish speaking before saying, "The French always have a plan. We'll alternate floors so there is no friendly fire. We take even floors, you take odd. Got it?"

I gave him a thumbs up, appreciating his no-nonsense approach. Müller turned and led his men toward the back of the lobby.

I passed the information to Belmont, and he radioed to the team outside to watch their fire as we would be moving upstairs. Belmont paused, looking to Henri as he said, "You're on point."

Our walk up the stairs was cautious and our inspection of the second floor resulted in nothing more than the discovery of a trio of dead bodies in the eastern side offices. Two clutched rifles even in death and wore a mismatch of civilian and antique military clothing. The third, a girl no older than twenty, wore a ballistic vest that was far too large for her and was slouched over on a couch. A handgun lay on the floor nearby.

I tried to erase the image, but it hung in the forefront of my mind even as we moved up to the fourth floor. Henri reached out and turned the handle, pushing open the door.

A rifle shot struck the doorframe, sending splinters and dust into the air.

We all stepped back onto the landing then, hearts pounding and adrenaline spiking. Belmont grabbed a grenade from his carrier and was set to pull the pin when a voice called out from down the hall.

"Our fight is not with you," the unseen combatant said in broken French. "We surrender."

Belmont looked at us to confirm what he heard. As several of us nodded, he looked at me and said, "Ask them to say it in German. Ensure they mean what they say."

I did, and after several seconds the voice replied, "Yes, we have no qualms with the French. We surrender to you."

I relayed the message to Belmont, who said, "Tell them to put their weapons on the ground and lie face down, facing the nearest wall." I opened my mouth to translate, but he held up a finger and his tone shifted to a snarl, "And tell them, if anyone does anything funny, I won't ask twice."

I translated what he said verbatim. The unseen voice called back that they understood, and all weapons had been dropped.

Then Belmont spoke German, odd pronunciation of the words but still clear as he asked, "How many of you?"

"Four," the voice called.

We were cautious as we moved around the doorway and into the hallway, our rifles pointing into each room as we methodically cleared the floor. Eventually we came across an office with a single occupant. His face was to the corner, and an antique bolt action rifle had been tossed to the far side of the room. The first thing I noticed was that he wore no military gear.

Belmont and Henri moved up and secured him while Meriam picked up the rifle. The remaining members of the squad secured the other offices further down the hall.

"We have no qualms with you," the sharpshooter repeated as Belmont secured his hands with flexicuffs.

Belmont rolled the man onto his side in a mock recovery position before saying, "That's not how it felt." His face was red as he looked to me to translate the remainder of what he said. "You shot at us, and killed several of our men."

"I wasn't aiming at you," the partisan said, his voice a trembling mess. "I was aiming at the SS."

"That's a lie," Belmont said, shaking his head. Apparently, he had understood enough to deduce what the man had said.

The sharpshooter flinched like he expected to be struck, but the blow never came.

The man looked at my face, straining his eyes to do so. "I could have shot you when you were talking to the girl. You were both exposed. I didn't; I only fired at the SS. The officer, I think."

No one in the room bothered to correct him.

Knowing that I had been in a rifle sight, one trigger pull away from death, brought on a disassociated sensation. I felt as if I was standing outside of myself. I hardly heard Belmont say, "What faction are you with? The loyalists?"

"They are sheep, just like the SS," the sharpshooter said, hacking out a cough. "We represent the silent majority—those who wish the Kaiser to return to Germany."

Belmont looked at me quizzically and I translated.

He shook his head. "Goddamned monarchist." I could see in his eyes he wanted to strike the man this time. "There aren't many of you, why fight for such a hopeless cause?"

"I don't see it that way," the partisan said, turning his head so he could see Belmont more clearly. "Why should we conform with liars and butchers? I would rather die for a true cause than sell my soul fighting for Adolf's bastard grandchildren."

Belmont opened his mouth to speak but held his tongue as the sound of approaching boots filled the hall. Müller entered then, accompanied by several of his SS companions.

"We will take it from here," Müller said, his eyes narrowing on the monarchist.

"No, no. I surrendered to the French," the sharpshooter said as he began to squirm under Belmont's grip.

"Leave him with me. We have some ... questions." Müller's pupils widened as his gaze fixed on the writhing prey.

Some of the SS riflemen moved forward and seized the sharpshooter, who began to scream, his shoe catching one of his captors in the thigh. The SS soldier shook off the blow and pinned the man to the floor, a pale fist meeting his face a moment later.

Belmont stood and motioned us out of the room. We headed toward the stairwell in silence, and I still found myself feeling distant from everything that was happening. We didn't get far before the gunshots echoed down the hall behind us.

One bullet for every monarchist.

# Chapter 12

## *A Flag Is but a Piece of Cloth*

I followed the fireteam down the street, thankful we had left Müller and his people several blocks behind. The windows in this part of the city shone brightly—clearly the conflict had not reached this district yet. As my boots clapped through puddles, I wondered if our presence here would disturb the fragile equilibrium and bring the war to this untouched pocket of the city.

Our squad entered a small courtyard, and I realized we had arrived at a community hall. The sound of a flag flapping in the breeze brought my eyes upward and I saw the Hitler Youth insignia flying above our heads.

I turned my attention to the building as a warm glow emanated from the open doors. A line of Foreign Legion members had formed, extending out from the entrance.

"I hope they feed us," Meriam said. "I'm starving."

I grunted in response, envisioning such delicacy delights as sawdust bread and mystery meat broth. I was painfully aware that our *Wehrmacht* defectors had not been seen since they had crossed into our lines, and I couldn't shake the image of them laughing with their SS counterparts over pints of golden beer and sizzling bratwurst.

The line continued to grow in size behind me, and after a moment I said, "I'm going for a smoke."

Meriam gave me a quick smile as a response and Belmont's face said what his mouth did not. He was hungry.

I cared little for the lack of company as I wanted to be alone. I moved past several dozen legionnaires and lit a cigarette. Upon reaching the open gate of the courtyard, I took a sharp right, heading down a small residential street. The buildings here were the familiar two-story homes; narrow, white structures constructed in the seventies to combat the housing crisis caused by the boom of newcomers who had flooded to the world capital. I studied the balconies on each home and figured these were properties designed for upper-middle-class families.

One house in particular had its windows open, and the smell of cooking chicken wafted into my nostrils. I pulled the cigarette from my lips to get the full effect of the scent. The airport food made me appreciate the delicate notes of something truly delicious. As my eyes met the well-lit patio, I saw the flag of France hanging over the railing.

I stood there for a moment, taking in the aroma and the sounds of the street before an aging man appeared on the balcony. He looked to be in his twilight years, but it was dark, and I couldn't be certain of his exact age. He was hunched over now, but I could tell by his shoulders that the man had been an absolute bull in his prime. The man leaned over the railing and the lights from inside showed me that he wore the face of boredom.

The man looked down at me, and upon seeing my French uniform, he straightened up. "Are you a Frenchman?" he called down in what I recognized as a Parisian accent.

"No, I'm Spanish," I replied.

"You are with the Foreign Legion though? My neighbour said you had come," he called back. I could sense the excitement in his tone.

"I am," I replied, my stomach rumbling as the smell of cooked food danced around my nose.

The man nodded. "Good enough. Come up; I've got enough dinner for extra company."

I began to step forward, but my mind turned to my squad members, Meriam and Belmont especially. "I have friends, let me grab them."

The man turned and pulled a bottle from the small table on the balcony. He balanced it on his shoulder as he entered the well-lit home. The sounds of French opera playing on a record player emanated out onto the damp street.

I bounded down the road and stopped as I approached the legionnaires who guarded the entrance. They had been assigned sentry duty and their faces looked as thrilled by the notion as one would expect. I nodded at each of them before moving through the courtyard and through the community hall doors. The line was nearly gone by now.

I entered the main room and saw a new line had formed along several long tables draped in red tablecloths. A group of aging civilians stood behind various pots as the legionnaires and a few SS riflemen stood with bowls in their hands, ready to receive whatever concoction waited for them in those boiling pots.

"Belmont! Sergeant Belmont," I called as I hurried past the legionnaires and over to him.

Meriam was directly ahead of him, and both turned around to look at me.

I moved closer to them and lowered my voice, not wanting the entire hall to hear of my discovery. "I found a Frenchman,"

I whispered. "A block away." As Meriam and Belmont looked at each other in confusion I added, "He's got chicken—enough for several guests."

Hearing this, Belmont and Meriam both left the line and placed their bowls on the nearby table. As they moved toward the entrance, I stopped for a moment, my eyes drifting to Henri, who stood several metres away, his bowl outstretched as a woman proceeded to fill it with a dark-coloured strew.

I shrugged, turned and exited the hall. I wanted to spend more time with Meriam and get into Belmont's good graces. I didn't need any competition from the likes of Henri.

I caught up to my companions and we passed by a few legionnaires who were still shuffling in. We paid them little mind, for chicken and wine and, if we were lucky, roasted potatoes with peppers awaited us just up the road.

---

The dinner was cooked to perfection, and we ate by candlelight. The entire meal reminded me of something my mother would have made. Our host, François, and his wife were lovely company. We chatted of various things, including weather, football and vacations.

Once François' wife retired to bed and the third bottle of wine was opened, I noticed our host began to talk more than he listened. François spoke of war, of the great German blitzkrieg and the unprecedented rate of their expansion over Europe. He sounded proud.

Meriam flicked the gathering ash of her cigarette into the ashtray as she said, "But it's all-ancient history, isn't it?"

François twirled the wine in his glass, appearing to look at Belmont for a moment before laughing to himself. "Ancient history? Hardly. It was all too recent." He leaned back in his chair, appearing to be lost in thought for a moment before saying, "You know, I had an older cousin in the French Resistance. Such a pointless affair. That moron got himself killed, and for what? Because the idea of a foreign invader coming and taking over? An invader who improved the country? Raised the standard of living? Treated us with respect, when really, they had no reason to? Both our sides bloodied each other in the First Great War, but they decimated us in the second. The Germans could have enslaved us, yet they showed leniency." François hoisted his wine glass into the air as a mock toast before taking a gulping sip. "But Gerard? Now there's a stain on my family name for a generation. I only pray my children's children will never hear that they had a Resistance fighter as a family member."

I fought with every fiber of my being to keep my face from showing any emotion other than the neutral expression plastered across it. Visions of my mother's side of the family filled my mind. The photos on the mantle. The stories I had heard of their warrior spirit.

François took another sip. "And you know, there are so-called freedom movements in Paris right now I'm told. They always claim they are the remnants of the Resistance. They believe their own propaganda, that the movement had hundreds of thousands of members in its prime." He pointed to me, but I could tell by his glassy eyes he was truly lost in memory. "I can tell you firsthand, I was a child in Paris during the height of their activity, and I never heard a gunshot nor bomb. It was a group of kids playing at war with more heart than brains, afraid of change and the future, still clinging to the long-extinguished embers of the revolution."

François picked up the remains of his cigarette from the ashtray and placed it at the corner of his mouth. He grabbed the wine bottle with gusto and poured himself another glass before topping Meriam and I off. Belmont's glass sat full, just as it had most of the night.

As the wine nearly overflowed past the rim of my glass, François said, "What's the matter, Spaniard? You're too quiet. This is the first time I've ever met a quiet Spaniard, I must say." François looked to Meriam, a humour filled expression on his face, but she did not match his joking mood.

I let a soft smile approach my lips. Sitting higher in my chair, I said, "I'm just listening." Judging by our host's face that he did not appreciate this answer, I added, "I'm embarrassed by my lack of French. I'm not able to articulate everything I mean sometimes."

I noticed the flash of a glance Meriam sent my way. It would be an easy lie to uncover, but François had been drinking heavily.

Our host looked at me, a shimmer of iron in his eyes as he placed the wine bottle down and said, "And what is it that you are struggling to say?"

The room turned quiet, and all eyes were on me.

I took a careful sip of my wine, thinking through the clouds of the alcohol as I attempted to construct a fabricated narrative about Franco and my family of jackboot-loving loyalists when François said, "It's called *you're welcome*." He pointed to the wine glass and laughed.

Taken aback by the sudden joke, my heart continued to thunder in my throat, my face remaining a blank canvas.

François wiped his face, adding, "But you saying you don't speak French well, it's all nonsense. You speak it better than many of my countrymen." He looked to Belmont and said, "Would you believe I was in Marseille last year and I saw a group of kids—teenagers, I think—at the café, and they were talking in so much *slang*, it is called, that I could hardly understand them. Half German too."

He turned to me and said in slurred German, "And I'm fluent in both, you understand. Just shows how much of a mockery they made of both languages. The languages of conquerors. We had our day, let me tell you, and the Germans are currently in theirs."

François looked around the table before switching back to French and continuing, "It will be a sad day when German inevitably replaces French, but I'll gladly speak German for the rest of my life before I speak a word of Italian. They may have been allies of the Reich, and I don't care if it's treason to say so, but they were morons. Complete incompetents. You know Ethiopia still celebrates the battle when they defeated the Italian army the first time. It's all a secret celebration, of course, but still, I would share that victory with them." He paused, holding his hands up. "I'm sorry, I'm just a rambling old man. Forgive my tangents. Tell me, Sergeant, what are your thoughts on this current conflict? The papers call it a string of coordinated terrorist attacks, but I hear the Swiss radio stations, and they report it as a civil war."

Sergeant Belmont watched as Meriam flicked more ash into the ceramic tray before retrieving a cigarette of his own. "Well, command has been informing us that Germania is not an isolated incident. This has been happening all over the German states. The Greater Reich, that is the commissariats, are unaffected I'm told, but this opposition was certainly organized. I just can't believe, with a conspiracy this large, the Gestapo or military intelligence didn't discover it and snuff it out before it could fester." Belmont hardened his tone before adding, "Were they really that inept?"

Meriam spoke next. "It's always hubris, isn't it?"

François took a quick sip of wine, eager to continue the thought. "Almost can't blame them. They were looking for communists or Arabic reformists. Not a huge swath of the

*Wehrmacht* to be traitors, and if the rumors are true that the Führer's own siblings are behind it..." Belmont put his hand over his glass as François picked up the bottle to top him off. Our host poured more into his own glass as he added, "And who's to say they didn't receive information about the plot, but the agents shared the same beliefs and became sympathisers to the cause, perhaps purposely misdirecting their colleagues?"

"The list of those involved could be endless," I offered to keep myself part of the conversation and avoid another bout of François' intense eye contact.

Our host waved a dismissive hand. "And they will be dealt with in time. Our Führer will be rescued; The SS are still loyal, and with their true Aryan heritage they will make short work of the traitors." He raised his glass. "To the SS and the sacred Reich."

I was quick to raise my glass, but not as quick as Belmont. Meriam hesitated, but luckily our host hadn't noticed. The shadows of the candlelight's flames danced across François' face as the conversation faded.

We lowered our glasses and Meriam said, "I expect we will wrap up the whole thing in a matter of—"

"I'll tell you something else," François interrupted, "the whole thing is complete shit, honestly. A bunch of bored virgin whiners following a second-born child and her little brother on a pointless crusade. I'm almost ashamed that these petty sibling rivalries can affect the Germanic people; I thought our leaders would be above such things, but such is not the case."

There was a lull. Clearly François thought those around him would cheer or salute, but when the three of us stayed quiet, he elaborated, "And so what? They don't like some of Otto's positions, it doesn't mean you stage a coup. If Karl was still alive, he would ... well, I lack the imagination to think what he would have done to those behind this embarrassment."

"But it's worth saying," Meriam said, her cigarette getting dangerously close to the filter. "If Karl was still around this never would have happened and never have been allowed to grow..."

François ignored her and added, "A little discontent and they do this and those in the *Wehrmacht*—the ones with empty skulls that follow that jealous sister—wanting to make the Reich what it was? We can't keep going and fighting the same old battles. You know why? Because we won them all. No battles left to fight except what lies ahead. This generation doesn't know how good they have it. The cities are safe, the money is flowing, and most importantly, the roads are whole and not a bombed-out ruin."

"But the *loyalists* destroyed all that," Meriam responded.

François raised his glass as if to say *touché* before adding, "I've fought in wars; Turkey didn't liberate itself. A little peace and quiet is pretty damned good, but this generation is bored, and it shows. But if they want to die on a fool's errand chasing a dream that already came true"—he pointed a trembling finger toward Belmont—"You oblige them." François patted the sergeant on the shoulder, and I could see how uncomfortable Belmont was.

The conversation died again, and I could tell our host was beginning to drift. Seeing this as well, Meriam said, "Thank you for the hospitality, François. The food was delicious. Please thank your wife for us."

François snapped back to reality and reached for the bottle. "No, no, the night is still young. Please, I have many bottles. Spaniard, I have a red from your country, a 2002. Great year, very expensive."

Belmont stood. "No, sir. Thank you, but it's late. The officers will be doing lights out at the centre soon. Don't want to be late. We will have an early morning."

"I'm sure. Conquest waits for no man." François laughed before letting out a wet cough.

We said our goodbyes, and while I shook François' hand, I did not thank him. I didn't have it in me to lie anymore.

As the three of us put on our jackets and exited the house, he waved and wished us luck in the coming weeks. As the door shut, I could hear the sounds of the French opera screech to life again.

We walked down the cobblestone boulevard, and I looked back at the French flag that hung from the balcony. I recalled my mother's words and knew them to be right. Flags were nothing but bits of cloth weak men hid behind to give them something to rally around. The colours on it did not matter, for their ideologies were a cancer that wore many different coats.

---

A half dozen flashlights blinded us as we approached the gate to the community centre.

"Legionnaires," Belmont called out, the three of us raising our hands in front of our faces.

"Down! Down on your knees," a voice shouted in French.

We complied, but I felt like this could all be avoided if the sentries opened their eyes and looked at our uniforms.

A collection of soldiers approached us, rifles at the ready. They looked us over, flashlights dancing over our prone bodies. Clearly, they weren't looking for weapons as our rifles were visible and slung across our backs. I suspected they were searching for explosives or bulges in our clothing.

After a few moments a legionnaire standing over Meriam said, "Get up." He sounded more relaxed now. "The commandant instructed no one to leave. What are you doing out?"

"We didn't receive that order," Belmont said.

There was some back and forth between Belmont and the sentries before they let us pass, but as we moved through the gate Belmont said, "I have to clear this up with my lieutenant. You two ... well, just don't leave and get me in more shit."

As Belmont turned to leave, one of the sentries called out, "They were asking for more people to head to the roof for the second watch. If you want to stay in the commandant's good graces, I would volunteer for that."

Belmont nodded, before looking at us. "Head to the roof, speak to whomever is in charge and keep watch. I'll meet you up there."

He headed toward the front entrance of the community centre, prompting Meriam and I to look at each other with dread. I knew I was feeling the wine, and I could see in her eyes that she was as well.

We found a staircase to the left of the foyer and followed it up. A large portrait of Otto Hitler greeted us from the first landing. His wide-set eyes stared past a small nose as he watched us ascend. Maybe it was the wine talking, but I could really see how much he took after his mother.

Without pause, we turned our backs to the photo and ascended another set of stairs. After navigating a short hall that looked as if it served as storage, we saw a ladder at the far end. I climbed up first, pushing open the hatch as I did so. As I pulled myself to the roof, I saw a pair of legionnaires look over their shoulders.

"How'd you get roped into this?" one of them asked, before turning back to face the surrounding buildings.

"Volunteered," I replied as I pulled myself onto the gravel-covered roof.

I turned my attention to Meriam and held my hand out to assist her, but she didn't take it, instead pulling herself up with ease.

"They feed us a terrible meal and then you volunteer to stand out here for most of the night. You must hate yourself," the legionnaire mumbled.

I gave a non-committal response before following Meriam over to the far end of the roof. The two sentries continued to speak to one another in hushed tones, and as I looked over my shoulder, I caught one of them gawking at Meriam's figure.

"I'm tired, Eduardo," she said after a moment.

"Me too," I replied, my mind not really present as I thought back to the large portions of chicken and potatoes along with the side of green beans and slice of chocolate cake for dessert. I had been ready for bed an hour ago.

Her voice softened, turned inward. "I don't mean physically. Well, yes, I do mean physically, but not only that. Mentally too. Knowing that those SS men shot those monarchists. Hearing those gunshots, they ... they have been in my head all night. It made me think about a lot of things."

I stayed silent, my eyes watching the approaching road and the parked cars that had been stuck in the same spot for days.

She cleared her throat and continued, "I've thought about it, and if that's how they treat their own, how did they treat those they saw as inferior?" She paused. "Have you been to the Reich History Museum?"

As I shook my head no, Meriam continued, "Let me tell you, they have an exhibit there showing the various houses for the 'Special Classes.' That was a name they gave the ones they once called "undesirables." They have seven or eight mock houses for Jews, Slavs, Gypsies. They claim these houses are out in the far east, or in Madagascar. But you know, I was wondering why I have never seen any photos of any Jews existing in their nice-looking houses..." She gave a laugh that oozed with disgust. "While I was in the museum, a pair of women were at the exhibit next to me. They said to each other that the Jewish house looked nicer than theirs. They sounded so bitter about it. I don't know, something—maybe it was how they said it—made me realize that these mock houses were a little too perfect. And I thought back to the required readings in school, of how much Adolf hated the *Untermensch*. It made me wonder, why relocate them at all?"

I looked down at her, my face souring. "You can't be suggesting we've been lied to for eighty years? They couldn't hide so much death. They... Someone would have found out..."

"People only find out if they are looking for it. I'm sure they doctored train logs to show millions of people being moved into the Moscow Commissariat or the Caucasus. But why go to all that trouble when a bullet works the same? Would be cheaper. That's if you don't work them to death."

"Meriam, I... I just think it's been too long. Someone would have uncovered this. What you're suggesting ... this is a conspiracy involving thousands, maybe hundreds of thousands, of people, from every facet of the government. Not just police or army, but train conductors, doctors, builders. Someone would have seen."

She shrugged. "Why? We have groups of people we are told to despise; makes it easier that way. Remember Germany lost the First War because of the Jews." Seeing my eyes dart back and forth she said, "Oh forgot about that one? Yeah, they don't talk about it anymore, but that was something Adolf and his Nazis pinned on them. They also caused the Depression. Anything bad to happen was because of the Jews. So, you make them disappear. Using slave labor, you construct whatever you need to, then kill the builders. After all, they are undesirables too. You put all of this in the middle of nowhere, so no one comes looking for it. They already euthanize cripples, are entire races of people really that much harder to fathom?"

My eyes darted back and forth. Even with her insinuation

that it was obvious, I found her argument to contain a huge leap in logic. Still, the Reich's slogan for dealing with disabled persons chimed in the back of my mind.

*We help those who can't help themselves.*

"Okay, but what about the guards at these sites you're talking about?" I said, my brain still picking at the holes in her theory.

"They're SS! We already know that they were in charge of relocating them. Goebbels let that exist in the history books. Those fanatics would do anything they were told to. And it wouldn't be hard—they hated whoever they were told to hate. But, Eduardo, let me prove my point. Before today, before this conversation, when was the last time you ever thought of the Jews?"

I felt my face become red with guilt. "I don't think ... ever."

"Exactly." She pushed a finger into my chest. "And that's not an attack on you, but an attack on all of us. On the world. No one goes looking because no one cares."

"Can we talk about something else?" I asked as she retracted her hand.

Meriam sighed, her eyes gravitating to the road. "What else is there to talk about?" Her words seemed to carry all the baggage of the Reich with them.

The flapping of the Hitler Youth flag somewhere behind us was the only sound for a long while.

# Chapter 13

## *Better Left Unsaid*

We were up and marching just as daylight crept around the *Volkshalle* far behind us. The rays of light shimmered around the dome, making it look almost biblical. I was feeling the march in every part of my body, due in no small part from sleeping on the tiled floor of the community centre with nothing but my thin mat and sleeping bag.

Despite our lack of sleep, Meriam appeared to be in moderately good spirits. I think she liked to be up and moving, accompanied by legionnaires and not the SS, who stayed behind to keep the sector secure. As we walked around the familiar looking streets, I wondered how much of the night prior she remembered. Her eyes looked ahead, suggesting she recalled nothing, but she had surprised me before. Those unassuming eyes contained secrets safely secured behind a well-guarded wall manned by fun times and a carefree attitude.

It wasn't long until we came across a large supermarket, the side street to our left serving as a shipping and receiving junction. Seeing the sign on top of the building prompted a few legionnaires to murmur to each other about the food we would find inside. I didn't want to overstep my bounds with Belmont, but I was hoping one of our squad mates, Henri perhaps, would suggest looting it for sustenance.

I looked down the side street and saw several dumpsters had been moved across the alley, as if they had been placed that way to conceal something. Belmont appeared to notice the peculiar placement as well and motioned for us to investigate. A closer look behind them caused us to stop in our tracks.

Ten bodies lay on the concrete, their hands bound and their skulls missing their frontal portion, what was once inside now splayed across the brick wall for all to see.

"SS, all of them," Belmont said, his eyes going up and down the line of corpses.

"You think the *Wehrmacht* did this?" Meriam asked. Her eyes shifted from the bodies and toward the roof of the supermarket.

"Possible, but it's odd they would go to such lengths to bind them, so I think it's unlikely," Belmont replied, his eyes lingering on the two females of the group. "Maybe they weren't sure what to do with them at first..." he added, seeming to speak to himself.

"You think it was another French squad that killed them?" I asked, attempting to navigate the confusing nature of the conflict.

"No, none of our people have been to this district. I think this may have been SS on SS justice. A form of friendly fire," Belmont replied.

Müller's catlike smile flashed before my eyes, his teeth the same colour as the bone fragments that rested near my boots.

"Except it wasn't so friendly," Meriam said. She had turned to face us again, her eyes fixed above Belmont in an attempt to shield herself from the remains. "I say these ones went against their unit. But which sibling..." She trailed off, leaving the remainder of the thought unsaid.

"I think Meriam had it right the first time—I think it was *Wehrmacht*," I said, but judging by the faces of the group, they had made up their minds. This was the work of the SS.

"Impossible to know," Belmont replied before stepping over a body and beginning to move down the alley. "Keep your eyes open for anything. Just because they wear friendly uniforms doesn't mean they are."

Meriam and I hurried to keep up with him, the remainder of our squad following behind. I looked back at the bodies. I didn't accept the agreed upon explanation, and thought the simplest answer was the correct one. The *Wehrmacht* weren't above killing their former comrades in cold blood any more than the SS were.

---

We came across another French unit not long after. It was the usual fare: hand signs followed by a response code and eventually Belmont ordering us forward to link up with the other team.

The squad leader sauntered forward, her body language relaxed. She and Belmont started talking about sectors and local landmarks, but my eyes gravitated to Meriam, who was looking across the block at a phone booth with a white eagle stencilled on the glass.

"Fan out," the other team's squad leader said after a moment. "Give us a wide defensive formation." She then turned and nodded to something Belmont was saying.

We followed a group of legionnaires across the street and Meriam moved beside the phone booth. "You think the lines are still up?" she asked after a moment.

I offered a shrug as a response.

She elbowed me in the side, saying, "Cover me."

Meriam hopped up and moved into the phone booth. The smile on her face told me she found the whole thing amusing. She pulled out a piece of paper and some coins from her pocket and began to dial.

"Who are you calling?" I mouthed the words, but she turned away.

I looked back and saw Belmont gesturing to a government building at the end of the street, the other squad leader shaking her head. I turned around to face Meriam, and she was now looking back at me, her lips moving, but I couldn't hear what she was saying through the privacy glass. She waved to me in a playful manner before continuing with her conversation.

*Who does she have to call so urgently?* I thought, my eyes narrowing.

She bit her lip before hanging the phone on the hook and exiting the booth.

"What was that?" I asked, an accusatory tone clinging to my words.

"Had to let someone know I'm safe." She studied my face before adding, "My mother, alright? She was expecting me back in Paris days ago. She's doing well, thank you for asking." She elbowed me again before gesturing with her chin toward the two sergeants. "Anything new?"

As I opened my mouth to speak, we heard a gunshot in the distance, followed by sounds of screeching tires. Belmont grabbed his radio and spoke into it, prompting the members of our team to quickly fall back across the street.

After a short back and forth, the sergeants came up with a plan. Our team would cover the right side of the road, the other team covering the left. The sound of another gunshot echoed past the concrete structures. Our teams moved north, passing several blocks, before we reached a major intersection and saw activity to the west.

A roadblock of sorts was set up in front of a blown-out library, multiple SS vehicles parked in front. A crowd had formed and was shouting at a formation of soldiers in SS camouflage. I estimated the size of the congregation to be in the hundreds.

Several people stood in military gear toward the back of the formation, swastika armbands on their biceps. They eyed us with caution as we approached, but none of them raised their weapons. It occurred to me that while the Brownshirts had all been a part of the loyalist faction, there would logically be civilians that backed Otto's government. Whether the SS had formed them into a militia, or if this group had joined up in their current state, I couldn't be sure.

I looked to the library steps and could see what was getting the crowd so worked up: A line of loyalist combatants were being paraded out of the pillared entrance, their hands on top of their heads. Several looked to have been beaten, while others were adorned with blood-soaked bandages.

Meriam approached one of the armband clad militiamen who turned to look at her. "What's this?" she asked.

"A mix of anarchists and some reserve *Wehrmacht* members, couple of off duty cops. Nothing we couldn't handle."

She sized the man up. "You aren't SS?"

"No, *Reichswehr*." He spoke as if the title was common knowledge, and I quickly translated what he said to mean "Reich Defence."

A group of militia members led the prisoners to the side of the library as several SS members followed them around the corner and out of sight. I trailed the formation at a fair distance, peering down the alleyway to see the loyalists being lined up against the wall, the fight in their eyes long extinguished.

I looked to my right and could see a SS rifleman sitting with his back against the wall of the neighbouring building, a fellow soldier crouching down beside him. I took a few steps forward to eavesdrop on what the man was saying, but kept my eyes on the library so it appeared I wasn't actively listening.

"They are still our countrymen," the SS rifleman said through sobs, his head in his hands. He looked young.

"They are traitors, Jan. They must be put away," the standing soldier replied, placing a hand on his friend's shoulder.

"What's the point of it all? All the killing. It doesn't solve a single thing."

The standing friend stayed silent, but the gunshots from the alleyway spoke louder than any words he could have said.

# Chapter 14

## *Life During War Time*

We finished our sweep of the sector in silence.

Upon returning to the community centre, I could see the SS had been busy in our absence. Trucks had been brought in from armouries around the city, and crews of soldiers unloaded barbed wire, sandbags, ammunition and, most importantly, food rations. The once mundane city block was now well on its way to becoming a fortress.

We navigated around the bustling army and as we reached the intersection, I could see a company-sized force of *Wehrmacht* soldiers. I tensed up, having been instructed to treat the uniform as a threat. It was then that I noticed the red armbands on each soldier's arm.

"I guess the defectors are back with us," Belmont said, sounding chipper. A certain level of respect hung unsaid behind his words. "Oh, and the remaining Foreign Legion members from the airport."

I heard the sound of revving engines and watched as a pair of tanks moved into the intersection, the *Wehrmacht* iron cross emblazoned on their sides.

"No one ever said anything about tanks," I mumbled to myself.

Belmont, thinking the comment was directed at him, replied, "The group that passed by us was only their western flank; the majority of the force took a different road. They are a grenadier battalion." He hit me on the back. "Good thing they defected; we wouldn't have stood a chance."

I let out a stunned breath, thinking about how many legionnaires would have been annihilated because the SS had given us bad intel. A third tank moved into the intersection then, a group of armband-clad *Wehrmacht* soldiers sitting atop the rumbling war machine as it moved out of sight.

"Someone should paint them with a different decal," Henri said as he turned to face Belmont. "It's going to get confusing if enemy armour shows up as well."

"I'm sure they thought of that," Belmont said, gesturing us forward.

As we moved past a trio of riflemen setting up a mortar position, a French officer approached. He wore the rank of a captain, and I noticed Belmont stiffen up as the officer neared. I could swear that the captain's face shifted, seemingly annoyed by Belmont's presence. I wondered if the two men had history.

"Sergeant, tell any other squad leaders you see that there will be a meeting in the main hall at fourteen hundred," the officer said with little patience in his voice.

"Yes, sir. Will it be the SS leading it or commandant—"

The captain's eyes lingered on Meriam before drifting over to me. As it did so, his look hardened with contempt. Something about my uniform seemed to irritate him.

"It shouldn't matter, should it?" the officer said before moving down the street.

We walked several steps toward the community centre and Meriam waited until the officer was out of earshot before saying, "I'm not a member, so I'll say it. That guy was an asshole."

Belmont said nothing but I noticed the corner of his mouth tug upward into a smile.

---

The main hall of the centre had been cleared of the tables and benches from the night before. The room was packed with SS, Foreign Legion and defected *Wehrmacht* alike. It occurred to me that a well-placed airstrike would serve as a crippling blow against the defense forces in this quarter of the city.

Meriam and I stood near the back of the hall. Belmont and the rest of the squad had disappeared into the mix of uniforms, and I had no desire to follow. Meriam was leaning against the wall, arms folded, watching the dusty ceiling fans twirl methodically.

The briefing started as an SS captain stood underneath a pair of crossed swastika flags mounted overhead. He was a short man, and from where we were standing, I could only see his uniform cap—the skull upon it looking this way and that as he began his instructions.

If I hadn't been standing, I would have fallen asleep, but Meriam's eyes cut like daggers. Every few seconds she would shake her head, then mumble to herself as the officer continued.

I adjusted my back against the wall, forcing myself to wake up and pay attention.

"This could be the decisive victory that brings the capital back under our control," the officer said. "And I would like to say, what a privilege it is that the French and our, um, true believer *Wehrmacht* forces can also be a part of it..."

He went on and on, tripping over his cadence and handing out filler "ums" and "ahs" every second sentence like they were free candy. He did not inspire confidence in Meriam or me, but as I peered around at the nearby SS members, they stood tall, hanging off every word.

*A Joseph Goebbels, he is not,* I thought as the man stuttered through some operation, confusing three different units and butchering the name of one of the French officers.

"I'll have no part in it," Meriam said under her breath.

I slid closer to her and asked, "What?"

The droning of the officer continued in the background as her words oozed with venom, "Haven't you been paying attention? There is an assault. Tonight. Against an uncounted number of *Wehrmacht*. This knob thinks they have armour..."

"At night?"

"Right. The whole thing is stupid. Why are we attacking when we have a perfectly good defensive position here?" She paused, craning her ear to listen to more before rolling her eyes. "It's just so this guy can get a medal while the French are the ones who bleed."

"The SS and defectors aren't coming with us?" I replied, looking past her to ensure no one was listening to us, while the blathering from the front of the hall continued on.

"The SS are coming in the second wave. It's us to the west and centre with the *Wehrmacht* defectors to the east." Her lips turned white with rage as she pressed them together before adding, "I'm not getting killed for some *Totenkopf*-wearing moron. I'll have no part in it."

---

Under the cover of night, the formation surged ahead, and Meriam, to her word, took no part. As Belmont and the rest of the squad pushed down the dreary street, Meriam and I slowed our pace to something that could be classified as a light jog only in the most liberal sense of the phrase.

As the last handful of legionnaires pushed by us, Meriam grabbed my wrist and pulled me into the overhang of a rundown store. "Let them fight it out."

I looked down the road. Seeing the camouflaged uniforms continue down the street filled me with a sense of guilt. They were going off to fight while I stood where I was, a beautiful woman gripping me tightly. I knew every man in that formation would wish to be where I was at that moment—something that made the feeling that much worse.

Gunfire erupted in the distance.

First the crack of a rifle shot, followed by the call and response of several dozen more. On and on the rifles sounded until their wish was granted and the tearing paper sound of a machine gun roared above all, drowning out the screams.

I looked into her eyes as a flare lit up the sky, illuminating her cheeks with a red glow.

"I think we should try to help—" I began to say, but never finished the sentence, as Meriam pulled me closer, her hand slipping up my back.

Then her lips were on mine.

With a free hand she felt for the door handle of the store, then pulled her head back and bit her lip at the existence of the locked door. She smirked, her eyes moving to my chest. She placed a hand over my heart and whispered, "Hold that thought."

Meriam unslung her rifle as the sounds of battle continued in the distance. She smashed the window of the door with the butt of her weapon before her hand navigated around the jagged glass and unlocked the handle.

The guilt had subsided now; her lips had seen to that. Now I wanted nothing but her.

She turned to me, the light of the flare disappearing behind the rooftops. I opened my mouth to speak, but she pushed her finger to my lips. I looked behind us to ensure no one was around, but my eyes didn't get far as she pulled me inside with surprising strength.

Shutting the door behind her she said, "We'll just wait a while. See where the night takes us."

It was my turn to be on the offensive. I wrapped my arms around her thin body as she ran her hands over my shoulders before they grazed the back of my neck. A shy laugh escaped her. We spun, our lips coming together, her tongue in my mouth.

She pushed me against the bookshelf and looked behind her. The road was still there and so was the battle, but those things were outside the confines of this room and therefore did not matter.

Sensing the coast was clear, she undid her carrier and began to unbutton her shirt. I did the same, and before I knew it, we were embracing again. She gestured with her body that we were to move down to the floor. Who was I to resist?

The boots came off next, followed by the pants. The sound of belt buckles scraping against hardwood drowned out the gunshots. She removed her hair ties and tossed them on top of her clothing.

The warmth of our naked bodies met, and she pressed her palms into my shoulders as she moved on top of me. Her brunette hair hung down over her breasts. The look of desire in her eyes told me she couldn't wait any longer. Her fingers wrapped around me, guiding me.

Her breathing changed.

She closed her eyes, but her mouth stayed open. As I grabbed her hips, I could tell she had been thinking of this moment for many days.

# Chapter 15

## *By Blood and Iron*

The door swung open.

The crashing noise stirred me from my sleep. I bolted up, the coat I was using as a blanket falling from my chest. In the doorway stood a group of SS members, their eyes peering down in disdain. Meriam had turned over and held a sweater over her exposed breasts.

"See, sir," the youngest of the men said. "French legionnaires screwing during battle."

An officer entered between the three men, and I could see the rank of lieutenant on his lapel. His jaw was clenched, and he looked to be in desperate need of sunlight. The officer studied the look of fear on our faces before turning his attention to the discarded uniforms beside us. "Up!" he snapped. "Both of you."

I was the first to stand. Meriam took several moments longer. While I was fully exposed, Meriam continued to clutch the sweater.

The officer looked between us before turning to one of his

men and saying, "At least he's laying with a woman. I thought all Frenchmen only loved the company of each other."

"I speak German," I said, my face hardening from the insult.

"Good," the officer replied as he turned, his beady eyes peering into me. "That means you'll understand me when I say *get dressed*. And if you aren't ready in the next thirty seconds, I'll shoot you both for dereliction of duty. Now move!" He raised his wrist and looked at the cheap watch upon it.

I heard the dull snap of rifle fire in the distance. The officer remained unphased, his eyes locked on the ticking second hand. "Twenty-five seconds left."

I bent down and collected my clothing. With haste, I started with the pants, but in her panic, Meriam let the sweater fall as she bent down to grab her underwear. She caught the garment but not before the soldiers locked eyes on her exposed body, a pleased smile touching their lips.

While I buttoned up my uniform shirt, hot fury came over me as I felt the need to defend her honour. I envisioned grabbing my rifle and shooting all of them for not giving her the decency to let her change in peace.

The heroic vision came and went as the officer said, "Ten seconds."

I pulled on my boots and the rage gave way to panic as I started to believe this officer may still shoot us and only wanted us dressed so his men didn't have to handle naked bodies.

Meriam and I finally put on our ballistic carriers and stood before the officer. I knew we had run out of time long ago.

An explosion from the west sounded off just as the officer said, "You two will be coming with me." He pivoted. "Perhaps you can make up for your degeneracy in combat."

"If you are going to take us to the street to shoot us, just do it now," I said.

The lieutenant turned, and his youngest subordinate adjusted the grip on his rifle, no doubt expecting the order to be given momentarily.

The officer laughed. "I'm not going to shoot you, but ask the *Wehrmacht*, I'm sure they will consider it." He paused, appearing to think about how much he was going to divulge to us. He licked his chapped lips before adding, "They are dug into those apartment complexes up the block. Our *Wehrmacht* unit didn't do enough to shake them from the area. Your French forces did even less. We are the second wave and *Hauptsturmführer* Peiper wants us to lead this thing personally."

I reflected on the name of the *Hauptsturmführer*; it sounded familiar, but I wasn't sure what history book his ancestor had crawled out from underneath in order for me to recognize it.

"We will take the apartment complex to the right, closest to our loyal *Wehrmacht* force," the lieutenant continued. "Most of my platoon will create a pincer movement while your French compatriots keep the traitors pinned down. I can radio and get the armour to shift fire as needed."

Another explosion erupted, this one closer than before. "Let's move!" the officer said, exasperation clear. Both Meriam and I snapped to and moved out onto the street.

I could sense the rifles of our SS counterparts pointed to our backs. I knew they suspected we would run at the first opportunity, and I would be lying if the idea wasn't at the forefront of my mind. Still, we moved up the street as ordered, and I tried to keep the images of the bloodbath we were walking into tucked down deep.

We marched for several minutes, finally seeing the end of the block and the group of riflemen that had taken cover behind several parked vehicles. I crouched down behind an aging Volkswagen that had taken a barrage of rounds. The lieutenant came up behind us and spoke with the sergeant, who was crouched beside me.

I used the opportunity to look through the shattered windows, noticing a row of apartment complexes across the double-wide roadway. Several bodies lay in the middle of the street, and by their placement I suspected they had been ambushed from a machine gun on the upper floors. My eyes fixed on a large hole that marked an apartment on the eighth floor, confirming my suspicion that something had been there and worth using an anti-tank round on.

I looked to the bodies again and realized they were all legionnaires. Meriam's quote flashed into the forefront of my mind: *The French are the ones who bleed.*

"That building is clear," the sergeant said, pointing to the one with the hole in it. "It's the one on the left that has the legionnaires pinned down, sir." He pointed to the right building next. "The *Wehrmacht* turncoats are in the process of clearing that one. Reports sounded good. Minimal resistance."

The lieutenant nodded. "We will head there first, link up with them and then push up the road to save the French." He looked over his shoulder. "Those with me, you know who you are. The rest of you to the centre building. Get ready to cut off the retreating force and help the French where you can."

Before I knew it, the lieutenant along with ten of us were moving to the right building while another twenty moved to the centre building. We ran in silence and my eyes found themselves moving to the copious windows that towered over us, expecting that at any moment they could erupt in gunfire.

We reached the side of the building, and I could hear rifle fire from down the road and to the east. The sergeant tried to pull open the fire escape door, but it was sealed from the inside.

He mumbled something but the lieutenant cut him off, saying, "The ground floor apartments, that's our way in." His eyes turned to Meriam. "You look fast. Break into one of them and open this door. And you..." His gaze gravitated to me. "You go with her. We don't want your mistress going anywhere alone now, do we?"

Meriam swore in French before muttering to herself, which the SS men found amusing. As I turned to face the edge of the building, someone shoved me, pushing me into Meriam. I held my tongue as I wanted to get our task over with.

As we turned the corner, I assessed the road ahead. Debris from a firefight and shredded vehicles sat atop a heavily pocked roadway. Meriam and I took several steps forward, her attention focused on the balcony of the ground floor apartment that lay a handful of metres away. At the far end of the road, I saw movement behind a sandbag wall.

"Shit," I said, attempting to speed up as my boots struggled to grip the rubble.

I saw one of the silhouettes point to us before another swung his weapon in our direction. The muzzle flash of a machine gun beckoned in the distance. Meriam and I dove over the railing of the balcony as a stream of bullets peppered the wall behind us. The crisp echo of the weapon followed.

I raised my weapon, firing it into the glass door of the balcony, and leapt into the apartment as shards rained down in every direction.

Meriam and I got our bearings, swinging our rifles to the corners of the room, ensuring no one was there. Satisfied, we moved toward the entrance of the apartment. Meriam unlocked the deadbolt and pulled the door open. She hesitated, her finger moving to the trigger of her rifle before she pointed the barrel out into the hallway. She looked right before pulling her head back and checking the opposite direction.

"It's clear. Let's let these bootlickers in, shall we?" she whispered before moving left toward the stairwell that served as the fire escape.

As we reached the door, Meriam pushed it open and we were met by the cold faces of SS members, their weapons leveled at us.

"What took you so long?" the lieutenant asked before gesturing for his men to lower their weapons.

The officer strolled forward, pushing past Meriam and I, his compliment of soldiers behind him. The door swung shut with a heavy thud, its echo reverberating up the flights of stairs over our heads.

The officer licked his lips before saying, "*Unterscharführer*, take four men up to the top floor. Work your way down and let me know when you make contact with our *Wehrmacht* force." He looked at Meriam and I before adding, "The rest of us will go to the second floor and work our way up."

"But what about that machine gun?" Meriam asked. A thin layer of sweat had coated her forehead. "Shouldn't we clear it?"

The lieutenant gestured for the sergeant to move out. As the bootsteps began to ascend the steps, he turned to Meriam. "We will, but from above them. They will be expecting us to come at them from the ground floor." He then mumbled something under his breath before leading us up to the next floor, Meriam and I lingering at the back of the formation.

The lieutenant pulled open the door and the six of us moved down the hall. The doors to the apartments were propped open with various tools, boxes and furniture. Our defectors had been busy.

"These rooms should be secure," the lieutenant said to the man closest to him.

I hardly heard him as my adrenaline had dissipated and I was growing tired of the whole thing. We took the time to look into each room, ensuring they had been cleared properly before moving onto the next.

As we neared the halfway point in the hall, we heard the creak of hinges, followed by the thud of a door in the distance. The SS squad pointed their weapons ahead, but as the *Wehrmacht* troops rounded the corner, their red armbands became visible.

The group relaxed and a dull sigh of relief escaped Meriam's lips.

"Your officer has been trying to reach you," the lieutenant said, his posture softening.

"We haven't heard a thing since the *Unteroffizier* got hit," the largest of the five *Wehrmacht* soldiers said.

Each of the men held a peculiar look that I couldn't quite place. I chalked it up to weariness from the battle.

"You're going the wrong way," the lieutenant said, pointing toward the group of advancing *Wehrmacht*. "We have to clear that machine gun nest and—"

In one moment the armband-clad *Wehrmacht* troops were sauntering forward in a slow methodical walk, and in the next they had taken cover in the doorways, their rifles pointed at us.

Gunshots erupted down the hall, slicing through the lieutenant and the corporal to his right.

I fumbled with my weapon as our SS complement opened fire, and I saw a few of the *Wehrmacht* troops tumble down as plaster and concrete dust filled the hallway. A round whizzed by my head, causing me to jump into the nearest room to my left. I landed hard on my shoulder and felt a surge of pain move up my side. I looked to the room across the hall and could see Meriam had done the same manoeuvre I had.

A half-dozen gunshots sounded off before silence filled the floor. Meriam looked at me, her eyes appearing to ask the same question I was thinking:

*Who won?*

I shook my head and began to roll onto my back.

I had hardly moved when I heard footsteps in the hall, followed by a whispering voice that said, "Check it."

I froze, my brain trying to decide if I recognized the voice or not. Slowly, I began to sit up. My finger was moving toward the trigger guard when the bootsteps started again. They were right outside the room.

A *Wehrmacht* soldier crept into view; the barrel of his rifle pressed to the doorframe as he attempted to clear the apartment. I froze. The determination in his eyes told me I didn't have a chance. But his pupils widened, and the surprise of seeing the French uniform bought me a moment more as the man remembered his orders.

*Were the French friend or foe?*

I had just taken one last inhale, thinking of all the life I still had to live, when the soldier's uniform erupted in a spray of blood. A burst of rounds pierced through him and embedded in the wall above my head.

The soldier collapsed with a wheeze, and my eyes swung to Meriam, who sitting up in the apartment across the hall, a thin trail of smoke emanating from her weapon.

A moment passed, just enough time for me to exhale the breath I had thought would be my last.

A dull thud came from the hall as a grenade bounced off the doorframe and tumbled into Meriam's apartment.

I stood, and without thinking, I charged. My rifle was level and my grip firm. I met the soldier head on, and the whites of his eyes grew in fear. He was still in the process of raising his weapon, which hung by the sling, as his hands had been busy prepping the grenade. His uniform was stained with blood, having been wounded in the firefight.

I fired. A single round escaped the muzzle and embedded into his rib cage.

The man's eyes turned from surprise to horror. I saw the soldier continue to raise his weapon, despite the growing pool of red that stained his uniform.

I pulled the trigger again and again, and a final time before the soldier collapsed with a choking death rattle escaping through his gritted teeth.

The grenade exploded then, forcing me to hunch over, my hands instinctively moving around my helmet to cover my head. I managed to keep my balance and looked behind me at the smoke that escaped the room.

"Meriam!"

I sprinted into the apartment, stepping over shattered tile and splintered wood. The spot Meriam had been in was empty, save for the remnants of the picture frames that had sprung from their nails. I moved left and entered a bedroom.

The mattress had been pulled from the bed and was now on the ground. As I approached, the barrel of a rifle began to peek out.

"Meriam it's me," I said as her face emerged, her expression shifting to one of relief. "Good thinking with the mattress," I added as she pushed it off of her and rose to her feet.

"I dove when I saw the grenade. Didn't even realize what I had done until I was under it." She paused, brushing herself off. "I heard the gunshots and hoped for the best but—" She stopped talking and I assumed she hadn't thought my chances were high. "Why did they turn on us like that?" she asked as she checked the gear on her carrier. "They had the red armbands."

I listened for a moment as I heard the building creak. The sounds of distant gunshots echoed up the block. "I think those were loyalists. They took the armbands to ambush us."

"Well, it worked," Meriam said. She let out an exasperated laugh. "Now we can't even trust our own people—we have to double check everyone."

"We have to warn the rest; more of them could have done the same thing. They could be pretending to fall back just to get behind our forces and..." I trailed off. Meriam's eyes were darting around my face, and she looked like she wanted to say something important.

"The radio," she said before starting toward the door.

I stuck out my hand to stop her. "The radio? Which—"

Meriam wrapped her fingers around my hand. "We use the radio on the officer and tell whoever is listening." I felt the realization as she said it, for I had forgotten about its existence entirely. "And while we're at it, we grab one of the dead *Wehrmacht*'s and listen to their chatter."

She appeared to see right through me and how impressed I was with her quick thinking, as she added, "Not bad for someone who just had a grenade thrown at them, huh?"

We moved into the hallway and, after checking to ensure it was clear, Meriam bent down over the lieutenant's body. She unclipped the radio from his carrier before looking at the speaker and saying, "You do it. Your German is better."

I grabbed the radio, but hesitated for a moment before saying, "We are in the middle of a battle—do we really want the SS second guessing their own allies? Could get a lot of innocent people killed."

"It's going to be a whole lot more confusing if an entire brigade of *Wehrmacht* loyalists assault SS positions wearing armbands. Now stop overthinking this and radio the officer in charge of this mess."

She gave me a shove, and I pressed the black button on the side with my thumb. "Hello, this is Legionnaire Domínguez. Who is on this frequency?"

"This is *Hauptsturmführer* Peiper," the shrill voice replied. "How did you get our frequency?"

"*Hauptsturmführer*, our SS squad has been wiped out. Be advised, loyalist forces have stolen red armbands and have dressed their *Wehrmacht* troops with them to ambush us."

There was a long pause, and I looked at Meriam, thinking, *He's wondering if there is any way he can verify I am who I say I am.*

"Legionnaire. Link up with another SS squad. I can't take the chance of... If you aren't who you say you are..."

I opened my mouth to reply when Meriam pointed upward and mouthed the words: *"The squad upstairs."*

In all the chaos I had forgotten about them as well.

"Yes, sir," I said into the radio. "You'll hear from us soon."

Meriam moved first, leading us down the hall and toward the far stairwell. She bent down and pulled one of the radios from a dead *Wehrmacht* soldier, trying not to look at the mortal wounds that covered his chest.

She joined me by the stairwell, radio in hand, and I pushed open the door. We moved up several floors, our assent as quiet as possible, not wanting to risk running into any other surprises.

As we neared the top floor, we heard the door to the landing above us open. We both raised our weapons at the sound of bootsteps descending from the stairs above. A group of men in SS uniforms arrived on the far landing, forcing Meriam and I to point our rifles into the air.

"Friendly," I said through gritted teeth, hoping these men weren't jumpy.

"Where is *Obersturmführer* Schuler?" the sergeant asked, looking genuinely confused.

"We were ambushed. The rest of the unit didn't make it," I replied with as much compassion as I could muster.

The sergeant's face twisted into a depressed visage as he

processed what I had said. "What floor?" he asked, pushing past me. As I answered he said, "Helmut, with me. The rest of you make sure they don't go anywhere."

There was a sound of heels clicking and the rest of the group turned to look at us. I watched the sergeant move down several flights before entering the second floor, the soldier he had identified as Helmut following him.

We stood there for several minutes. Meriam and I looked at each other, and I wondered if the sergeant would blame us for his commander's death, or even more likely, believe we were behind it.

The sergeant and Helmut bounded up the stairs soon after, their faces red with exertion. As the two men arrived at the landing below us, I said, "I have your *Obersturmführer's* radio, and I spoke with *Hauptsturmführer* Peiper but he wouldn't give us orders until he verified—"

"We have our orders." The sergeant's voice was biting now. "Take this block."

"Things have changed," Meriam said, pointing to the floor below us. "The *Wehrmacht* loyalists have taken the armbands of our turncoats and are disguising themselves."

The sergeant shook his head, his gaze flashing to the radio on the webbing of my carrier. "Give me that."

I handed over the device and watched as the sergeant proceeded to pull the earpiece from his radio and plug it into the one I had given him. "Yes, sir," the sergeant said after identifying himself to the commanding officer. "Yes, with two legionnaires. Yes, sir."

A minute passed with some back and forth before the sergeant looked at us, saying, "We are to head to the roof."

Our squad pivoted and we moved up the stairwell, the sergeant still nodding to the orders flooding into his earpiece. A rifleman pushed open the door at the top of the stairs and our team fanned out.

The soldiers were careful to look to the adjacent rooftops to ensure there were no snipers. Satisfied, we neared the far edge and scanned the streets below. Peering to the north, I could see a column of six tanks, with four trucks trailing behind. My eyes darted to the hundred or so troops that moved up the block parallel to the armour, their heads bobbing in and out of storefronts and alleyways as they looked for explosives or enemy combatants.

"There's the main force, just as *Hauptsturmführer* Pieper said," the sergeant mumbled. He sounded exhausted.

I could sense the unease of the squad around us. Whether it was due to the loss of their officer or the number of advancing troops, I could not be sure.

The sergeant grabbed the radio from his carrier and spoke into it again, identifying the sight of the enemy force. He gestured for one of his men to hand him a map.

As the soldier struggled to pull the paper from his side pack, the sergeant paused, hand in the air. "But, sir, you are aware that we still have troops in contact all around the area?" The map was thrust into the sergeant's hand and he found our location with a finger. After a pause, he nodded and said into the radio, "Yes, sir, I understand."

The sergeant read off the coordinates and waited for a response, turning away from the advancing force as he did so, his eyes looking southward in the direction of friendly lines. "Yes, sir. Understood, sir," he said after a moment.

The sergeant released his grip on the radio. Then, turning to us, announced, "We fall back before this block becomes a crater."

"Crater? What did you call in? Artillery?" Meriam asked, her eyes darting skyward.

The sergeant gestured us toward the stairwell, his face flushed. "Yes. Peiper says there is a reserve unit that arrived in the city this morning. All they needed was a fire mission."

As we reached the stairwell, I looked to the east and the block beyond. I could see a pair of *Wehrmacht* tanks retreating toward the SS-controlled zone, a dozen armband-wearing soldiers scurrying behind them. I hoped those men were the rightful owners of those insignias and not a ruse by the loyalists.

We made our way down the stairwell and out onto the street, our team retreating across the road. As we bounded down the street, I noticed the sounds of rifle fire had become nearly non-existent.

Several blocks raced by without a word from anyone. Every few metres, the sergeant would raise his hand to his ear, but he never replied, his eyes always facing forward.

My knees began to burn as we arrived at a sandbag-ladened intersection. A machine gun position lay ahead with two soldiers peering over the barrel—the SS decals on their helmets a welcome sight for once.

"Where did you get the Frenchmen?" one of the gunners asked as he lit a cigarette.

"We caught them—" a private began to say, but the sergeant gave him a stern look with the snap of his head. The private didn't dare say anything else.

"We *found* them fighting, cut off from their unit," the sergeant said, turning to face the two men.

The machine gunner pocketed his lighter as he gestured to his left. "Any French units still alive were instructed to fall back to the butcher shop on the corner of Rhine *Allee* and Assembly *Straße*."

"That's the one next to Zimmer's Beer Hall?" the sergeant asked.

"One and the same," the gunner replied, the cigarette bobbing in his mouth.

"Are there many French troops left?" Meriam asked, and I could hear the worry in her voice.

The machine gunner shrugged. "I don't know; you're the first two I've seen. I heard they took a beating." He looked over at his spotter before adding, "But I also heard on the radio that they gave those traitors a hell of a fight. So..." He shrugged again.

The sergeant turned to us and said, "Go on, go find your comrades." He gave us a peculiar look before adding, "I hope you find them in better shape than I found mine." He turned before gesturing for those under his command to move around the sandbags and up the block.

Meriam and I pivoted and began a brisk walk down the boulevard, passing formations of SS troops who fumbled with ammo and equipment.

The sound of artillery strikes impacting in the distance echoed up the boulevards, and after several blocks, we heard the stolen *Wehrmacht* radio on Meriam's chest begin to fill with chatter.

"Anyone left on this frequency?" the voice asked, panic coating each word.

I could see in my peripheral that Meriam's head lowered to look at the radio, but I kept my gaze forward.

"This is *Hauptmann* Kofler ordering anyone that is able, please respond..."

We walked on in silence.

"Second Platoon, what's your combat status? *Oberleutnant*, I need a report..."

The dull thumps of the artillery continued on, and I found that I cared little about the souls being annihilated then, for I was hungry, and my throat ached for a drink.

# Chapter 16

## *By Liquor and Wood*

Locating the beer hall was of little issue as we could hear the French troops long before we saw them. Inside the dimly lit hall we found almost a hundred legionnaires forming a half-moon congregation around the bar. At first, I thought everyone was already drunk, but soon noticed no one was holding a stein. The crowd was growing restless and there was some shoving as the hollering became louder by the second.

Meriam and I pushed our way through the crowd, ending up against the side of the bar. Through the jostling group I could see several soldiers behind the counter, rifles in hand, yelling at their compatriots to get back. Belmont was among them, but he looked to be less than enthused about the assignment. I suspected he was in dire need of a drink as well.

The shoving continued and I was surprised by the troop's blatant disregard for discipline. I thought back to what the machine gunner on the road had said and recalled the legionnaires had taken heavy losses. I looked around and noticed a startling lack of officers, and I guessed none of the soldiers were in the mood to be told "no" at the moment.

I made eye contact with Belmont and yelled to be heard over the uproar, saying, "Need any help?"

Belmont shook his head. "I thought you two left," he said, taking his eye off of a legionnaire who looked like he was about to hop the bar.

"It occurred to us, but we were too busy," Meriam said. Her hand slid to my lower back before letting it fall to her side.

"Ya what a disaster," a legionnaire said beside us. His eyes were wild. "I got separated too."

Meriam ignored what the soldier had said, her eyes returning to Belmont. "We thought you might be dead after we heard about how bad the losses were."

"Using us as cannon fodder," the legionnaire beside Meriam said, before swearing to himself and moving to a table near the back. He appeared to realize that the kegs would not be pouring beer any time soon.

"Even the SS guys at the checkpoint were talking about it," Meriam added after a moment.

Several corporals and a sergeant farther down the bar threatened to make arrests and the crowd slowly began to dissipate. Each legionnaire looked more depressed than the last.

"Command is aware," Belmont said, his voice returning to a normal level. "The rumor going around is that the officers are meeting to discuss how botched of an operation our whole involvement has been. The SS left us to take the brunt, and command well, we were only meant to assist. Guard a government building here, secure a street there, not lead a charge on a dug in and battle-hardened force. We are too few for that."

"And even fewer now," Meriam said, her eyes scanning the faces of those who remained.

I did the same, and while I recognized most, there were several familiar faces missing from the group—Henri among them.

"Any idea what our next move is?" I said, keeping my observations to myself.

Belmont pointed vaguely toward the entrance of the beer hall. "That lies with the officers, but I don't think we will be the tip of the spear for the foreseeable future. Not unless we get a significant number of reinforcements. The radio station is saying the loyalists are making advances in almost every major city."

"The SS have always been better at abusing civilians in the colonies than actually fighting," Meriam said, which caught me off guard.

Belmont fogged the statement by saying, "I just hope we don't get cut off."

The words had hardly escaped his lips before someone announced the presence of an officer and the entire room snapped to attention. Meriam and I took a full second longer to change our stature.

I looked to the entrance, and I watched as the major approached, several officers parading in behind him.

"At ease, legionnaires," the major said upon taking a position at the head of the beer hall. The fact that an officer of his stature was addressing us personally was not lost on anyone.

The major waited for his officers to form around him, and I noticed that Belmont had moved from around the bar to stand beside us. His face was flushed with anxiety.

The major tapped his finger on the wooden table in front of him, before letting out a quiet sigh and saying, "I'm proud of all of you today. It's a shame *Hauptsturmführer* Pieper called in that artillery strike; there's no doubt in my mind that the Foreign Legion would have dislodged the enemy force and routed them."

The room stayed silent; the major's attempt to raise morale

had failed. No one was feeling particularly boisterous at the moment.

The major cleared his throat and continued, "Our mission here is ... at an end for now. I have word from Paris that the terrorist group *Fils de la Republique* have launched a large-scale campaign across Northern France. We are being recalled home to assist in any operation the government requires of us."

He paused again, looking around the room once more, a hand running through his close-cropped brunette hair. "Now, our train for France leaves tomorrow morning, first thing, oh-six-hundred. I want everyone packed and ready to move by oh-three thirty. Officers will brief squad leaders about the location and a rally point in case we get separated or ambushed."

His face mellowed before he corrected it with a thin smile. "But enough about that. I want everyone to celebrate the victory today. So, drink up. I trust each legionnaire will be responsible with their consumption, of course. Drunkenness will not be tolerated. Now let's see if we can wrestle up something to eat from that butcher shop across the street."

The legionnaires beside me began muttering to each other, but the major hesitated to depart. Turning back, he added, "And remember, stay in the vicinity of the building and don't tell our SS counterparts we are going anywhere. It would just create confusion in their lower ranks." He nodded at the room before pivoting and exiting the beer hall.

His junior officers began identifying squad leaders and talking to them while the rest of the men headed toward the beer kegs.

I had a feeling that the access to alcohol was not to improve the mood of the troops, but to ensure the soldiers didn't ask too many questions. An old quote came to me then: *Keep your population drunk and their need to rebel will become nonexistent.*

I couldn't remember where I had read that, but as a legionnaire handed me a mug of frothy beer and the crisp beverage met my lips, I found I no longer cared.

---

I awoke to the sounds of boots scuffing hardwood next to my face. My eyes shot open to reveal that the formation of soldiers was awake, or in the process of such. I had hardly remembered unpacking my gear and laying out the thin mat that was the only thing saving my back from the cold floor. My sleeping bag was zipped up tight, and again, I could hardly remember setting it up.

I sat upright, my head a little tender, and I suspected I was on the outskirts of a hangover. I recalled the first drink leading to the second, and the second leading to a third, when the garlic sausages arrived followed by cuts of pork and ham—a lot of ham. I remember drinking a fourth pint followed by a trio of shots while talking to a legionnaire about Spain and his trip to Barcelona five years prior. It had made me miss home all the more.

I kicked my sleeping bag away and began to stand. I could see Meriam was already up, as she sat at the bar. I looked around and noticed that everyone was gingerly packing up their gear. I felt I had time.

I shuffled forward, attempting to crack my neck to relieve some of the stiffness I was feeling, but the ache persisted. I moved up to the bar and took a seat beside Meriam.

"A little early for a drink, no?" I said in Spanish.

She turned, a sly grin on her face. "You know, I wouldn't have been opposed to you coming up and kissing me on the neck."

I sat there in stunned silence for a moment. I hadn't

expected that reply. Eventually I said, "But it could have been any of these guys. Could have caused a scene."

"I know what your lips feel like," she replied with an infectious smirk.

She turned her attention to a legionnaire who came over with a coffee mug on a saucer, placing it in front of her.

"Someone found a coffee machine in the breakroom in the back," Meriam said, her eyes drifting from me and over to the legionnaire. "Freddy here was being a sweetheart, weren't you, Freddy?"

The legionnaire nodded, his face showing his youth, and I suspected he had not seen the majority of his twenties yet. Meriam touched the porcelain mug with a finger before adding, "He was just telling me about the States. He's American, you know."

Fred nodded again. He spoke, his southern drawl coating the French as it exited his lips, "Born and raised Stateside. Was in the Army Rangers two years before I joined the Legion."

"Why'd you leave, if you don't mind me asking?" I replied, my eyes shifted to Meriam's coffee, which I found myself coveting.

"Let me get a cup of my own and I'll tell you," Fred said as he pivoted, heading toward the end of the bar.

Before he disappeared from sight I called out, "Can I have one as well, please?"

"Me too," a soldier said as he passed by.

"Fred, don't forget me," another legionnaire added.

A sergeant looked toward the bar as he rolled up his sleeping bag. "Me as well!" he said.

"See, this is why you don't do anything nice. Everyone wants one," Fred mumbled before switching to English and rounding the corner.

I turned to Meriam, who was passing a coaster between her fingers, something that reminded me of Ernesto, as I had seen him perform the same nervous habit many times before. I felt a sense of shame as I realized I had not thought of him in many days.

*I wonder if he's alright...*

I felt the thought grow cold in my head and instead focused on Meriam's hands and the coaster that was being passed between them. The chipped white nail polish on her thin fingers stood in contrast to the advertisement in front of us showing a brown-uniformed young man holding a stein of light-coloured beer from Vienna.

Meriam turned her attention to me, and I suspected she spoke only to avoid the silence that surrounded us. "What are you looking at? You can't be dreaming; we have to march soon."

"I was thinking of my brother. He lived here in Germania." Seeing Meriam's expression shift to one of a quizzical nature prompted me to add, "Don't worry, we aren't close."

"But you told me that, remember? Outside the museum..."

I racked my brain, trying to recall what I had said and gave an unsure shake of my head.

Meriam blew on her coffee before saying, "Still, he's your brother, so you are bound to worry."

It was not what she said, but *how* she said it. The tenderness of the words. I found myself appreciating her even more then. This thought distracted me from what really tumbled around my brain. I had visions of my brother dead at the side of the road, a rifle clutched in his hands, dirt caked under his fingernails as rainwater slowly filled the ditch and submerged his dyed blond hair.

"I'm an only child so I never got to experience having a sibling," Meriam said after an unknown amount of time. Her hands returned to the coaster. "I have always wondered what it would be like to have a little sister." She laughed to herself quietly. "Sometimes I wonder if I could have raised her better than I was raised. Given her a fighting chance, you know?"

Her words surprised me. As my hand rested on her lower back, I said, "What do you mean? You have a good job—and a nice apartment in Paris you told me about. Sounds like you are doing well."

Now it was Meriam's turn to give me a non-committal tilt of her head. "I guess, but those are just *things*. Objects, you know? None of them define me. I don't know, I'm rambling... I've been working on myself over the last year." She looked around again. "That's why I'm here; part of my sightseeing trip. I took a month off, using all the vacation time I had saved up, but I don't know if I'll go back." She let out a nervous chuckle. "I— Well, I mean if this coup didn't happen of course. No telling how Europe will look in a few months when this thing is over."

"If it lasts that long," I said, hardly realizing I had said anything. Quickly, I added, "But you're right—life is all about experiences, constantly learning, bettering yourself. And it's like you said, if it makes a good story then it's worth doing."

She tilted her head. "So many of these things I had to teach myself. Life would have been easier if someone had taken the time to teach them to me when I was young, but instead I had to trip and stumble around in the dark."

Meriam looked up and stared straight through the advertisement. "When I have kids, I'm telling them to be positive. I'll tell them that negativity ... it's a cancer. First it comes to you as a coping mechanism, then it shifts to humor, but soon it is all consuming. I won't let my children be like that, like my family was. I'll ask them every day after school to name something positive that happened to them that day, you know? I won't let it cost them like it cost me and my relationships."

Her expression changed then, and I feared it was because she felt she had revealed a vulnerable side of herself that she had sworn to hide away.

Meriam's gaze softened as her eyes met mine. "But you're a positive guy, I can tell." She sounded sincere, but I could see the pain lurking just out of sight. She looked toward the far side of the bar. "There he is, our savior," she said, and I turned to see Fred carrying a tray with seven cups of coffee on it.

He set the tray down on the bar before lifting up a mug and placing it in front of me. He looked over my shoulder and said, "Bains, Corrion, coffee! Oh, and yours too, Sergeant."

I smiled in appreciation of his delivery service before asking, "Any milk back there?"

"No, you get black; that's it. This isn't the Ritz," Fred snapped. Clearly, this was not the first time he had been asked this.

I held up a hand to apologize before asking, "So why join the Foreign Legion? Why leave the Marines?"

"Army Rangers," he corrected, his accent becoming obvious again. "It's relatively new, but a different thing. I wanted to join an army with a proud history, a long set of traditions. America ... well, I don't agree with our isolationism."

Fred moved a cup of his own closer to him as he added, "Funny, really—the Chinese emperors did that, and it cost them dearly. I did always like the shared histories of France and the States ... so I guess that's my answer to your question." Fred sipped his coffee and winced at the heat. "But the French have a great programme here; they welcomed me for my experience, and I get to be a part of something greater—a country that actually uses its army for something. I plan to see the world, not just military bases Stateside or dealing with the riots in Lower California and Havana.

"You know, before I shipped off to Paris, friends of mine, they said, 'Why join them? They lost the war.' And I said, 'At least they fought in it.' But now that I've thought about it more, I realize there ain't no shame in the loss. People back home like to sit on their high horses because the Reich never conquered the States, like in some way, our lack of participation put us above the whole thing. But the truth is, if we had gotten involved, we would have been conquered. Japanese on one side, Reich on the other. But I guess they were right at the time; staying out of the war really was the best thing to keep America whole."

Meriam blinked a few times as she looked at Fred, clearly wanting to ask something, but kept her lips sealed. Fred noticed this and asked, "What? Is it an American question? Ask away."

"What about that bomb your people and those exiled Germans made? That could have turned the course of the war," Meriam said.

Fred shrugged. "We go over it in school. It wouldn't have been ready to make a difference. The war was already over. Besides, how could we even get it anywhere? The Luftwaffe would have shot down any bomber that dared carry it, and that's assuming we could even get it across the Atlantic. But it's hardly unique now; every empire that matters has their version of the bomb."

"Except the New Roman Empire," I said in an offhand remark.

"That's why I said, 'Every empire that matters,'" Fred retorted with a smirk. "And as terrible as a weapon it is, I think it's the only thing keeping the world together. Still, ever since Japan dropped it in northern China, I don't think anyone is eager to see it in action again."

"The Germans used those small ones in Siberia in the sixties," I said.

"Sure, and then they signed those pacts to never use them again after all the international pressure. It's funny though, Japan was the first one to use it and now it's just the sick old man of Asia. A once great empire, just a shadow of what it was."

"There's a lot of that going around," Meriam muttered under her breath.

As I went to take a sip of coffee, I heard movement at the entrance to the beer hall. An officer entered, prompting us all to bolt up and stand at attention.

"The commandant wants us to be underway inside of ten minutes. Pack up your stuff and line up outside for inspection," the officer shouted. A hint of exhaustion hid behind the words.

Everyone moved then, but I took a moment to look longingly at my coffee. I decided I would pack as quickly as possible and down the beverage. Scalding hot or not, I had a feeling I would be needing it today.

I stood and joined the others as they rolled up their mats and shoved items into their rucksacks. I could see a group of legionnaires sitting at a long table, their weapons in front of them as they filled magazines with rounds, a tin of ammo between them. Clearly the war was far from over for them.

I saw several of the men around me had pints of beer on the ground next to them as they prepared to leave. The sweat from the chilled glasses formed puddles around the bases of the steins.

---

Once everyone was assembled, we departed the beer hall and moved down the dark streets in a weary march. I was situated close to Belmont, with Meriam directly on my right. As we reached the next block, I could hear several soldiers whispering amongst each other from somewhere behind me.

"We were guarding their northern flank. If we leave, they'll be exposed," the legionnaire said.

"The officers have it handled," another voice said, sounding annoyed with her squad mate. "Trust the commandant; he knows what he's doing."

I looked to the head of the formation and saw the major along with one of his lieutenants and the captain Belmont disliked. The remainder of the officers were scattered around the formation.

We marched on in relative silence for close to an hour.

The night was calm—unnaturally so. I did not hear the crack of a rifle or the dull thud of artillery. The streetlamps basked us in a warm glow and the puddles that lined the gutters reflected the window lights with a cozy warmth. While I'm sure many in the formation worried about snipers, I didn't share their sentiment. I had a feeling everything was going to be fine, for I was on my way home, headed back toward my beloved Spain with Meriam at my side.

We marched a little further, until the major held up his hand. The formation ceased its movement immediately. He gestured to one of his sergeants, who came forward. The major whispered something to his subordinate, but they were too far ahead to hear. The sergeant nodded and handed his weapon over before moving down the block and disappearing from sight.

"Where's he off too?" Meriam asked Belmont, who was studying our surroundings, clearly not enjoying the location we had decided to stop.

Belmont stayed silent, ignoring Meriam's question, and I suspected it was because he didn't know either.

Several minutes passed before the sergeant returned. He approached slowly, his hands above his head so as to not spook any of us. He moved over to the major and spoke in hushed tones as another officer handed the sergeant his weapon.

After the conversation ceased, the major waved us forward. As the formation moved on, one of his lieutenants stayed still, waiting for us to pass.

As we moved by the officer, he said, "All rifles are to be slung. No one fires unless fired upon, regardless of who is ahead."

I nodded at the command and proceeded to move my rifle to my back. I could hear the group behind me asking questions to one another, their whispers being interrupted as their squad leader snapped at them to maintain silence.

With each step forward, I became increasingly aware of how peculiar the entire operation was. Our departure in the middle of the night, the fact we were not allowed to discuss our redeployment with the SS soldiers we had just fought beside, or how we were leaving their flank wide open. Not to mention sending an unarmed soldier into the dark, only to be told to sling our weapons once he returned.

The street widened as we rounded a bend, and I could see a train station to the right of a plaza. There were no lights, but the moon was bright enough that the outline of the concrete structure met my gaze. I could see the silhouettes of soldiers, sandbags and machine gun emplacements surrounding the building.

At first, I assumed this was an SS garrison, but as we neared, I could see the men ahead were wearing a uniform that certainly wasn't that of an SS member. As we passed the first group, I could see the Luftwaffe insignia on their tunics. I trained my eyes forward and felt my pulse thunder in my neck.

It became so clear to me then. The major had secured a

deal with the loyalist faction. Passage home in exchange for us to end our fight. Whether the Luftwaffe had been chosen as our reception because they already had a garrison at the train station or because they were more agreeable as we had not bloodied each other, it was impossible to know.

*Could the commandant have acted alone?* I thought. *If we're caught ... this could be treason.*

The notion didn't last long. No, the logistics of how he had managed to broker this deal would have been impossible unless the French government had stepped in. They must have realized that if the Führer was dead, the *Reichswehr's* days were numbered. Combined with how frivolously SS command had been in their use of the French forces, and the choice had probably been an easy one.

We entered the train station, and a heavy presence of guards stood around an ammo cache of sorts. While the airmen outside had been regular Luftwaffe-enlisted personnel, the soldiers on the inside wore paratrooper uniforms and carried themselves like they would be able to annihilate our entire unit with little effort.

Seeing the wealth of ammo and rations out in the open stood in stark contrast to how little gear the SS had at their disposal. If this insignificant garrison had access to this much of a stockpile, the SS truly had no chance of victory.

The French generals in Paris were making the correct choice.

We boarded the aging train without comment and Belmont chose a seat in the fourth car from the front. Meriam took a seat across from him and I beside her. The cars were the standard passenger fare: sixty seats, two on each side of the aisle that split the car down the middle. Despite the abundance of room, I noticed that only a handful of legionnaires chose to sit in our cabin. I didn't take offense to this, figuring everyone wanted to be left alone.

It would not be long until the train shunted forward, and we would be on our way to France, leaving the horror that had befallen the Reich behind us. Then, God willing, I would find a way home to Spain.

# A Change in Perspective:

## The Remnant

The air was cold and biting, much more than it should have been for that time of year, but the summer was long gone and only the cruel mistress that was the Siberian winter lay ahead.

Sasha navigated the pothole-laden road that snaked up toward the mausoleum. A group of men warmed their hands over the fire that danced from the mouth of a dented barrel. Sasha recognized the insignia on their armbands: a red star against a black background.

He felt intimidated upon seeing the battle-hardened shock troopers of the Marxist-Leninist Popular Front faction, a dwindling number after their headquarters had been hit with several German missile strikes last June. Still, seeing the famed freedom fighters gave Sasha hope that the reports were true; members from all across what remained of the once great Soviet Union were answering Comrade Kravchenko's call.

As Sasha continued up the hill, the crowds became nonexistent, and he was alone. He looked to the grey skies. The heavy storm clouds overhead ensured there was no threat of Japanese air assault. But even if there hadn't been a storm brewing, Japanese planes hadn't been reported overhead in months. The comrades in China had been keeping them busy, and the death toll to the Imperial Japanese occupation force was reaching a breaking point after decades of guerrilla warfare and terror campaigns. But while the true believers in China kept the Japanese busy, Sasha had a different mission, and a different enemy.

The entrance to the tomb lay open, just as it had since its first desecration in the decades before Sasha had been born. His eyes drifted from the brickwork and toward a pail of cleaning supplies that lay beside the door. Sasha knew who they belonged to, for she had always taken care of Comrade Stalin's final resting place.

Sasha walked into the crypt and saw the middle-aged woman hunched beside the long-empty sarcophagus. Stalin's body had been long stolen and hacked apart by disenfranchised veterans who had too much time on their hands and alcohol in their stomachs. Not even the great leader's medals had been spared; Sasha recalled hearing a tale about how they had been melted down to make ammunition.

The woman was scrubbing at the latest batch of graffiti, courtesy of the locals. Sweat pooled on her brow as she worked to remove the remnants of the word "butcher," which had been painted on the side of the sarcophagus.

Sasha looked up to see that the vandals had been particularly prolific in their debauchery this time. Such phrases as: "Traitor to the Soviet Union," and "Who needed enemies when we had Stalin?" were sprayed onto the stonewall.

"They've been busy," Sasha said to the woman as she rubbed the back of her hand against her cheek.

"There is nothing I can do but scrub," she replied, huffing. "I just worry that when I get too old ... who will do it?"

"We have to hope that by then we will have won, and we can build him the grand state tomb he deserves."

"I don't understand why they hate him," she said, looking at the small photo of the former leader she had set up beside the smashed death mask. "He led us against an enemy the world has never known, an evil..." Her voice turned to hatred as she trailed off. "Before they can judge him, they must ask what they would do in his situation."

"I agree," Sasha replied, adjusting his grip on the sling that held his weapon. "But people always want to find someone to blame. They want to second guess every decision he made. But none of them ask, 'Why didn't the generals do this?' or 'Who was the logistics officer in charge that resulted in the shortages?'" Sasha shook his head. "No, it is easier to blame the boss. They don't want to think it was the soldiers of the Red Army that let us down."

"Such is life. But those weak men weren't true communists. They were corrupt and that's why comrade Stalin had to purge them. I weep thinking of how our countrymen could be so dishonest that they would let their ego get in the way of fighting the true enemy." She pulled a cigarette from her breast pocket, and Sasha watched as small flakes of tobacco tumbled from the end.

He took the opportunity to retrieve a cigarette of his own before passing his matchbook to her. "A war on two fronts," he said, striking a match. "Never easy."

"Three, if you include the Turks," she replied, holding her face close to the flame. "Allowed another avenue for Germany to flank around our forces while the Japanese slowly but surely whittled down our comrades in the east. But such is life," she said, and Sasha recognized those last four words to be her comfort phrase.

The woman's eyes turned upward, looking at the words

that littered the walls, no doubt thinking how much work she had in store for her. The light from the candles she had placed around flickered along the bones of her thin face. “Why are you here, Sasha?”

“I came to pray. I wish Comrade Stalin will grant me luck and bravery in the weeks ahead.”

“Another offensive?” she asked, her eyes navigating to the barrel of the rifle that stuck out over Sasha’s shoulder. “I lost my brother in one of Comrade Menshikov’s offensives some years ago. I wish you luck, but...”

The wind outside picked up, taking the remainder of her thought with it.

“I’ve been listening to my father, and they have been telling me of reports that the evil Reich is collapsing. The jackals turned on each other,” Sasha said, hardly able to contain his enthusiasm. “We will use this opportunity to strike. Cells in Moscow and Kiev and Minsk, all over the land that is rightfully ours, are ready too.”

“I see,” she said, puffing on her cigarette. “Careful when you talk that way about land. Those Germans have lived behind the Urals for seventy years. Their mothers are buried in that ground and the soldiers were born there. It is their land in their hearts, just as much as it was ours. Never think they won’t fight to hold on with as much desire as you have to take it. Maybe even more.”

Sasha felt a warmth in his face as he sensed her ignorance. The entire world knew the Soviet people had been robbed, and even the blond gorillas that patrolled the Urals knew in their small black hearts who the rightful owners were.

Sasha knew he had the will to win, and his comrades would not stop until the final victory was achieved. Kravchenko was more of a tactician than Menshikov ever was. This time, the offensive would succeed.

"Can you give me a moment alone?" Sasha asked as the conversation faded.

She nodded, holding out her hands so the young man could help her up.

As Sasha assisted her to her feet, she said, "I need to check on the baby anyway."

She moved out of the tomb, her hand moving to the square of her back as she did so. Clearly, she had overworked herself.

Sasha removed his helmet and placed it beside the photo of Comrade Stalin. The great leader's face was that of steel, which gave the young fighter solace. He bowed his head and prayed to the God of his father that his aim would be true and that he would make it through the coming fire in one piece.

As Sasha made the sign of the cross, he envisioned the jack-boot jackals, the blood of all his countrymen on their heels, staining the snow outside the gates of the Kremlin. Sasha prayed that he would be able to kill every German he could get his hands on. He vowed he would do this for the motherland who had suffered so much under their occupation.

As Sasha stood, he returned his helmet to his head and touched the frame of the photo. He wished Comrade Stalin was with him now, leading the gallant soldiers in what he dreamed would be a chain of decisive victories.

Sasha retracted his hand and moved out of the crypt.

As he began his journey down the hill, he saw a group of soldiers approaching. Their uniforms were faded, and he knew these men had participated in many raids in the past. The fact they had been baptized in combat made Sasha both envious and in awe of them.

The group of veterans looked to the young revolutionary as they passed. "For luck?" one of them asked.

Sasha nodded, his helmet shifting on his head as he did so. He gestured toward the tomb. "For luck."

He adjusted his scarf as the beginnings of the winter gusts moved across the hillsides. In the coming weeks the squall would venture past the Ural Mountains and into the Reich, as it had for nearly a century.

Except this time, the wind would not be alone...

# Act III

## The Sun Always Sets on the Third Reich

"One death is a tragedy; a million is a statistic."

— Commonly attributed to Joseph Stalin

# Chapter 17

## *And That's All There Was*

The train slammed to a halt.

Meriam swore, and I gripped the armrests to ensure I didn't fly forward.

"It can't be the border yet," she said, alarm coating her words.

"No, it's not," I replied as I began to stand. I looked over to Sergeant Belmont, who was waving for me to sit down. "Any idea—"

I was cut off by a voice over the loudspeaker. My gaze snapped upward as the major said, "All soldiers, please remain seated. We are being inspected by members of the SS. I will brief you further when I know more."

My eyes stayed locked on the overhead speaker, but no more words sprung from it.

Meriam looked at me then, her eyes showing panic. "They are boarding the train?" she asked. As I opened my mouth to reply, she added, "They must be looking for deserters."

"They will leave us alone," Belmont began to say. "You are with us—"

"It won't matter," I said. "The Germans don't work that way."

I heard the door to the cabin open behind me. Two SS soldiers along with a low-level officer stood in the doorway. The junior lieutenant's gaze ran across Belmont's face before coming to rest on Meriam and me. He appeared to be wondering to himself why there was something different about us, but he couldn't quite place it yet.

"All of you, identification please." His voice was as cold and crisp as his uniform.

"We are soldiers of the French Foreign Legion," Belmont said. "Our uniforms should be enough for you."

"Identification, now!" the officer pressed. He moved beside our seats and paused before his attention snapped to Belmont, adding, "Your rank?"

"Sergeant."

The officer looked at me, his eyes narrowed on my boots. "And you? Steal those off a dead man?"

"I'm a ... corporal," I said, the words almost refusing to come out as the officer's gaze immediately pierced the lie.

He grabbed the sleeve of my shirt, looking up and down for a rank insignia. "No markings," he said, directing the comment toward the two SS men waiting behind him.

The officer snatched my wrist and began to pull. Meriam stood up, placing her hands on the officer's chest. "You can't take him! He's with me. Please, I'm pregnant and he's the father. Please!"

The officer and I both looked at her in surprise. I could tell by the way the man had stiffened that he was assessing if what she said was the truth or the boldest lie he had ever heard.

"You aren't showing, *Fräulein*," the officer said as he gave her a once over. Noting the lack of insignia on her arm, he added, "You are not a soldier either. Imposters, the lot of you."

The officer began to pull me again, prompting Meriam to scream. The SS soldiers moved forward and grabbed her as well. As they tugged, the officer said, "If you're pregnant, you can't be separated from the father." His face was smeared with a sick smile. "You must stay together, like a family."

I heard Belmont raise his voice, prompting one of the SS soldiers to yell in broken French at him. I was thankful Belmont was speaking up in our defense, but I expected that's all he would do. God knows that's more than I would have done if I had found myself in his position.

Both Meriam and I were brought into the aisle, hands gripping our shoulders. Several French soldiers stood from their seats, blocking the exit.

"These are deserters!" the officer shouted in German. "Stay out of our way or there will be violence!"

The French soldiers remained where they stood, their boots rooted firmly in place. Each man kept their gaze fixed on the three SS men.

Seeing the look on the soldiers' faces prompted the officer to pull out his pistol with his free hand and shout, "I'm warning you!"

I watched as one of the Frenchmen near the back of the cabin slowly reached over to the seat beside him, and I suspected he was going for his rifle. The SS officer was distracted and did not see this. He looked between Meriam and I before his eyes rested on the far entrance of the car. "Commandant, your men are interfering with an operation of Hitler's SS."

Hearing this prompted me to turn and look to the French commander standing in the doorway behind us.

The major looked past the SS men and said to the legionnaires, "Everyone stand down!" He narrowed his eyes as they returned to the SS officer's thin face. "Why do you have your hands on two of my soldiers?"

"They are not soldiers; they are deserters. Filthy cowards hiding behind the uniform," the officer said, jostling me a little as if hoping the motion would somehow shake loose my disguise. "His uniform is all mismatched, no insignia. And her ... look at it. I think she stole it from one of your dead men."

The major looked between us for a moment, and I knew he only had the vaguest idea of who we could be. He paused, chewing his lip for a moment. "They are no soldiers of France, but I can assure you that they were given that equipment by my own people."

I felt the officer's grip loosen slightly on my shirt. "Explain yourself," he said to the major.

"The SS forces in the capital conscripted many people into their ranks, as well as my own. All the others that were mingled with the Foreign Legion either ended up dead or ran off. These two were following my orders. I told them to board the train."

The SS officer's grip tightened again. "Well then they are excellent soldiers for remaining at their post, but now the Reich has new orders for them."

Meriam and I were pulled again, and I looked back at the major. "As you were," he said, his words directed to the SS men.

The major's gaze met mine, but he quickly looked away. He pivoted and headed back into the train car he had come from. I knew he wanted this to be over so he and his people could return to their families.

Belmont looked between us, and I could see he was wrestling with himself. A moment passed before he too brought his gaze downward. The sergeant had his orders and like a good soldier he followed them. I did not hate him, but I suspected the man would relive this memory for years to come.

We were marched to the back of the train car and pushed out onto the gravel below. I pulled my arm free from the officer's clutches and said, "Relax. I'm not going anywhere."

The officer grabbed Meriam's wrist and shoved her beside me. I could see several military trucks on the road beside the train. A dozen SS members stood beside them. They had set up a roadblock along the street and I could see that it was they who had flagged down the train.

I turned my attention to a squad of SS soldiers who climbed from the train several cars ahead. "Just these two?" the officer asked the approaching men.

As the group of soldiers nodded in response, Meriam looked to the officer and said, "Shouldn't you all be fighting the war? Not rounding up innocent people?"

The group of soldiers shook their heads in annoyance before the officer replied, "There are no innocents here." He pushed us toward the row of trucks, and I began to walk.

"Are we fighting again or are you going to shoot us?" I asked, trying my best to mask the fear in my voice.

"Perhaps both. But for now, we go into the city and let the *Standartenführer* decide," the officer replied, shoving us harder toward the trucks.

"What's the matter, jackboot? Can't make decisions for yourself?" Meriam snapped as she grimaced at the man with disgust. "If it doesn't involve shooting *Untermensch* you don't know what to do?"

"Dumb French bitch!" the officer snarled, clearly refraining himself from striking her.

"That's right, I'm French—so why did you take us off the train? We aren't Germans, you moron. We can't be deserters if it isn't our country." She smirked up at him. "Are you sure the *Waffen* in *Waffen* SS doesn't mean 'fucking idiot'?"

The officer took a deep breath and was about to yell when

the train whistle cried out across the countryside. There was a pause and then the massive engine began to shunt forward. It pained me to watch our ticket home leave us behind.

"Don't mind him," a voice came from beside us as we were pushed beside the trucks. I turned to see an SS sergeant holding open a pack of cigarettes. "His wife is missing in Hamburg. He wants to be there but—"

The officer shook his head saying, "That doesn't concern them, Felix." I felt his hand slide away as he released us from his grip.

I took a cigarette, prompting Meriam to do the same. She moved her head closer to the waving flame as the man held out a lighter.

"And to answer your question," the sergeant said, "we are all fighting for the same Reich."

I felt a droplet of water on my head. As I looked up to the sky, I heard the sound of the rain begin to patter on the cloth coverings of the transport trucks.

"This day couldn't get any worse," I said, as the flame from the lighter ignited my cigarette. I took a drag, my face becoming warm with anger now that the fear had dispersed and I had become acutely aware of where I was, and most importantly, where I was *not* headed.

Meriam mumbled something in French, one arm under her elbow as she held the cigarette in the air, the rain beginning to soak our clothes.

"Why did you do that?" I asked, my voice rising to speak over the rising downpour. "Why stand up for me? Why say you're pregnant?"

Meriam shrugged. "I don't know. I thought they would believe it." She offered a soft smile before she continued, "Maybe they wouldn't force you to go if they thought you were going to be a father." She took another drag of her cigarette, appearing to savor it before adding, "I guess I forgot who I was dealing with. Maybe if they were *Wehrmacht* or the loyalists it would have worked. Or if they were anyone but Germans."

I let the conversation die, instead focusing on the train as I watched it disappear off into the distance.

My eyes darted back as Meriam said, "Why are we just standing here? Let us get on the trucks and out of the rain at least."

I could see several SS soldiers talking a fair bit away. They looked tired.

"I don't think they are in a hurry to get back into the city," I said, hoping it would calm her.

Meriam flicked some cigarette ash to her boot, studied how the rain mixed with it and said, "One thing we have in common with them, I suppose."

We stood there for a while longer as the rain continued to hammer down on us. I heard a voice from around the truck and knew it was time to go. As we moved to the back of the vehicle, I could see a field ahead, and beyond it, a farmhouse and barn. Seeing the muted greens of the grass made me realize that this was the first bit of nature I had laid eyes on since entering Germania.

"Come on, you two," the sergeant who gave us the cigarette said. "An offensive is coming up."

I took a step, then another, my arm rising to hoist myself up into the back of the truck. My fingers made contact with the steel bed of the vehicle just as the sounds of rifle fire broke out from the field.

A trio of soldiers farther down the road collapsed in a heap.

I saw the sergeant in front of me turn, raising his rifle before taking a round to the chest. I lost focus on him and dove under the truck.

I turned my head to call out to Meriam, but saw her tumble

down onto the road, her hands clutching her thigh. The rifle fire was drowned out by the roar of a machine gun opening up from the field.

Meriam screamed, coddling her wound.

A SS member fired from beside the truck before breaking cover to drag Meriam to safety. He grabbed her by the vest but took a bullet to the throat. He toppled over, spraying blood onto Meriam's face.

A barrage of machine gun fire chewed through the truck, and I felt every muscle in my body lock up. I wanted to rush out and save Meriam, but I couldn't move, no matter what I ordered my limbs to do.

The firing ceased in an instant and the road took on a silence that hung until Meriam's clenched-teeth scream shattered the obscene peace.

I heard bootsteps approaching and placed my head flat on the pavement. I prayed they would spare Meriam, perhaps get her medical attention when they realized she wasn't SS. The footsteps stopped beside the truck, and I could see the mix of camouflage patterns of their pants.

The men looked down at her with contempt.

"What's with her uniform?" one of them asked.

"Help me!" Meriam screamed. Her pleading eyes darted between the group of Brownshirts.

"French flag on her shoulder," a blond loyalist said, his coat was that of a *Wehrmacht* officer from the Great War.

"Must have stolen it. She isn't French Army. They couldn't have invaded without us knowing," the first man replied.

"I—" Meriam cried before clutching at her wound again, tears streaming down her face. "I'm not SS!"

"Doesn't matter," the blond man said before pulling out his pistol. He looked to the fighter closest to him. "Have to put her out of her misery; it's the decent thing to do."

Meriam raised her free hand to shield herself, but in that last moment our eyes met. A thousand lifetimes existed in that instant, and the gunshot ended them all.

Her lifeless body slumped over.

I closed my eyes and put my head flat to the road, my entire body trembling as I held back tears. All her experiences, her loves and passions, gone with the pull of a trigger and a cheap bullet. How's that for justice?

I heard the voices dissipate as they moved toward the front of the truck. Through my ragged breaths I could only make out the final bit of the conversation.

"Leave them; they will serve as a warning. Only take the ammo." It was the blond bastard who spoke.

My eyes shut again. My fear and sadness swallowed up by an all-consuming fury.

*I'm going to kill him,* I thought, my hands moving out from under me as I began to push myself from the hiding spot.

*I'll kill him and I don't care what happens to me.*

My mind filled with images of me rushing forward, bullets tearing through my body, a knife finding its way into my hands. The steel plunging into his chest, twisting.

I moved out from under the truck, and I could see the group was farther down the road, pulling equipment from the beds of the other trucks. I turned, my eyes finding Meriam's body, her blood mixing with that of the SS soldier and the rain before flowing away toward the ditch at the side of the road.

I shivered, and with it, all my rage vanished.

Seeing the bodies, I knew the same thing would happen to me. And for what? I couldn't bring her back. The primal being withdrew into the depths of my skull and told me that I wasn't ready to die. Not yet.

I retreated back under the truck, disgusted with myself.

# Chapter 18

## *Draped in the Soils of Revolution*

The loyalists were gone for some time before I overcame my grief enough to slide out from under the truck. As I stood, I focused my eyes away from Meriam's body. By keeping her out of sight, I felt I could push the truth deep down and pretend her death had not become a reality.

I looked in the distance to the aging farmhouse, eyeing the property for any sign of movement. It was then I realized the rain had stopped.

I turned my head and peered into the back of the truck. A camouflage jacket lay on the bench inside. I grabbed it, my eyes lingering on the SS lightning bolts on the collar. Pulling the knife from the belt of a dead soldier, I cut off the insignias and turned, laying the jacket on top of Meriam's body. My eyes were forward, watching the road and keeping my mind free from what I was doing.

I took a step left and grabbed the rifle that sat on the road. I wiped the blood from the frame before ensuring the weapon was in battery and ready to fire. I took a deep breath and turned to face the house once more.

I walked forward, down the short embankment on the side of the road and across the tall grass of the field. I was giving myself the order of investigating the house. A small, almost mundane task, but something that would distract me from what waited behind me.

I completed my journey in a daze. It wasn't until my boots hit the faded and stained steps of the porch that I became aware that I had reached the house. I took a deep breath and tried the handle, finding it locked. I sighed and looked to the doorframe to see if I could shoulder my way in. It appeared well-constructed. Taking a step back, I eyed the living room window and deduced that a rock through the glass would be my best course of action.

I looked around for something heavy and saw a small statue of a rabbit sitting on its haunches farther down the porch. As I picked up the object, I noticed that it was lighter than it had initially appeared. I turned the statue over in my hands and saw a small outline on the bottom, I pressed my thumb against the marking and slid a plastic compartment open. Inside was a key.

As I pulled out the small piece of silver, I shifted my eyes to the window, thinking it should be grateful, for it had not known how close it had been to being shattered.

I lowered the rabbit to the porch and turned the key in the lock. The door swung open without a sound. As I stepped inside, I noticed the musty smell of stale air along with the sour notes of rotting fruit.

I kept my rifle down at my side as I moved through the small entrance way and turned into the living room. I saw the aging furniture, antique vases and of course the familiar framed photograph of the Great Führer mounted above the fireplace.

My gaze met his cold black eyes.

I took a step forward and peered to my right, eyes landing

on the kitchen. A wide-mouthed bowl sat on a heavy wooden table, a storm of flies buzzing around its rim with excitement.

I pivoted and returned to the entrance, looking at the stairwell at the back of the hall. A dull red carpet met my gaze. I moved up the steps slowly, listening for an indication that I was not alone. Reaching the top, I headed toward the end of the narrow hall where an open window sat, looking out toward the roadway. The white curtains swung as the breeze took hold of them.

I took my attention from the window and noticed a desk under the windowsill. An overflowing ashtray sat at the edge of the table, the red lipstick on the filters telling me they had belonged to a woman.

I imagined the owner of the house, sitting on the edge of the desk, peering out the window, wondering what the world was coming to. I lifted the curtain with my free hand and looked toward the sky. It was turning orange in the dusk.

My eyes shifted to the raised country road in the distance, the drainage ditch beside it and the overgrown weeds that jutted out, trying to strangle the road in its clutches. My eyes moved over the lumps that represented the bodies. As my gaze met the jacket that covered Meriam, I looked away.

I moved into the adjacent room and could tell by the items inside that it had belonged to a young man.

*The woman's son?*

A collection of posters hung on the walls. Posters of *Wehrmacht* soldiers admiring the Great Führer during a rally in Kiev's stadium; a late nineties Volkswagen roadster completing a circuit; and Hermann Kotch, the international boxing champion, mid-fight. I moved to the dresser and pulled open the drawers. Only underwear and socks looked back at me.

Frowning, I went to open another drawer when my eyes focused on an object on the dresser in front of me. A Hitler Youth knife in its scabbard, sitting propped up in a sort of display. The dust covering the case told me the man had been out of the organization for some time.

I could almost hear the remnants of the conversation between him and his mother, her begging him not to go, him saying he must fight for the Führer, reciting the various oaths soldiers had sworn over the years.

*But which Führer would he commit his blood to?*

I blinked as my mind filled with questions.

*Was that why she was smoking so much? Was she waiting for her son to return home? Where is she now? Did the Brown-shirt thugs drag her out back and...*

The house creaked, causing me to look toward the door. No one was there.

I took a calming breath and, looking at the Hitler Youth knife one last time, pulled open another drawer. This one contained a dozen folded shirts. I lifted a few out, holding them up to my chest to ensure they fit. They would be a little loose, but nothing too drastic. I tossed two on the bed before opening up the bottom drawer and finding more shirts.

I moved to the closet and eyed several pairs of dress pants that were folded neatly over their hangers. I checked the labels on several and saw that they would fit. I tossed a pair onto the bed and moved out of the room.

I looked across the hall and could see a bathroom. The shower curtain had been pulled back, showing a spacious area, and the enamel-coloured backsplash invited me inside. My body relaxed in anticipation of the sensation of warm water running down my skin. I imagined the feeling of changing into clean clothing after I had toweled off and I could think of no sweeter sensation.

While I knew I really didn't have time for a shower, I cared little at the moment. I longed for nothing but the sound of hot water flowing over me as my thoughts were carried away with the mud.

---

It was dark by the time I left the house. The shower and subsequent dressing had allowed me time to come to a decision.

*Meriam must be buried.*

While I had originally envisioned taking her to France and giving her a proper funeral, the risk of crossing the border with her was too great. If she was discovered, they would assume I had murdered her, and in these turbulent times a trial would be a luxury I doubted I would be afforded.

I ventured outside and headed back toward the road. The cold air forced me to rub my arms as the chill crept through the sweater I had put on. I reached the body and lifted her into the back of the nearest truck. I was trembling now as I headed to the driver side door. I pulled myself inside and found the keys in the ignition. I drove the truck down the gravel driveway and behind the farmhouse.

I exited the vehicle and entered the nearby barn. As I stood in the doorway, the lights from the truck behind me revealed the grill of a dusty sedan parked toward the rear of the barn. I pushed the knowledge of its presence toward the back of my mind and grabbed a shovel from the wall.

I returned to the backyard and picked a spot in the centre of the area where the dirt looked the softest. I dug and I dug. I tried to make the grave six feet deep, but I became too tired.

I felt the tears then, feeling ashamed of the terrible job I was performing of giving Meriam a dignified final resting place. The grave was shallow, and worse, it was uneven at the bottom. She didn't deserve that. She deserved a state funeral, a cenotaph overlooking a grand mausoleum, constructed of intricate stonework and golden features...

Yet all I could provide her with was this pitiful excuse for a ditch.

I leaned on my shovel, the sweat stinging my eyes as my shoulders ached from the hundreds of shovelfuls of dirt I had thrown to the sides of the hole. Through my agony, I thought of resting through the night and resuming my task at first light. But as my eyes gravitated to the bumper of the truck, I knew that it would not do to leave Meriam alone in the dark, her body left to rot.

Images of wild animals wandering from the distant trees, the soft patter of their paws echoing about the property as they approached the truck. The scent of her body entering their nostrils as their stomachs rumbled with hunger.

I dug more, the mental creations providing me with newfound strength. I dug until I couldn't bear it anymore—and then I dug some more.

I estimated the hole to be a little under five feet as I pulled myself out of it. My shaking limbs disobeyed me as I tried to push myself to my feet. My arms gave out then and I collapsed on the grass. I lay there for several minutes, my chest rising and falling, rising and falling, rising...

I was with Meriam in Paris.

We ordered wine and laughed at a joke I would never know. She wore a large-brimmed sunhat, and her white dress swelled in the wind. The sounds of a city at peace rustled in the distance. It was the most peaceful I had ever been.

"More wine, monsieur?" a waiter asked, his tuxedo appearing to absorb the sunlight.

"Please. And another for the lady as well," I said, gesturing to Meriam, who rested her chin on her hands, leaning toward me.

"I'll switch to Cointreau," she said, a thin smile flashing across her lips.

"Excellent choice, mademoiselle," the waiter spoke again before lowering his head and departing.

The city of Paris grew quiet, the patrons slowly disappearing around us.

"You can't stay here, Eduardo," Meriam said after a moment, her brown eyes filled with sadness.

"Why not? We are having a grand time. I will take you to Madrid the day after tomorrow. I will show you my favorite places. I know many people who would love to meet you."

"That sounds nice," she said, looking down at the white gold watch that I had not noticed before, yet knew it had somehow always been there. "It's time to go, Eduardo."

I gasped myself to consciousness.

I shivered as the sweat on my body cooled and the night winds tumbled over me. As the dream melted away, I was left feeling more alone than I ever thought possible. I blinked, attempting to figure out how long I was asleep before giving up and standing, my aching muscles screaming out.

I moved to the back of the truck and, as carefully as possible, grabbed Meriam's body. I took several deliberate steps to not disturb her or the coat that was draped across her. I wished for the last memory I had of Meriam to be the dream in Paris, not her as she was now.

With as much care as I could manage, I lowered her into the grave.

I looked down at the coat for a moment, the sounds of the night behind me. I tried to think of something to say, but no matter how hard I thought, nothing came.

Maybe I could say that she died with honour? But how

could I even utter the words when there had been nothing honourable about it? No, Meriam had been like so many other unfortunates, those born and subsequently killed before their rightful time through no fault of their own.

Realizing the words would never come, I loaded the shovel with dirt, and after a moment of hesitation, tossed the soil into the hole. Tears dropped along with it.

# Chapter 19

## *Papers Will Set You Free*

I drove down the road in my stolen car, keeping the headlights off in an attempt to conceal my advance toward the French border.

I thought back to the keys sitting on the small hook by the closet in the house. Most of the spots were empty and the tire tracks to the left of the house told me the owners had once owned multiple vehicles. The one I was driving, despite being in storage in the barn, drove fine. I worried about being pulled over, and while the visions of handing soldiers the ownership information intimidated me, I hoped I would be able to come up with a convincing lie.

A loaded weapon lay on the passenger seat. I didn't care who I came across next, SS or loyalist, I would fight my way out if they got in my way, and if need be, die trying.

A set of headlights came over the hill ahead. I gulped and adjusted my grip on the steering wheel. Another set of lights followed behind it before a third pair joined the pack. As the lights came closer, I realized they belonged to trucks—military transports, if I was to bet on it. I looked at the rifle, its black metallic frame seeming stoic in the darkness, the headlights rising up its body as they approached. I felt a layer of sweat form on my forehead.

The lights were almost on me now, but I kept my foot on the gas, eyes forward, looking like I had driven this road hundreds of times. As the vehicles passed me, I felt a chill, but as I peered to the rearview mirror and saw their taillights moving off into the distance, I allowed myself to exhale.

I found myself wondering what faction they had been with, but as the taillights disappeared around a bend, I realized it did not matter.

I switched on the radio in an attempt to calm myself. I flipped through several stations of dead air before stopping at a frequency that was broadcasting its emergency chime.

I waited a moment before a voice interrupted the droning noise by saying, "Please monitor this station, a message from the Führer will be broadcast shortly."

I turned the dial and landed on a station playing old French pop music. I let my hand slip from the dial and listened to a song that I had not heard in years. The singer reminded me of simpler times and the promised land ahead.

I drove for at least an hour, passing several towns, each appearing sleepier than the last. All was calm with no talk of treason behind brick walls or impromptu executions in dreary wine cellars. I was beginning to feel like the worst was behind me. Knowing that the entire Reich was not a war-torn hellscape allowed me to feel like the world might soon return to some degree of normalcy. But as I drove on, my newfound peace was whittled away by a constant, nagging thought. The unseen yet all too real final obstacle ahead.

The border.

I knew the *Zollgrenzschutz* force was large, so large that even in peacetime they examined all traffic, both inbound and departing, but during a civil war? Who knew how many guards would be on duty or how scrutinized I would be for leaving the Reich. I had heard stories of how effective of a force they were, recalling that since the war, France had put their complete trust in the Germans to patrol their eastern border for them. The thinking being that if the Riech was okay with authorizing someone to leave, who were the French to argue?

Images of my vehicle being rifled through, the evidence that it was stolen soon being discovered, the gaps in story becoming wider and wider with each subsequent question flashed through my mind. The blindfold and post appeared to be racing toward me, its speed increasing with each rotation of the tires.

My hand returned to the radio as the songs began to lose me. I scanned the stations again, stopping at a voice I vaguely recognized. Within the first few words I knew they belonged to Magda.

"...I want to remind the people of the Reich that he was my brother, long before he was our Führer. He confided in me time and time again that he felt he was not the right man for the job. I must inform the people that the reports from the SS that Otto is dead are false. I urge every citizen to come to the side of loyalty to the regime. By fighting against me you are fighting against Otto's wishes. The SS and their *Reichswehr* militia are nothing but radicals, those who wish to push their own agenda in selfish acts instead of serving the needs of the fatherland. But I promise you this, the treason of the SS will be dealt with in time and my wrath will be fierce." The uproar of applause was deafening. "This is a point in history that all shall—"

I switched off the radio, my grip tightening on the wheel. I wondered if the cheers were of real followers or lifted from a historical speech of Dr. Goebbels in the *Volkshalle* in an attempt to give Magda's words more credence.

A sign ahead informed me that the French border was approaching in a few dozen kilometres. Seeing the rifle on the seat beside me sent a shiver through my body. Having a weapon in the vehicle was a surefire way to get myself arrested before a single question was asked. I switched off the headlights, pulled over to the side of the road and exited the vehicle. The silence of the night crept along with me as I moved to the passenger side of the car. I pulled open the door, grabbed the rifle and tossed it into the weeds.

I walked in front of the vehicle, and after looking down the road to ensure no one had seen me, I got back in and turned on the headlights once more. The sound of the tires leaving the gravel of the shoulder before gripping the pavement filled my ears.

---

The lights of the border made it look like I was entering a military facility.

Spotlights lit the surrounding fields, showing the barbed wire fences and tank obstacles. A large concrete structure was perched to the left with several *Zollgrenzschutz* vehicles parked neatly beside it. A paved parking area sat adjacent to the facility behind a tall chain link fence with more than a dozen vehicles locked behind it. I suspected these vehicles had been seized and found myself wondering where their owners had gone or what crime they had committed. I began to second guess the entire plan.

As I continued to slowly approach the border, I could see a mix of uniforms as various personnel moved about the perimeter. Other than the *Zollgrenzschutz* officers, I immediately recognized the *Wehrmacht* uniforms and wondered where their allegiance truly lay. I had not anticipated the army being here and felt my pulse quicken.

I turned my attention forward and watched as a border guard authorized a small car through the gate before holding up his hand at an approaching van and walking to the driver's side window. The guard flipped through a passport, his mouth opening and closing as he asked a question. I rolled down my window, as I was next in line.

The guard asked another question, but I could not hear it over the sound of the van's engine. The guard nodded, before pointing toward the structure and the examination area illuminated by the bright overhead fluorescent bulbs. The van moved to where it was ordered and as I followed it with my gaze, I could see a group of soldiers emerge from the structure and move to intercept the vehicle.

I was next.

I drove up in a slow approach until the guard raised his hand in front of his stern face. I handed him my passport and he did a double take as he looked at the Spanish coat of arms emblazoned across the red cover.

"Are you a citizen of the Reich as well?" he asked, before flipping open the passport and looking to see if the picture matched.

"No, I'm just trying to get home," I replied.

My eyes focused on the road ahead and the dark countryside beyond it. I could almost see the invisible line that existed where the Reich transformed into France.

"And that's Spain?" he asked, looking into the back windows of the vehicle before his eyes gravitated toward the passenger seat.

I nodded as I said, "I was only here for business when all this started." I surprised myself with how confident my voice sounded.

The officer moved to the front of the vehicle, my passport still clutched in his hand. He looked at the Reich license plate again before returning to my window. "And this is your vehicle?" He phrased it more as a statement before adding, "Why do you own a Reich-plated vehicle if you reside in Spain?"

"I own a business in both nations. This is the car I use to get around while I'm in Germany. I flew in, but with the airports closed I figured it would be best to drive home. I will return when all this settles down," I gestured vaguely as if the whole thing was nothing but a minor inconvenience.

"What sort of work are you in?" the guard asked, staring deep into my eyes.

"Textiles, but if you want me to be more specific, import and export." I was thankful I had listened to my uncle's babbling during the holidays.

The guard nodded and closed my passport. I instinctively reached for it, but the officer kept it close to him. His face hardened again as he asked, "And who is the Führer of the Reich?"

I took in a breath and decided to cease guessing what faction this garrison belonged to. I replied with the truth. "The Führer who inherited the position by birth right, of course."

"And who is that?" he asked, and I saw him stiffen slightly as if he was ready to reach for his holstered firearm.

"Otto Hitler. First born grandson of the Great Führer," I spoke plainly.

The guard let out a soft smile, his eyes attempting to look over his shoulder, and I suspected he held different opinions than that of the *Wehrmacht* soldiers they had sent to assist the *Zollgrenzschutz*.

The officer tapped the roof of the car before heading into his booth and stamping one of the pages of my passport. He then pressed a button on his desk, and I watched as the gate arm in front of my vehicle rose into the air.

The guard returned to the side of my vehicle, handed me my passport and said, "Heil Hitler," in a nonchalant tone, his heels clicking lightly together.

"Thank you," I replied, a small smile on my lips.

As I put the car in drive, I could hear the guard say to the soldiers, "No, it's okay; he was Spanish..." The rest was drowned out by my engine as I began to move up the road.

I drove past another series of barbed wire fences and looked to my left, toward the Reich's inbound border inspection point. A long line of vehicles waited to enter.

My face soured. *Everyone should be trying to leave. Why are so many people going back?*

Then I remembered Magda's radio broadcast, and I wondered how many she and her rival—Dr. Fertig, the current acting Führer—had given in the previous days. No doubt they had both been ordering the citizens of the Reich home to fight.

As I crossed over the line into France, my mind turned to thoughts of Meriam. Again, I felt the shame of having to leave her buried in a shallow grave in a country she loathed. I wished more than anything she was with me now.

"Welcome home, Meriam," I whispered to myself as I passed a bilingual road marker—French on top, German on the bottom.

# Chapter 20

## *Another City, Another Language*

With the border far behind me and the sun approaching noon, I diverted from my route and headed toward Paris. I wished to see a capital engaged in conversation and music, not engulfed in flame and anarchy. At least that was the lie I told myself.

If I was to be honest and truthful with myself, it would be to say that I wished to see the city through Meriam's eyes. As someone who had lived there, studied there, laughed and cried there, made love and suffered heartbreak there. I wanted to experience the smell of the bakeries and the heat of the cafés, just as Meriam had. Doing so would bring me closer to her and bring her back to life, even if it was for a fleeting moment.

As the outskirts gave way to the government buildings and cathedrals of the downtown core, I found a parking garage and drove my vehicle inside, the bright sky disappearing behind grey concrete and yellow-painted markings. I found a spot in the spacious structure, and after parking, moved over to the ticket booth. I inserted a series of coins and waited for the steel box to dispense a ticket.

I realized then that I would give nearly anything to speak to a physical person. Someone who wasn't questioning my allegiances or race. I wanted to hear the mundane details of someone's day, a new restaurant they had heard about or an interesting book they had read. That was living and that was where true life began. The shared experience, the journey, just as important as the destination. The adventure of it all before the spectre of death came and shot you dead in the road.

I returned to my vehicle and placed the ticket on the dashboard. Upon doing so, I realized I had been lost in thought for some time. I wandered out of the garage in a daze, stopping at a restaurant down the block.

I entered, the sound of a British drinking song playing from the far end of the bar. A group of tourists sang and drank. A couple in the corner groped at each other, the man slipping his hand down the blouse of the redheaded girl, all the while a picture of a youthful Queen Elizabeth II looked on with a thin smile—her exile having ended some forty years ago with the death of her uncle.

"You want a seat at the bar, mate?" a muscular man in a black shirt asked as he swung a white cloth over his shoulder.

My English was not very good, but I understood the question all the same. I shook my head no, before mumbling that it was too noisy and left. The door shutting left the sounds of the party behind me.

I walked down the block, embarrassed that of all the places in Paris I could have picked, I had walked into an English pub. I couldn't think of anything farther from Meriam than a place like that. I wanted somewhere that had deep ties to the city. A place that had been passed on from generation to generation, where none of the signs were in German, not attempting to cater to the tourists. But most importantly, I wanted something quiet.

I saw a patio restaurant on the right side of the street and crossed, a trio of cars passing behind me as I did so. One of them may have honked, but I was not present enough to have heard it. I sat on the patio and watched as the Paris crowd moved by, paying me no mind, their focus solely on the routine intricacies of their lives. I envied them.

"Good day, monsieur," a voice from beside me said in French. "Will it just be yourself dining with us today?"

I looked up and saw the clean-shaven face of the waiter. "Yes," I said, hardly aware I had spoken. I looked at the wine list on the thin menu in front of me. I pointed to something at random and said, "A glass of the twenty-twelve Cabernet Franc from Bordeaux."

"Unfortunately, monsieur, we just uncorked the last bottle an hour ago..."

"Cointreau then," I said. "Neat."

"Excellent choice, monsieur," the waiter said with a smile, before pivoting and moving to the bar area inside.

I listened to the mundane conversations of the other patrons around me. It was nice to hear the French language and not the aggressiveness of the German tongue. I was feeling in the mood to get quite drunk, but as I looked over the wine list again, I realized that I would be leaving with a much lighter wallet if I continued to drink here.

I felt then that I cared little for money, and if a gust of wind would have come and rid me of every Reichsmark to my name, I would not have shed a tear.

By the time the waiter returned with my order, the couple closest to me had begun to talk about the war. As I sipped my drink, I continued to listen, but became agitated by how easily they were able to get all the details wrong. Their opinions were pedestrian, regurgitated nonsense from the news outlets, yet they spoke as if they were fonts of wisdom such that people from far and wide should seek out and kneel at their feet.

I shook my head, frustrated and empty.

I finished my Cointreau, hardly even tasting it, and placed down a twenty-Reichsmark bill, the Great Führer's sullen face staring up at me. I moved out of the patio and down the road in search of another restaurant. One where the occupants didn't speak of the war and where the drinks were as cheap as the conversation.

# Chapter 21

## *You Can Never Truly Go Home*

While the German-French border had been heavily secured, the Spanish border contained little in the way of arms. An ageing structure in desperate need of a facelift sat at the side of the road with a few small booths where the road forked off running alongside them.

A line of approximately ten vehicles idled in front of me, split in half as two lanes were open. I looked to the rearview mirror and could see in the distance the modest French checkpoint in the opposite direction.

I knew I was on Spanish soil and had been for a hundred metres at least, but I wasn't truly home until I was past this checkpoint and in my apartment in Madrid, drinking from the bottle of vermouth I had bought before the trip in celebration of a successful business meeting in the mouth of the lion's den.

It all seemed so trivial now.

After some minutes it was my turn to be processed. I forced myself to smile, since I knew to be surly would increase my chances of being referred inside for additional questioning. I grabbed the passport from my pocket and admired the coat of arms before reaching the booth and handing it to the outstretched hand.

"Where do you live?" the officer asked, his voice softer than the aging face behind the mustache suggested.

"Spain," I said quickly, happy to hear my mother tongue. A moment passed before I corrected myself, "Madrid, specifically."

"This is a German-plated vehicle, is it not?"

"It is," I replied. I knew he expected me to elaborate, but I kept my response the way it was.

"Are you coming from Germany now or were you only in France?"

"Germany. I was on a business trip." The way he tilted his head prompted me to add, "I've been in the Reich since the fourth."

"You've been in the Reich since the fourth?" he repeated, his eyes narrowing. "The battle's been going since the sixth, I read."

I nodded, my eyes darting forward as I remembered the coffee shop and the calm afternoon before all the chaos that ensued.

"What business could have taken that long?" the officer asked, his voice becoming accusatory.

I sighed. "I was trapped. My business was in Germania. Some of the fiercest fighting is there." I paused for a while before adding, "I just want to be home."

"One second," he said before shutting the window to his booth and grabbing the phone from the wall. He held the receiver in the crook of his neck as his fingers dialed a series of unseen numbers.

I began to sweat. *He's calling for backup. The Gestapo or the SS must have reported me as a terrorist. Spain will extradite me. If the Reich wants someone, they get them, doesn't matter—*

The officer slid the window open again and said, "My supervisor wants to speak to you. Pull over to the area under the canopy." He pointed to the side of the building before adding, "You're not declaring anything are you?"

When I shook my head no, he stamped my passport before handing it back and pointing toward the inspection area.

I could see the open road ahead of me and I strongly considered gunning it and taking my chances. But I knew fleeing was not the answer. I understood that if I complied, I could argue that the SS were confused, or that the war made communications unreliable and they were looking for my brother.

*No, it's best not to mention him. The secret police may show up to inquire about him.*

Slowly and with a pounding heart, I turned into the inspection area and parked my car. I looked to the doors of the station and saw a man in a more elaborate uniform approach. He was alone, which calmed me a little, but I still felt the sweat running down my neck and soaking into the stolen shirt.

The officer, who I took to be the supervisor, greeted me by saying, "Were you in Germania?" I nodded, prompting him to add, "And you'd been there since the fourth?"

I nodded again.

The supervisor removed his uniform cap and brushed his hair aside; he was sweating as well. "My wife and daughter were there visiting. Their flight was out of Erich Hartmann Airport. I haven't heard anything since she called me the night of the fifth. Please tell me, is it as bad as they say? You're the only one we've had come through here from Germania."

*They don't want to search me,* I thought, the feeling of panic melting away as my fingers loosened on the steering wheel.

I noticed the pleading expression in the supervisor's eyes and realized I was his only source of news from the Germania front lines. It came down to me to give this man assurances that everything would be fine. That he would see his wife and child again. The uniform he wore and the power he wielded as a result were inconsequential; they did nothing to rid him of his fear for his loved one's safety.

I chose my words with surgical precision, not wishing to terrify this man any more than he already was. "I went to the airport on the seventh to try and get home. There had been a battle there, and the SS made it a staging area."

The man looked at his boots. Clearly the news grieved him. Seeing this, I added, "But that was on the seventh, like I said. I had gone there because I heard they were sending out flights full of refugees. Maybe your wife and daughter got out and landed in another city?"

"And the Hotel Guderian? Did you see that? That's where they were staying."

"I'm not sure where that is, *señor*. I'm sorry."

"I heard the area was shelled and the *Wehrmacht* brought tanks. Do you think anyone could have made it out?"

"I do," I said, and I truly believed it. "There are civilian gathering points around the city, I stayed in one for a night and some of the train stations are still running, that's how I-I um..." The man looked at me with a peculiar glance, prompting me to adjust my story mid-sentence. "...How I got to my second property and got my car."

The man nodded in a way that assured me he believed what I had told him. "But the phone lines have been down for days. I tried calling everywhere, and nothing gets through."

"I don't know. I'm sorry."

The man looked through me for a moment before saying, "I've thought of going. I don't know how I'll get there, but ... I've thought of it. I need to go look for them. I can't stand not knowing. Sitting on the sidelines while my girls are lost in a strange city... They don't speak the language that well." His face showed his grief.

I stayed silent, not knowing how to console the man. His eyes focused again, and I could see him switch from grieving father and husband back to an officer once more. "Thank you for the information, you were very helpful," he said, before pivoting and retreating to the front doors of the building.

The officer held the stature of a broken man desperately trying to hold himself together until he was out of view.

I understood him, more than most, but there was nothing I could do. I put my vehicle into drive and moved out of the inspection station, following the lane to the highway.

I could see the hills ahead, and while I had been in the area many times in my life, they looked different now, holding an aura of beauty that I could not describe. Everything looked more vibrant, and more importantly, alive.

The sweet air of the Spanish countryside filled me with a sense of calm accomplishment. I had made it.

---

I slipped the spare key I had hidden in the mailroom into the lock of my apartment door. I used the familiar trick to grab the handle as I turned the steel in the lock that grew more stubborn with every use.

As I pushed the door open, a rush of air exited the apartment. The familiar scent of a place one had not been in for some time entered my nostrils and granted me a miniscule boost to my mood. I was thankful I had remembered to remove the trash before my journey, or the smell of home would not have been so welcoming at all.

I walked over to the kitchen and hesitated, looking at my living room, the feeling that I was home slowly becoming more and more real. I forced myself to smile, recalling that doing so could increase the endorphins flowing through one's mind.

I felt nothing.

I turned, pulling a glass from the cabinet before retrieving the bottle of vermouth from the rack nearby. I filled the glass with ice and some bitters before pouring myself a drink. I moved to the window over the sink and looked out at the warm afternoon.

The yellowing wall of the apartment building next door met my gaze. The storm shutters on many windows were closed and several laundry lines swayed in a soft breeze. A dog barked in the distance, and I could hear a man on the street talking with someone about the beautiful day.

I was home, and if I was being honest, I didn't know what to do with myself.

I took a sip of the drink and moved over to the phone, seeing that, according to the flashing number on the display, I had twelve missed messages. I pressed the button on the base of the receiver and sat on my couch, letting the recordings play.

The first few were from Lorena in scheduling, wondering where I was and why I had been missing work. I felt my blood pressure rise. No one had cared enough to open a newspaper or turn on the TV and see I was in the middle of a collapsing empire lashing out against itself. The messages from work stopped soon after and I assumed that someone had realized that Germania was on fire and perhaps, just maybe, that was a valid reason for my delayed return from the trip.

Next was an appointment from the bank I had failed to attend, and another asking for donations to refugees fleeing the "Reich Crisis." I couldn't help but laugh to myself at that one. I had no date stamp, but in an educated guess I would say it was no more than half a week after the coup d'etat and already the charities had their sweaty mitts out for cash.

The messages continued. Sipping my drink, I hardly paid attention. That was until there was a message from a Captain Garcia at the local armoury. He stated my name had been drawn to reinstate my military service. He mumbled a time and date to report: September sixteenth at oh nine hundred hours. Without looking at the calendar, I knew I was late. Over twenty-four hours late.

I sipped my drink, the ice hitting my lips.

*Arrest me then.*

I had seen enough killing to last ten consecutive life sentences.

Then the final message began. My eyes widened, and I became still.

It was Meriam's voice.

I felt everything then. The images of our time together, of her smile, her humor—all of it came to me as I listened to the message.

"I know we exchanged numbers again at the airport, but I don't know what the future holds for us, or how this war will turn out. I thought I would call and leave you this message with my number in case you lost the one I gave you. I would hate for us to never see each other again because a little piece of paper got lost in a war." She laughed and added, "That could be a plot to a romance novel. Maybe I'll write it."

Then there was a pause, and I remembered her entering the phone booth when we had been patrolling the city. "But I see you looking at me. You're probably wondering who I'm calling. How should I play this, do you think? Say it's a boyfriend perhaps, or maybe a husband? No, I won't be that cruel. I'm waving at you now. You're smiling. But I can see it on your face, you're wondering who I could be talking to."

She read off her number before concluding the message with, "Goodbye, Eduardo. I'm going to be speaking with you in a moment, but maybe the message will be a nice surprise when you get home from this war. And who knows, maybe I'll be there with you when you listen to it?"

I heard the phone click and felt my heart shatter along with it.

I jumped up and scrambled to the machine, pressing the button to save the last message. I stood over the device, knowing that this piece of plastic and circuity housed the only recording I had of Meriam's voice. It had, within a few ticks of the second hand, become the most priceless item I owned.

The time I had known her could have been measured in hours, but that was inconsequential. Meriam had been someone I had fought with, laughed with, been at the end of my rope with. I would never forget her, a woman whose last name I didn't even know...

I realized then that I loved her.

And now she was gone.

# Chapter 22

## *Coda*

Through the scope of my rifle, I searched the street below.

The rain had stopped, and I sensed I would not have to wait long. I adjusted my aim to the alleyway on the left side of the road as a woman emerged into the overcast day. She walked with a little boy beside her, their hands clasped together, a small raincoat in her free hand. I recognized them both, but I was not sure where I had seen them before. Yet I sensed I had known them both all my life.

The little boy jumped in a puddle before gesturing ahead, his finger going up, up, up to a window on the fourth floor. Right at me...

Right at my rifle.

The mother grabbed the yellow raincoat and flung it over her child's back. I suppose she suspected it would rain again. I thought little of this, as I knew they were the enemy, and the fact that one of them was a child bothered me little.

As my finger drifted to the trigger, the change was immediate.

Now I stood where I had been when it had happened.

Müller had his boot on the back of the monarchist, but the man was not who he had been when it had been real. No, now I recognized him as Ernesto. His hair had returned to his natural brown and he looked several years younger.

The fear in his eyes caused me to tremble.

The two other SS members fought to keep my brother restrained. A fist was raised, then lowered.

"Eduardo, help me!" my brother called out. His voice was distant and distorted, sounding as if it had come from under water.

"Let's go," the shadow that was taking on the role of Belmont said.

We turned and departed the room. The walk down the hall lasted an eternity as I waited for the sound of the gunshots to echo past me. Each step became agonizing and deliberate, as if my shoes were full of cement. I walked on, following the rippling spectre of Belmont as he led me down the rotting and mildew-encrusted hall. The cusp of the gunshot began to approach. I couldn't take it.

It all shifted again.

I lay on my back in the apartment, the *Wehrmacht* soldier towering over me, his rifle firmly in his grasp. I knew I was dead, but the face of the soldier was not how I remembered it, for it had changed as well. Now Ernesto stood in his place. His eyes... I had never seen him look at me with such hate.

Meriam fired from behind Ernesto, and he began to topple forward. The blood exploding forth hovered in midair.

I tried to look to where I knew Meriam lay, but my brother's corpse, still falling, blocked my view. As his body neared the floor, I strained my eyes to be able to see Meriam's face again, but the images shifted this way and that. Crumpling together as one before flattening themselves into something thinner than paper.

Now I was in the hallway.

Ernesto stood in front of me. He had just thrown a grenade into the apartment Meriam had taken cover in. He fumbled with the sling of his rifle in a vain attempt to level his weapon toward me.

I fired. Ernesto's stunned eyes were locked onto my emotionless visage.

I fired again, feeling nothing—not for my brother, not for ending a life and certainly not for an ideology.

I was cold, ruthless and, most importantly, I was human.

---

I awoke to the sound of a thundering at my door. In the brief moment between the noise entering my ears and my dream shattering, I believed in my heart that it was the SS. As I opened my eyes and recognized the ceiling, I became aware again that I was home, and a moment of peace came over me. This sensation lasted until there was another series of raps on my door.

I stood, unsure of who it could be, but hedging an educated guess that it would have to do with one of the messages I received, I moved out of my bedroom and down the hall. I looked through the peephole and saw a pair of men, both in military uniform, but thankfully no weapons in their grasp.

I lowered my hand to the doorknob, but hesitated, imagining a reality where I did not answer and what that would mean. Another series of blows to my door caused me to abandon this fantasy and pull back the bolt. I opened the door and did my best to look presentable, despite being in my white undershirt and shorts.

"What is your name, *señor*?" the taller of the two men asked. I could see the rank of a sergeant on his sleeve.

"Eduardo Domínguez," I replied, pushing the door open further in an attempt to show them I was alone.

"*Señor* Domínguez, I am Sergeant Alvarez with the *Regimento de Infanteria Asturias numero treinta y uno*. May we come in?" he asked, removing his cap and placing it under his arm.

I nodded. Whenever the army came to one's home, they always wanted to come inside.

I gestured for the men to enter and saw the rank of a corporal on the sleeve of the second man.

"Would you like anything? Water?" I asked, already knowing the answer but offering as a courtesy.

"No, thank you," both men replied.

Sergeant Alvarez sat on the couch, while the unnamed corporal stood in the entranceway to the living room, the look in his eye suggesting that some of the people they had visited had tried to run. I sat down in my chair across from the couch and let out a sigh. I was already bored with this conversation and wanted it over with.

"What can I help you with, gentlemen?"

Alvarez took his eye from the empty bottle of vermouth on the table and blinked, appearing to understand the story it told. "Is anyone else home?"

"No, just me," I replied. I craved a cigarette.

Alvarez nodded. I could tell he was doing his best to be polite, but I sensed he wished to be far from this assignment. "*Señor* Domínguez, I understand you served with my regiment in the past, correct?"

"Yes, I completed my mandatory service. One year."

"And you understand that you would be on a standby list for a period of fifteen years from the completion of your duties."

"I am aware." I could hear the defeat in my voice.

"We placed a call to the number you provided on the last census. Why did you not call back or report as instructed?"

"I... Well, I didn't feel like it."

Alvarez blinked. Clearly, he had been expecting the same lies he had heard a hundred times so far and not whatever it was I was doing.

"You ... didn't feel like it?" he repeated, blinking again.

"That's correct." The craving for a cigarette intensified and I crossed my arms, wanting them to hurry up and arrest me already.

Alvarez chuckled, and something about his demeanour told me that he didn't do that often. "You are aware that failing to report when ordered is a crime in the military code if you are still within the standby period?"

"I am, but what if I told you I was away when the call was placed and..." I sighed again, knowing I was wasting my breath. "And I'm in no shape to fight."

Alvarez gestured to me. "You look fine. Healthy, even. Who says you are not fit to fight for his Majesty?"

"I say," I replied, my tone softening as I recalled Meriam's body slumping to the street.

Alvarez looked to the corporal, who shifted his weight to the balls of his feet, ready to arrest me on his sergeant's order. A peculiar look appeared in Alvarez's eye then, and I sensed he was impressed by my boldness.

He cleared his throat. "You say you were away. Where did you go?"

"Germania," I replied.

The corporal let out a quiet snort as he clearly did not believe me. Alvarez kept his eyes on me.

"Germania?" he asked, his voice softening. "When you say Germania, you of course mean Germany, the Reich?"

"No, I mean Germania," I replied.

Alvarez opened his mouth to speak but hesitated, appearing to mull over the details I had given. He then proceeded with, “How long were you there?”

“The fourth of September until...” I paused, looking at the ceiling for an answer, before asking, “What day is it?”

“The twenty-fourth.”

“Then I’ve been back since the seventeenth. The last week has been ... not good.”

Alverez blinked again. “You were there on the fourth? Two days before the fighting?”

“I was,” I said, which prompted Alvarez to look to the corporal, and I could tell they were thinking I had been involved in the initial attack somehow.

“Do you have proof of this? Entry and exit stamps?”

“I do,” I replied. “Reich ones, Spanish ones...” I stood to retrieve my passport, and the corporal took a step forward. Alvarez held his hand out for his subordinate to stay put.

“Please show us,” Alvarez said. He looked curious.

I moved over to the dining room table and pushed aside the mail that I had collected from the postage box the day before yesterday. Underneath the pile was the red of my Spanish passport. I handed it to Alvarez before saying, “A drink, gentlemen? I have another bottle of vermouth.”

“No drinks; we are on duty. But...” He hesitated, and upon opening my passport and seeing the stamps, he said, “But you are welcome to one, of course.”

The corporal moved out of the way, and I entered the kitchen and pulled a bottle down. My eyes darted to the pack of cigarettes on the table. I pulled one out and lit it with a nearby match. I returned to the living room to see Alvarez holding the passport up to the light, as if to verify that the stamps were genuine.

I plopped down, poured myself a healthy portion of the

liquid and puffed on my cigarette. The corporal stared at me the entire time. A minute passed, then two, before Alvarez cleared his throat.

"*Señor* Domínguez, tell me please about your experience there. Tell me everything."

So, I told him. Every grisly detail, in full and without care to keep the words delicate. I told him of the business trip, told him about the police officer who was gunned down by Brownshirts and my fleeing to the train station. Told him about the Gestapo and them detaining me before a raid on the building which forced me to flee again. I told him of Kurt, the Gestapo officer, and how I retrieved my passport. I told him of the airport, and the SS and the French Foreign Legion. I told him of the rounds I fired, the people I had seen killed and the utter waste of life such a civil war brought upon the Reich. I told them, finally, of Meriam. My voice became a stern, hardened mess when I mentioned her name.

With every shocking detail, Alvarez's eyes widened more and more until finally I stopped speaking and snuffed out my cigarette in the empty soda bottle I had made into an ashtray. Several ticks of the analogue clock above my head sounded out until the corporal broke the silence.

"Do you have any proof?"

"Just the memories," I replied, my eyes burning a hole in the hardwood floor.

Alvarez nodded. He stood and sized me up before placing his hands into his uniform pockets and removing a pack of cigarettes of his own. He pulled one out and lit it, his eyes fixed on me.

"Quite the story," he said after a moment. He paused, appearing to choose his words carefully as he added, "*Señor* Domínguez, I'll be filing a report with my commanding officer about this."

I stayed silent for a moment, figuring the arrest order would be coming my way momentarily.

But I was caught off guard when Alvarez continued, "I will be reporting that I found you a compliant and loyal servant of the King, but unfortunately you have had numerous accidents and appear physically unfit to serve. I will also be mentioning that you have gained considerable weight, and it would be inhumane to allow you to train as doing so would put your life at unneeded risk. We can't have you experiencing a heart attack while on parade."

He gestured to his corporal to move out of the way before extending his hand toward me. "Thank you for your time, *Señor* Domínguez, and take care of yourself."

I shook his hand and offered a thankful smile as my response. Sergeant Alvarez led the way while the corporal followed him.

They proceeded to exit into the hall, and as they departed, I heard the corporal say, "Sergeant, he has no proof—"

The door shut before I could hear anything further.

I returned to my seat, poured another overflowing portion of alcohol into the glass and did not leave the spot until the bottle was done.

# A Change in Perspective:
## The Student

María Jose Weber took a sip of coffee from her thermos. History of Empires was her first class of the day, and she had never been much of a morning person. She looked toward the professor, who stood at the head of the auditorium below, his hands moving from his leather bag as he organized a series of papers on the desk in front of him.

María Jose's eyes glimpsed the digital whiteboard which had been pushed to the side, revealing the antique blackboard underneath. The professor was quite a bit older than her other instructors, and she suspected he appreciated the old-fashioned things in life.

He grabbed a piece of chalk and wrote: THE FALL OF THE THIRD REICH, 2015-2018.

The professor turned as he said, "Good morning, class. I expect everyone had a good weekend?"

There was a murmur from the audience, and judging by the professor's thin smile, he accepted that as a positive answer.

María Jose admired the tricolours of the Spanish Republic flag that hung over the blackboard. The Third Spanish

Republic was entering its eighteenth year of existence that summer, the anniversary date signifying when the monarchy had stepped down after acknowledging the ties it possessed to the fascists, courtesy of Franco. The king's resignation had been met with much glee across the country.

"Now, last class we ended on the start of the German Civil War," the professor said, his voice projecting to the far corners of the auditorium. "We talked about the factors that lead to its cause and the domino effect that could be traced all the way back to the death of the first Führer..."

María Jose took another sip of her coffee. She knew all this already, not only because the professor had covered it in detail, but because she had studied the Third Reich for as long as she could remember. Growing up, her father had always talked history to her, showing her historical films and documentaries, and each time, she had eaten it up.

"Today we will be covering a great deal of content, and I'm afraid we will have to move fairly quickly," the professor said.

María Jose sat up in her seat. Her pen met paper, eager to jot down notes. The fatigue from staying up late the night prior to complete her readings dissipated for a moment.

"Magda Hitler was assassinated in March of 2015," the professor said, forcing María Jose to begin scribbling down a note. "She was killed by a pair of her bodyguards in her headquarters in Hamburg. This is just days after the loyalist factions had claimed Germania was under their complete control. An interesting turn of fate, as you'll remember that she ordered Otto to be assassinated in his *Berghof* some six months earlier..."

María Jose zoned out again, knowing where this was going, having recalled a documentary on Magda she had watched earlier in the year. She felt the brain fog swirl about her again and mentally kicked herself for staying up so late trying to keep up with her readings.

"...With Wolfgang, her younger brother, now in charge of the loyalist faction, it didn't take long for them to splinter. The largest and most important of those groups to break off declared their loyalty to the Prussian State."

The professor wrote the name of the group on the blackboard before adding, "The Canadian Historian, Joseph Mellanox once said: 'The death of Magda was the death of the Reich.' While I tend to agree, I do believe he is over-simplifying it a bit. So, let's break it down..."

María Jose wrote down a few bullet points, but knew they would be nearly useless; she would have to go over them again when she got to her dorm to make them more concise and legible, and—if she had time—substantiate them with facts from the text.

"The Prussian Forces and the remaining loyalist faction fought each other around the country, with the largest battles occurring in the western and northern areas. For more information on them, chapter twenty-one of the text dives into the Battle of Konigsberg, which is a good read."

A hand flew up near the front of the auditorium. María Jose recognized the arm, as it belonged to Hector Fernández, a surprisingly daft individual in her eyes. He was someone who asked the most innocuous questions and who she suspected only was taking the course because he thought it would bump up his average. Still, despite her annoyance at him, she could see the professor looked delighted by the opportunity to answer a question on history.

"Can you explain why the loyalists broke up once Magda was assassinated?" Hector asked. "If they had all been of the same before, why should it matter if Wolfgang took over? He was still part of that family. They still could have followed his orders."

The professor smirked. "A civil war within a civil war." His eyes passed over the class before focusing on Hector. "Wolfgang, much like his older brother, was not seen as a particularly bright individual, nor passionate. He was regarded as a poor public speaker for his time and many scholars agree that he was the least gifted of the three."

The professor paused, seeming to peer inward to access his vault of personal knowledge. María Jose suspected that the professor had forgotten more about this era of history than she could ever know of it.

"Magda was the most like her grandfather; cunning, ruthless, blood thirsty, a risk taker and completely devoted to the party values that she felt should be continued. I've long thought that if Adolf had been alive to see Magda, he would have named her his successor. Wolfgang was none of those things." The professor paused again. Clearly something was tugging at him. He rolled the chalk between his hands, the light catching on his wedding ring for a moment as he eyed the student. "I hope that answers the question," he said finally.

Hector gave a non-committal shrug, which prompted the professor to continue.

"Now, we will jump ahead to October 2015, when the French decided it was a good time to take advantage of the situation. Under the guise that they were protecting the sovereignty of the Reich and expelling Prussian forces in Western Germany, they moved in. This marks the second time French troops were on German soil as belligerents during this conflict.

"They invade—or should I say 'liberate'—large portions of the country, getting as far north as Cologne and as far east as Frankfurt, stopping just short of Munich. No resistance is offered as the locals accept the propaganda that the French have been spreading about them saving the Reich.

"Now, I've reviewed first and second account sources, and found no indication that any groups other than loyalist forces existed in the regions the French moved into. The SS and *Reichswehr* didn't have a presence there either as they had been pushed back and were making their stronghold in Kiev, which—on paper—was seen as the capital of the Reich for a while. It's interesting of course that..."

María Jose ceased writing again, knowing about the three-faction battles that continued for months in the colonies. A continuous tug of war as each side took land, just to be forced back several weeks later.

"Enter 2016, a year of great change. The Siberian Free Corps and the Marxist-Leninist Popular Front organize the largest attack yet. You'll remember me talking about them last class, and while those skirmishes are worth noting, their gains in 2016 put those to shame. They directly assault the forts in the Urals that the Germans have manned since the end of the Second World War. At this point these forts are poorly guarded as large portions of their numbers continue to be pulled back westward to assist in the Civil War. This is also ignoring the purges these bases experienced at the start of the conflict."

Hector shot his hand up again, and while the professor looked at it with delight, he continued, "Over the course of the year, the communist rebels have a great number of victories. Their determination prompts various uprisings in the colonies, and the rise of the Moscow Liberation Movement. The most successful of these rebellions was in Croatia. which declared its independence in December of 2016. Greece is next in early 2017 and finally Serbia, in late April or early May of the same year, depending on the source."

Hector lowered his hand and María Jose assumed his question had been answered. The professor jotted down several notes on the blackboard before he turned and looked at the clock at the back of the room.

Seeing that he was running out of time he said, "By the end of 2017, the Reich is getting rather small. I'm speeding ahead here in the interest of time, but the resistance movements of the former Soviet areas pick up more speed, and within a year, everything up to Minsk is firmly in their grasp. The loyalist forces splinter again into several smaller groups and continue to fight each other. This results in Wolfgang attempting to flee to Norway, as the government has offered him protection. Denmark, oddly enough, declares they are allies with the self-identifying Prussian state and loudly announced that if Wolfgang attempted to transit through their territory, he would be arrested."

María Jose crossed out a bullet point as the professor elaborated on a thought. She jotted down another note before looking up from her notebook.

Seeing that the bell was about to go off, the professor said, "The Reich as we know it ended when Austria declared its independence just days before the Ukrainian state was split between Soviet and Prussian forces."

He began to write on the board as he spoke, "Please read chapters twelve to fifteen of the text, which covers these last few months in a relatively straightforward manner. The part on Czechoslovakia's separation is the most fascinating in my mind, and it spawned a great many important figures."

The bell rang and everyone remained in their seats until the professor said, "Those readings are required for next class and will give more insight into the mind of those communist resistance movements and how their influence is still felt in the Soviet state today. Thank you, everyone. You're dismissed."

The auditorium slowly emptied, but María Jose did not feel

the need to rush. She packed up her notebook and pens before hoisting her bag over her shoulder and descending the steps to approach the professor.

He was in the process of erasing the board when he turned, apparently hearing María Jose's steps. "Questions?" he asked, a look of intrigue flashing in his eye.

"Yes, professor. You said that when the French liberated western Germany, that was the second time they had forces in the conflict. What did you mean by that?"

The professor's face changed; the interest scattered, and he appeared to look far within himself. As he spoke, it sounded as if he was choosing his words carefully. "The history books never mention it, and I think it's because they simply don't know, but I assure you it happened. The French Foreign Legion was in Germania during the opening days of the conflict, but soon Paris called them home. The French government was convinced the loyalists would win, and not wanting to be on the wrong side of history, they pulled their forces out."

"I had no idea. I've— I've never heard of this," María Jose said, thinking back to the copious number of documentaries, fiction and articles she had studied, all dedicated to the fall of the Third Reich.

"As I said, it isn't common knowledge. I don't blame the historians; no one reported it because no one looked for it. Who would think the French Foreign Legion was there? I just... Well, I'm saddened for the men and women who died in the streets of Germania. No one remembers their names or knows of their sacrifice."

María Jose could see the sadness forming in the professor's eyes, but he quickly composed himself. He smiled and, appearing to recognize how interested María Jose was in the conversation, pulled a hardcover book from his bag.

"Here," he said, passing the text to María Jose, who

accepted it. She looked at the worn dust cover and read over the title: A STAGNANT REICH: ITS FINAL DAYS

"It goes into more detail on the matter," the professor said. "It's well researched, I can assure you."

"But, professor, if you have this textbook available, why make us read the other one?" María Jose asked, her voice betraying her true feelings at just how poorly written the class assigned text was.

The professor looked to the ceiling. "Oh, because it didn't reach approval by the board. They said it has too many unverified accounts, but I can tell you they are all authentic."

María Jose could hear the voices of the next class entering from the hall at the back of the auditorium. The professor's eyes drifting over her head confirmed this.

"You can review the chapters in this book as your readings," the professor said after a moment. "Chapters fifteen to eighteen should do, I believe. I think it covers everything more succinctly and has a little more flavor to it than *Señor* Richard offers in his book. I know he can be dry at times." A kind smile moved across his lips.

"I'll return it next class. Do you mind if I make photocopies of it?"

"You can keep it; I have a few copies at home. It was produced in a limited run by a small publisher. Don't worry about returning it."

"Well, thank you, professor. I should be going though. Can't take up all your time."

"No trouble at all, and let me know if you find anything new in there. I would be happy to talk about it."

María Jose thanked the professor again before muscling up the stairs with newfound vigor. She was eager to head to the library during her spare period and dive into the book to see what new insights and accounts it could potentially offer.

Before heading through the door, she looked behind her and saw the professor leaning over his desk, palms flat on the wood, eyes blurred as if he was lost in thought. He stayed that way for several moments until he snapped back to reality and welcomed his next class to the lecture.

As María Jose walked down the hall, she found herself opening the text. She flipped past the title sheet and copyright information before landing on the dedications page.

Atop the cream-coloured paper, jutting up in raised black ink, two words stood alone:

For Meriam

# A Note from the Author:

The city of Germania, while fictitious in our reality, was all too close to occurring had the Allied powers lost the Second World War. The city portrayed in the novel is in line with what Hitler and Albert Speer planned to build. Many models and sketches of their vision to rework Berlin into a suffocating world capital still exist and are now housed in museums for all to see. These remnants serve as a terrifying reminder of what almost was...

# Did You Enjoy the Book?

If you liked this book, or if you've been a fan of mine for a while, please consider leaving a review and a high star rating over at Amazon.

Doing so really helps other readers like yourself discover my works and find out if this book would be something they would enjoy. It is also nice to hear from my readers about what they liked most in each of my works.

# Acknowledgments

I would like to take the opportunity to thank all the people who not only helped to make this novel a reality, but also stuck with me and showed their support through the entire process.

I would like to start with giving a huge thank you to my beta reader team, consisting of:

Colleen Atkinson, for catching all those pesky typos and sharing all her positive thoughts on the story.

Dennis Atkinson, for reading the manuscript cover to cover twice so he could provide me so many wonderful notes and comments, and for once again renewing my love of the game.

Veronica Martinez Soto, for having such a keen eye for the details and pointing out the little things that slipped by.

I would also like to thank my creative team of:

My editor, Christie, for all her helpful suggestions, sentence fixes and overall hard work.

My cover artist, Ronnie at *Tegnemaskin.no*, for creating such a striking cover. He took my vague idea and brought it to life in a way that I didn't think was possible.

I would also like to take the time to thank all those who helped me along the way including: Nathan Olmstead, Allison Tremblay, Adam Kudryk and Gabriela Hernandez Maltos. Even just asking me about my latest projects or letting me bounce ideas off you is something that means so much. Thank you for everything you do!

To those listed above and others who helped me through the lengthy creative cycle of taking a scrap of an idea and turning it into a finished novel, I give you one last giant thank you!

--Robert J. Bradshaw<br>January 2025

# What's Next for Bradshaw?

Did you enjoy the novel and can't wait to find out what I'm working on next? Maybe you've been a fan since reading one of my other works and can't wait for updates on my next release?

I have some great news for you. My newsletter, "Bradshaw Monthly," has been going strong since December of 2020. Each month, I update my readers with my progress, unveiling cover art for upcoming releases, and sales to my back catalogue. But all of that is just scratching the surface.

Best of all? It's completely free!

For easy access, head over to my website:

www.writingwithbradshaw.ca

There has never been a better time than now to join the Bradshaw Camp. I hope to see you there!

# Also by Robert J. Bradshaw

## Nebulous Seas

*A Thriller Novella*

*Can Either Truly Be Trusted?*

For Everette Davis, a vacation in a cozy cabin by the lake sounds like exactly the sort of thing he needs to let the stress of life melt away. Everything is going according to plan until an unwelcome guest arrives. Everette soon realizes that he is now trapped in a personal hell with someone who is standing in the way of the vacation he desperately craved...

Art Billings is trying to help out his ailing friend by winterizing his secluded cottage. A chance to get away and relax by the water before the cold winds sweep the countryside. There's just one problem: Someone is already there. Art soon begins to suspect that his housemate might be up to something. Something sinister...

## A Stone's Throw Away From Paradise:

*A Collection of Science Fiction Short Stories*

A research vessel is tasked with locating the end of space. A fully-terraformed Mars is not enough to combat the dreaded midlife crisis. An alien race believes it is their civilization's mission to uplift any life it encounters.

Twelve stories of thrilling science fiction that will bring you to the distant future, the long-forgotten past, and everywhere in between.

In this anthology, technological expansion, ghosts in the machine, and the meaning of the soul are only the beginning...

Twelve stories of thrilling science fiction that will bring you to the distant future, the long-forgotten past, and everywhere in between. Venture through the portal and find what awaits beyond.

After all, it's only a stone's throw away...

# A Monarch Among Kings:

*A Colonization Space Opera*

*Dune* meets *A Game of Thrones* and *Starship Troopers* in this epic space opera.

Far off in the Andromeda Galaxy, thousands of colonists have carved out a life for themselves on the remote world of Seryhenya.

However, as a young officer in the Colonial Guard Corps will soon discover, the planet might just hold more life than expected...

Follow multiple viewpoints as each character struggles to navigate the unfolding crisis. Some want to destroy this potential threat before it can fester; others want to live and let live. It is up for debate who is correct in their assessment of the situation.

But keeping an eye on the horizon might not be the only thing the colonists have to worry about...

# About the Author

Robert J. Bradshaw is a Canadian author born and raised in St. Catharines, Ontario. He relocated to British Columbia, seeking adventure. He currently lives in the Fraser Valley region.

Bradshaw has released six books to date. These include the science fiction anthology, *A Stone's Throw Away from Paradise*, and the psychological thriller novella *Nebulous Seas*. His debut novel, *A Monarch Among Kings*, an epic space opera was released in 2022. His first two pulse pounding anthologies, *Songs of The Abyss* and *Shadows At Midnight*, were rereleased by Velox Books in 2025.

He is currently hard at work on his third novel as well as another gathering of horror tales.

Printed in Dunstable, United Kingdom

77349976R00160